The Lottery Winner

Julie Bradley Garrett

ISBN 978-1-68526-330-0 (Paperback)
ISBN 978-1-68526-487-1 (Hardcover)
ISBN 978-1-68526-331-7 (Digital)

Covenant Books
11661 Hwy 707
Murrells Inlet, SC 29576
www.covenantbooks.com

The Queen Mary World cruise itinerary 2013 includes ports in Spain, Greece and Egypt (including a Suez Canal crossing), UAE, India and Sri Lanka, Malaysia, Singapore, Thailand, Vietnam, China, Australia and New Zealand, Mauritius, South Africa, Namibia, Canary Islands and Portugal, before returning to its home-port Southampton in England.

Queen Mary 2 World Tour ports of calls: Barcelona, Athens (from Piraeus), Port Said, Suez Canal (January 19), Port Suez, Port Sokhna, Safaga, Dubai (January 27), Abu Dhabi, India (Cochin), Sri Lanka (Colombo), Malaysia (Langkawi and Kuala Lumpur (from Klang), Singapore (February 9), Thailand (Ko Samui and Bangkok (from Laem Chabang), Vietnam (Ho Chi Minh), China (Hong Kong (February 17) and Shanghai), in **Australia** (Yorky's, Brisbane and Sydney (March 7), New Zealand (Bay of Islands, Auckland (March 11), Wellington, Christchurch and Fjordland), AU again with Sydney (March 19), Melbourne, Adelaide and Fremantle), Mauritius (Port Louis), in **South Africa** (Durban (April 6), Port Elizabeth, Cape Town (April 9), Namibia (Walvis Bay), **Canary Islands** (Gran Canaria, April 21), Madeira (Funchal), Vigo

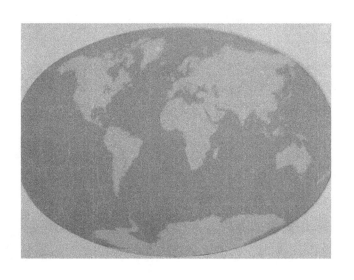

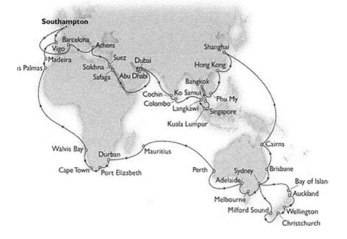

Acknowledgments

No author writes alone or can take credit without the encouragement and support of others. This novel couldn't be written without the love and patient advice of my husband, Mark, a far better writer than I am, and who has always believed in me as a writer. To my friends, Harriett Ford, a published writer and inspiration to many; to Kathy, Elaine, Desma, my daughter Holly, and my son Aaron who believe in me; to Les and Rita, and Suzy Carr, Lyn Skews, and Michelle Holmes of Covenant Books who have been patient with my lack of computer skills and constant editing, and who have been great encouragers to me as a life-long writer, but first-time novelist. Thanks to you all!

I want to thank the people in Linn, Missouri, three hours from my home, who talked to me and answered my questions about their small town in the two days I visited there. They were open and honest. Most of the places in this book are real places in and around Linn, except for Grace Community Church which is totally fictional. All characters are drawn from my imagination and are not based on any real person in Linn. Any resemblance to anyone in Linn is purely coincidental.

A large amount of research went into this novel, and I want to thank the website Wikipedia for the research I did. I know so much more about the geography and people from all cultures because of it. This website is invaluable for writers.

I am in debt to the great writers who have influenced me over the years, whose books I read and re-read—Margaret Mitchell, Edna Ferber, Willa Cather, Taylor Caldwell, Mark Twain, Pearl Buck, Olive Ann Burns, Victoria Holt, Nicholas Sparks— all accomplished storytellers who turned me into a passionate reader as well as a writer.

Finally, I want to thank God for speaking to me through His Holy Spirit on June 29, 2021, as I sat on my back patio in the early morning watching the birds eating their sunflower seeds from our feeders. He told me He wanted me to finish the book I had started thirteen years ago and had forgotten about as it lay in a dusty briefcase under a pile of clothes in my closet. To you, the reader, I pray this novel encourages you, inspires you, entertains you, and ultimately draws you into a closer relationship with your Creator. I have always loved this expression and taken it into my heart—He loves you so much; if you were the only person in the world, He would have died for you. That's the greatest love anyone can give.

1

Damaris

Every life has challenges and trials, and no one's life is immune from pain. Children shouldn't have to experience deep loss or suffering. In an ideal world, they should be free to live as children—playing, exploring investigating, and always trusting in their parents' love and continued presence in their lives. Sadly life isn't always fair. Sickness, disease, financial problems, divorce, or death often hang like haunting specters over innocent lives; and in a moment, their childhood world is destroyed by an engulfing tragedy hitting them like a giant wave.

A tsunami hit fifteen-year-old Damaris Kelly's family three years ago. Until then, she lived life on a calm, peaceful ocean. Her parents, Phillip and Georgia Kelly, had a loving marriage and were committed to their children—Damaris, fifteen, and her brother, seventeen-year-old Bryan. They lived in the city of Linn, a small town of 1,500 in central Missouri, close to the capital, Jefferson City.

Phillip was a traveling salesman for a farm equipment company, which provided an adequate living for his family. He was a good salesman primarily because of his rugged good looks, infectious personality, and ability as a storyteller. With a slight Irish brogue inherited from parents who immigrated to America when he was ten and his enthusiasm for his products, he joyously drove down country roads through Missouri, Kansas, and Oklahoma during the week, preparing for the next sale. He occasionally took Damaris on his road trips when she wasn't in school, visiting farms and small implement stores. He carried a huge bullhorn in the front seat of his van; and as he drove down farmers' gravel driveways, he yelled into the bullhorn, "It's me, Phillip Kelly! Get that lemonade ready!"

Farmers leaned on their shovels or stopped their tractors, smiling because Phillip Kelly was coming up the road. Wives took fresh lemonade out of the refrigerator, filled glasses with ice, and dusted off front-porch rocking chairs, knowing they could count on a great joke or long-winded story as they perused his equipment catalogs. On days she tagged along with her dad, Damaris played with the farm children in the hayloft, chased their cats, or sat happily on the front steps, scratching a scruffy farm dog's ear as she listened to her dad spin his yarns, which breathed cool, fresh air into the monotonous predictability of their farm lives.

If he didn't get an order, he drove back onto the highway shouting with enthusiasm, "If life hands you a lemon, turn it into lemonade, Damaris!" The farmer and his wife would wave goodbye, happy for his visit. If they didn't place an order that day, Phillip was still optimistic. He was confident a sale awaited him at the next farm. His sales were good because his ebullient personality made him friends and his friends gave him orders.

Damaris's mother, Georgia, was the opposite of her husband, shy and somewhat of a loner. After twenty years of marriage, they acted like they were still on their honeymoon. Always the romantic, Phillip predictably brought her a bouquet of flowers when he arrived home each Friday night and served her breakfast in bed on Saturday mornings. Before the tragedy soon to come, she had a shapely figure and was always well groomed and well dressed, especially on Fridays when she knew her husband was coming home from his travels. She had few friends, which was probably why Damaris, too, was somewhat of a recluse.

Georgia earned a two-year degree from Stephens, a private girls' school in Columbia, attending there because it was her mother's alma mater in the 1940s and she wanted Georgia to attend too. Her mother died of cancer when Georgia was in her twenties. Six weeks later, her father died of a heart attack at fifty-eight probably because he was a heavy smoker. Damaris was a baby and had no memory of her grandparents. They left Georgia a small inheritance; and with it, she bought Phillip a new van and made a down payment on a small house in Linn, where they now lived. The rest of the inheritance, Phillip carelessly and spontaneously frittered away. Her parents' untimely death left her feeling insecure, and she clung to her husband as she would a lifejacket. She truly believed, if something happened to him, she would not want to live. In a few months, those prophetic thoughts would come true.

Damaris's brother, Bryan, was born with musical gifts that weren't inherited. There were no musicians in his family history except for his dad who had a strong tenor voice. Bryan didn't read musical notes, but at five, he could play tunes on their small spinet piano in the dining room. His father bought him a used guitar at a pawnshop; and at six years old, without lessons or formal training, Bryan played chords and sang songs he heard on the radio. As a child, he sang with his school choirs in full voice and perfect pitch. In junior high and high school, he was chosen for leading male roles in school musicals and given solos in school choirs and ensembles, learning his parts quickly and with ease. He entered school talent shows, singing and playing songs he had written for both piano and guitar. He baffled his teachers. He could pick up any instrument and, in a couple of days, teach himself to play it with ease. His music teacher in junior high entered him in the *America's Got Talent* show as a pianist, singer, and guitar player; and he came in second place. He didn't care about coming in second or even first place. He played and sang for the mere joy of it.

In junior high, he decided to learn classical guitar; so night after night, he listened to Spanish guitarist Andre Segovia on YouTube and practiced until he could play very difficult guitar pieces by ear. A representative from New York's Juilliard School of Music heard about this gifted adolescent and visited Linn to hear him play both guitar and piano. The visit was written up in their local newspaper, the *Osage County Unterrified Democrat*, but Bryan wanted nothing to do with Juilliard. His musical talents and his vision were his own and inviolate. As he entered high school, he found four kindred musicians with his same musical vision, and they formed a band, the Rogues. They practiced daily in the garage of one of the band members. In the beginning, they played for school assemblies and parties, eventually enlarging their venues in the Jefferson City and Columbia areas. His careless good looks, deep dimples, and auburn-streaked brown hair made him popular with girls; but he was not the least interested in romance. Girls were a distraction that took him away from what he truly cared about—his music. Damaris's whole family had pride in his talents, having no idea where these gifts originated.

Damaris was a beauty but didn't know it. Basically a tomboy, she wore baggy T-shirts and faded blue jeans most of the time. She usually wore her blond hair in a ponytail, which kept it out of her eyes when she rode her bike around town. She rarely wore makeup. Even with her opaque-blue eyes, long eyelashes, and deep dimples like Bryan's, she didn't stand out in a crowd. She felt the girls in high school were too obsessed with their looks, so she underplayed her own good looks. The few friends she had were like her, tomboys and outsiders. She was shy around groups of people and often felt awkward in social situations. A loner by nature, she preferred to read books, write, or draw. She had some artistic talent and loved architecture and sketching buildings. Her architectural drawings won some school art-contest awards.

Her parents thought she was the prettiest girl in school, but Damaris believe they said that because they loved her and wanted her to feel better about herself but not because it was true. She accepted the fact she was a plain girl with limited assets. A thoughtless boy once teased her about how thick and full her lips were, so she constantly hid them with her hands. She was shy about her body and hated taking communal showers after high school gym class because, in her nakedness, she felt inferior to the other girls with their voluptuous curves and full breasts. She was on the thin side. She rode her bike miles each day, and food didn't interest her.

She finally accepted that she was ordinary and unattractive. She didn't give any signals to boys in her high school that would prompt them to ask her on a date. She didn't attend the prom because the only boy who asked her was the homeliest boy in school, and she apologetically turned him down. She would rather stay at home and read than spend an evening in an awkward social situation. She occasionally went the river or the lake with a few friends. Her best friend, Kris, the one she spent the most time with in high school, had moved to California after graduation. They exchanged letters and called one another on the phone and hoped one day they would see each other again. Damaris didn't really care about the lack of friends. Family times filled her weekends. Her brother's band was well known in central Missouri, and oftentimes she and her parents attended his concerts. Bryan always saved front row seats for them, and that made her feel special. She was Bryan Kelly's sister, and she didn't mind living in the shadows of his growing popularity. She was basically a happy young girl.

Times were good, but then came the tsunami.

2

Tragedy

Damaris's dad considered himself a good driver, but he was careless. He spent impulsively but not on keeping his car in good running order. They needed tires, but instead he drove his family to Branson for dinner and a show. He needed brakes, but instead they went to the Lake of the Ozarks and rented Jet Skis. They needed a new refrigerator, but he bought another guitar for Bryan. The clothes dryer wouldn't dry and needed servicing, but he bought the whole family tickets to a University of Missouri football game. As he drove, he loved singing passionate Irish ballads in full voice and often ran stop signs on country roads because of that.

On that fateful crisp fall day, he headed down Highway D for an appointment a few miles east of Sedalia, his windows down and his hair blowing freely in the breeze. Georgia warned him the brakes were not working as they should and reminded him he needed to get them fixed with his next commission check. Phillip, a great procrastinator, put off important responsibilities until the last minute. He didn't think much about safety because, in his mind, he was invincible. As he drove, he loudly sang "The Wearing o' the Green" while admiring the farms he passed, trying to remember if he needed to pay a call to that farmer whose name was on the mailbox. Today his appointment book sat open on the passenger seat, and he glanced at it to remind him of his appointment time and address of the farmer he would see in an hour or so. As usual, he was speeding.

A seventy-eight-year-old farmer was leaving the cornfield on a dirt road that emptied onto Highway D. It had been a long day, especially for a man his age. He had been up since dawn operating his tractor. His aging wife hadn't been feeling well, and he wanted to get home as quickly as possible to see if she needed anything. The tall corn impeded his view of the highway. He didn't expect the speeding brown van barreling toward him at a high rate of speed. As the old man pulled out to make a left turn, Phillip looked up from his planner, and directly in front of him was a faded-green Ford pickup. For an instant, he saw the farmer's eyes wide open with astonishment and surprise. Phillip slammed on the brakes. The last thing he heard was the sliding squeal of the tires against the black asphalt; and the last thing he felt was his car sliding sideways in the direction of the old man's truck stopped in the middle of the road, as if the farmer was in shock, incapable of pulling forward or backing up. Trying to miss the truck, Phillip yanked his steering wheel to the left, hoping to avoid the farmer. The crash was inevitable. Phillip's van spun in a complete circle and hit the old man head-on, smashing the entire driver's side of the old man's truck. The impact was so great the front of Phillip's van was crushed, throwing Phillip through the front windshield, nearly decapitating him with broken glass, killing both drivers instantly.

*****

Hours later, two sheriffs parked their vehicles in front of the small Benton Avenue house, knocked on Georgia's door, and asked to speak with her. She was preparing dinner for the family and went into the kitchen to turn off the burners, wondering why they were there. Damaris came out of her room, a bath towel wrapped around her head. She invited the officers inside. Both deputies looked uncomfortable as they waited to speak. Deputy Corey Gardner cleared his throat and reluctantly spoke first.

"Mrs. Kelly, Damaris, this is very difficult for me. We're bringing you some bad news. Your husband, your dad…"

Damaris and Georgia froze in their places. Georgia remembered the doctor's words when they told her of her parents' deaths.

"This morning, your husband was driving near Sedalia, and an elderly man pulled out in front of him."

"No!" cried Georgia. "I don't want to hear it. I can't hear it. Please, no!"

"Your husband and the old man were killed instantly. I am so sorry…"

Damaris ran to her mom and held her, not knowing what else to do. Not her dad! Full of life and love, only forty years old! Not Dad! This was a dream, not reality. Her mother stood as if paralyzed.

"Officer Gardner, are you sure it was my dad? Phillip Kelly, born in 1973 in Galway, Ireland?" said Damaris hopefully, trying to be strong for her mother.

"Yes. The Sedalia police checked his identification and registration. We know how hard this is for the both of you."

"Where is he now? Can we see him?" cried Damaris, unleashing her emotions.

Not her dad! His strong life force and enthusiasm promised a long life ahead!

"He and the other man were transported by ambulance to the coroner's office in Sedalia. You'll have to identify his body and sign papers, then make arrangements to bring him back to Linn. Here is the address and phone number."

"We don't have a car now. Bryan is at practice," said Georgia mechanically.

"Is this some kind of a joke, Deputy? He is in his forties with a family that loves him. Can this be a mistake? Could it be someone else? He can't be dead!" Damaris cried, sitting next to her mother on the sofa, gently placing her arm around her.

Deputy Gardner offered to take them to Sedalia tomorrow on his day off and gave them a card with his personal phone number if they needed him.

"This is the hardest part of my job, delivering messages like this. We have families too." He patted Damaris on the shoulder, trying to be as professional as possible.

There was a long uncomfortable silence.

"Mom, Dad is gone. He's not coming back." The words choked in her throat like large, painful rocks, as she held back her own tears, still in a state of shock.

"That's a lie!" she wailed.

A neighbor came out of his house and stood on his front porch, wondering about the crying and wailing and the parked sheriff's car in front of the Kelly's house.

"Mom, what are we going to do? How do we get him back here?"

"How do I know? Why are you asking me? Call Bryan on his phone. He'll know what to do," Georgia ordered. "Tell him to get home as soon as possible. I'm going into our bedroom now. When your dad gets home, tell him dinner will be ready soon. He said he would be here at six o'clock." She stumbled into her bedroom, murmuring, "I can't walk into a cold building and see him there. He isn't dead. He's coming home for dinner."

Damaris and the deputies looked at one another, realizing Georgia couldn't face the fact her husband was dead.

Georgia slowly stumbled into her bedroom numbly closing the door behind her as if she was sleepwalking. They heard her sobbing into her pillow. Deputy Gardner wanted to put his arms around both the women but knew it wouldn't be appropriate. They left the house with heavy hearts burdened with the Kelly family's pain.

Damaris sat on the old sofa after the deputies left, trying to gain the courage to call her brother at his practice. Finally, she picked up the phone which felt like a piece of lead in her hand. Bryan said he was too busy to talk.

"Bryan, it's important."

"Damaris, we have a concert in a week. Can't this wait?" he asked, irritated. "I'll come home later tonight, and we can talk then."

"Mom and I need you now. It's too terrible. I can't tell you on the phone, and this can't wait."

"It can't be that terrible, can it?"

"It is, Bryan. It is." She couldn't hold back her tears any longer.

*****

As is usual for small Midwest towns, Linn had compassion for the Kellys. Fundraisers and collection plates in the churches paid for Phillip's body to be transported back to Linn and for his cremation. Phillip's small insurance policy covered the costs for his cremated remains to be buried in the Linn Cemetery and for a small granite headstone. The Kellys weren't churchgoers and had few friends in Linn. The funeral parlor director said a few words at the gravesite. Residents brought them meals for a couple of weeks. Car insurance money bought them a new van. After his death, Phillip's social security was only $1,100 a month, and their house payment was $700.

Damaris knew she had to bring in money so began working a part-time job at BJ's Lounge and Grill, a popular place for eating, drinking, and socializing. She was too young to serve alcohol; but she could serve food, bus tables, help wash dishes, or work as a hostess. BJ's knew her financial predicament and gave her a twenty-three-hour workweek during the school year. She also earned money from housecleaning and babysitting jobs. Most of her money went for household expenses.

Bryan didn't earn much money with his band yet but pitched in when he could. He needed to use the van, and BJ's was close enough to home. Damaris could ride her bike to work or hitch rides. When people drove by her on Main Street as she rode her bike, their hearts were heavy for Bryan and Damaris who were only teenagers. She opened up her own checking account. Only she and Bryan had access. She hid her mother's checkbook, paid the bills, and worried about her mother who started drinking too much and losing interest in cooking, shopping, cleaning, or taking care of herself. Thankfully BJ's customers knew that Damaris helped support her family while finishing high school and left generous tips for her even when she was washing dishes in the kitchen. Little did they know those tips meant keeping their home from foreclosure, the utilities on, and food on the table.

Her mother started staying out all night, carousing with the losers in town. She caused scenes in local restaurants and businesses when she was drunk. It seemed she had a complete nervous breakdown. Sometimes she wouldn't come home for days at a time, and often Damaris didn't know whether her mom was alive or dead. Ashamed and embarrassed, Damaris became a recluse apart from her school attendance and jobs. Her mother had a seventy-five-year-old great-aunt Janie in Texas, a spinster who lived on social security and would have helped them financially if she could. She sent small checks occasionally, and Damaris saved them for paying past-due bills. Damaris and Bryan had to buy their clothes and shoes in thrift stores, which was fine with Bryan but embarrassing to Damaris. If someone in town saw her buying used clothing or shoes in the thrift store, she would hide in a dressing room until they left.

After graduation, Damaris received a small academic scholarship from the State Technical College of Missouri, on the eastern outskirts of Linn, one of the best trade schools in the nation which had put Linn on the map. After high school graduation, she still had to work at BJ's but found time in the mornings to take two courses in architecture and interior design. Often she hitchhiked to her classes or asked for rides from fellow classmates. When Deputy Gardner was out on patrol, he would often see her hitchhiking to the college on Highway 50 and offer her a ride. He warned her about the dangers of hitchhiking.

She would stare out her window and sadly whisper, "I have no choice."

His heart ached when he heard her say those words. Luckily she loved her architecture and design classes and dreamed that, one day, she could design her own house and decorate it with style. She didn't know it then, but that day soon was approaching. Right now, all she had were her dreams, which sadly were fading by the day.

The last several years, Bryan's music reputation grew; and with the help of a Jefferson City recording studio, his band released a popular alternative-rock song. Surprisingly it hit a spot on the Top 100 Billboard chart, which earned the band a small sum of money. His band was disciplined and harmonious, unusual for a band with such young musicians. Bryan had a definite musical vision and was a good leader.

They booked touring gigs in small venues and arenas, indoors now because it was winter. Bryan knew the time was coming to hire a manager. The business aspect sapped his creative energy. He knew he needed someone to manage the details. Damaris wished she could help him. Their father's death didn't appear to bother him much. He had his music.

As much as she loved her brother, Damaris wanted her own life, tired of the responsibility laid on her at such a young age. At the end of her day after attending classes, working at BJ's, and taking care of bills and housework, she threw herself on the bed in exhaustion. She missed her dad. She ached for his presence. She was still angry with him because he had been careless and irresponsible. She had loved him, but something had to change. Her mother's life was out of control. Damaris was losing hope and felt like a very old woman. She had a hard time concentrating in school and at her job. Sometimes she felt like the living dead, moving mindlessly through each day, one foot in front of the other just to get to the next destination. She desperately wanted to fly to California and live with her friend Kris in her apartment near Newport Beach. She was tired of looking after her mother, tired of responsibility, and tired of the heavy load thrust upon her as a teenager.

3

Dave

Linn had only one main street extending a mile with no streetlights or stop signs. Sidewalks were laid intermittently. Some were good. Some were cracked and uneven. Some were just dirt. Damaris borrowed Bryan's van when necessary for grocery shopping at Thriftway, east of town, because it was too far for a bike ride and there were no sidewalks leading to the grocery store. Today she passed by the small white Grace Community Church on Main Street. The rose bushes lining the church sidewalk bloomed fragrantly, and she smiled as she stopped her bike, listening to the white-haired elderly gentleman singing a joyful song in a strong bass voice as he pruned the rose bushes.

"Hi!" she interrupted. "Your roses are beautiful and smell so good. You have a wonderful voice!"

He laid down his clippers on the front steps and walked down the sidewalk toward her.

"Thanks, young lady! They really are prolific this year. I can barely hold back their growth." He smiled, deepening the laugh lines around his eyes. "We haven't met. I'm Dave Bergman, the pastor. Everyone calls me Pastor Dave. And you're?"

"Damaris, Damaris Kelly. I live on Benton Avenue, around the corner and down the hill, with my mom and brother."

"I've heard your name around town."

Changing the subject, she said, "I bike by here a lot. I thought you were the gardener, not the pastor!"

"Well, I am kind of a gardener. I tend the people in my congregation like I tend my roses."

"You sure have a cute little church. It just needs a steeple!" she said as she smiled.

He laughed. "We have started a fund to buy a steeple with an electronic bell that will play hymns several times a day and before church on Sundays. Do you attend a church, Damaris?"

"No. We were never churchgoers. In fact, I have never been in a church."

"Really? Well, how about a tour of ours?"

She hesitated for a moment, then said she had a few minutes to check it out. Pastor Dave put her bike in the foyer while he showed her around.

Out of nowhere, she said to the pastor, "You have probably heard my name before because my brother is a well-known musician around here, Bryan

Kelly. Have you heard of him? Also our dad was killed in a car accident three years ago, and I think your church was one that brought food to our house. That was nice."

"Oh, yes, I remember." Quietly he put his hand gently on her shoulder and said in a gentle voice, "I'm so sorry, Damaris."

"I'm sorry too," she said, trying not to cry.

He led her to a pew where they sat together. He didn't say much, but she felt she could trust him with the churning feelings and emotions she had constantly kept in check since her father's death. She felt absolute love from this gentle pastor and finally began to cry without restraint. She told him about her life before her father's death and how her mother started drinking heavily afterward. She told him about their money situation and how beaten down she felt. She unloaded every burden onto Dave's shoulders, and he listened sympathetically.

After a while, he gently handed her some Kleenex and asked her if she was ready to see the church.

In the sanctuary above the altar with its simple gold cross set on a white linen tablecloth, a huge stained-glass window, probably fifteen feet high and ten feet across, allowed sunlight to flood the church with rainbow colors. The church emanated peace with its smell of incense and roses. She had only seen the inside of churches in movies or in her architecture class in college when they studied the great cathedrals of Europe. The beauty, artistry, and intricacy of this stained glass touched her sensitive spirit.

Pastor Dave proceeded to tell her its history. "One of our people inherited a large sum of money. He thought our church needed something spectacular inside to spruce up our rather-plain interior. He researched stained-glass artists and commissioned this man to create a large image of Jesus in white robes standing in a sheep pen surrounded by white lambs."

Outside the gate of the pen stood a little black lamb, looking up expectantly to Jesus as He reached out His hand, inviting the black sheep to walk through the gate into the pen. Damaris thought how happy the black sheep would feel if he walked into the pen, especially if Jesus was like Pastor Dave who made her feel safe, comforted, and accepted.

Dave showed her the baptismal fount behind the altar. By pressing a button, the cover rolled back. At either end of the pool were some steps. Dave explained what baptism meant—a giving of your life to Christ, accepting His forgiveness and love, and rising to new life. A new life sounded wonderful to Damaris. She thought how great it would be just to jump into the pool and come out a whole new person with a brand-new life with no sorrow, worries, or fears. He took her into the fellowship hall where people met after church services. The church fed lunch to fifty needy people a day, five days a week, supplied and staffed by church members who also took time for conversation and prayer with those who needed fellowship. Several members were cleaning up and gave Damaris a big smile as Pastor Dave introduced Damaris to them. The adjacent rooms were used for Sunday school and Bible study. One huge closet was for food distribution to the needy.

This was foreign territory to Damaris. She appreciated the generosity and charity of the congregation who provided these meals. She was glad to know about the meals. There were times when she only had bread and peanut butter in the refrigerator. She wondered why her mom and dad never took her to a nice place like this. Why weren't they interested in going to church or even talking about God to her and Bryan?

Pastor Dave opened the back door and pointed to a little house behind the church with a rose-bush-lined sidewalk like the one in front. He told her the story of his house.

"You see, Damaris, ten years ago, my wife of nearly thirty years died of cancer. My deep depression and lack of will to live ran deep. I lived a couple miles from here, and my congregation worried about me feeling isolated, so with generous donations and their own hands, they built me this little house with a bedroom, bathroom, a small living room, a kitchen, and a one-car garage. It saved me from loneliness. Now, when I work out in front, I connect with the people in Linn. They often park in the side parking lot and start a conversation like I did with you as you rode by. You would be surprised how many people I have met just because I was out here pruning. Oftentimes they begin attending this church where they are loved and nurtured like my roses. I guess you might say I am a gardener of people. I pull out the weeds of their lives, enrich the dirt with the fertilizer of God's Word, and when the dead branches are cut away, what emerges is their true beauty, the way God intended them to be in this world, a fragrant aroma and a channel for His love."

Damaris loved that story told from his loving and sincere heart. She didn't quite understand what he meant, but she thought about his words.

"I should be going, Pastor Dave."

He brought her bike to her.

"Thanks for showing me the church and for talking with me. I can't say I've never been in a church now!" She laughed.

Pastor Dave appreciated how beautiful she looked when she forgot her troubles.

As she sat on her bike, Dave touched her arm. "Damaris, I know about your family and your dad's tragic death. I know about your mom and her struggles with alcohol. It's a small town. When your father died, our church reached out to you on many different levels with money, food, cards, and phone calls, which were often unanswered. We understood. Sadly the Lord has allowed these heavy burdens to fall on your shoulders. Here is my card and phone number.

You know where I live. I am always here and never too busy to listen."

She took his card and read the words "Come unto me you are weary and heavy-laden and I will give you rest."

"That's from the Bible?" she asked.

She thought to herself that she was weary and heavy-laden and needed rest. She didn't know anything about God, but He sounded like a good friend to have. If He was like Dave, He must be easy to talk to.

"Of course! It's the fertilizer I use to enhance the beauty and aroma of each person God puts in my life." He looked directly into her eyes.

She put the card in her pocket. "Thanks for everything. I feel better," she said with a melancholy smile.

She rode off, looking back with a big wave, her long blond ponytail flying in the wind.

The pastor attacked the weeds vigorously, thinking about Damaris, the loss of her dad, and her mom's alcoholism. He and his church would pray for her and reach out to her. He truly believed she would one day recognize a new purpose for her life. He could tell she was ready for change. This was a good start. He asked the Holy Spirit to lead her into faith. The sweet-smelling roses assured him his prayers would be lifted heavenward by the unseen hand of God who would be with this beautiful, fragile young woman carrying such a heavy load on her young shoulders.

4

Change

Linn's nickname was the "Longest Little Town in America." All the businesses were on one stretch of road, Main Street, which was also Highway 50, with some typical businesses found in small towns across America—a Casey's gas station and mini-mart, a flea market, a tire store, a Dollar Tree, Subway, a newspaper office, an attorney's office, a community pool right in the middle of town, one bar (BJ's), a pizza parlor, a beauty salon, community health center, a city office building (smaller than most residences), the tiny police department building also housing the license bureau and the water department, an attractive four-pillared courthouse built in 1923, the Legends Bank (since 1913), the Legends Park with its new white gazebo surrounded by grass, and the Ten Commandments etched on a huge stone slab in a garden area next to the gazebo.

The west end of town had a car dealership, McDonald's, and the Linn Cemetery. At the east end of Main was the Thriftway grocery store; an elementary school, middle school, and high school complex; and Linn's claim to fame, Missouri State Technical College, with its modern architecture and nicely landscaped campus. Another claim to fame was the Where the Pigs Fly museum, gift shop, and farm. The Stone Hearth Inn was the only hotel in town and did a brisk business because of the trade school's families and frequent weddings in the Linn area. Most of the dwellings on east Main (also designated Highway 50) were plainly built apartments where many trade school students lived during the school year. Caspers 66 was a local restaurant and gas station, a hangout for the men's coffee club which met at the same table by the coffee machine each morning for fellowship, friendship, breakfast, and local gossip.

Across from BJ's Lounge and Grill, in the central part of town, was the Osage County sheriff's department and jail. There hadn't been a homicide in Linn for twenty years; but law enforcement kept busy shutting down meth labs in the forest, issuing traffic tickets, arresting petty burglars, and handling domestic violence cases. Many people in Linn worked in Jefferson City, the capital about twenty miles from Linn. Highway 50, the highway name for Main Street, was the main thoroughfare to St. Louis and heavily traveled but without a single stoplight or stop sign the entire length of the city.

German immigrants, practicing Catholics, settled Osage County at the turn of the century; and it was considered Catholic country. St. George's Church and its school and huge brick rectory took up almost an entire block along Main. There were several Protestant churches, all vital assets to this small, compact town. The Osage, Gasconade, and Missouri rivers close by provided outdoor recreation, along with the nearby Lake of the Ozarks, popular places for Missouri's favorite pastime—fishin' (the correct Missouri pronunciation). Vast acres of forest and rich farmland surrounded Linn. Corn, soybeans, peas, and beans were the main agricultural products; and cattle, hogs, poultry, and sheep provided a good living for the farmers in the area. The strong Missouri work ethic spoke loudly here in central Missouri in this little piece of America, tucked away in a forested area between the two great cities of St. Louis, about 100 miles away, and Kansas City, 170 miles. Linn was a small city quietly and happily existing in relative obscurity with few changes over time.

As she rode her bike to Casey's on this December day in 2014, she felt good after talking to Pastor Dave, but she was tired of Linn. She wanted to travel and see the world. The farthest she had been from home was Branson, about three hours away. She wanted to get away from her mother's drinking, but love for her mom and brother kept her in Linn. She needed milk today and didn't really want to wait; but as she did, she listened to the excited conversations in the line of people about one of the largest lottery jackpots in lottery history, the drawing tonight for $960 million! For weeks, millions of Americans watched the jackpot grow larger as no one claimed to have the winning ticket. People enthusiastically bought handfuls of tickets, and an unbridled lottery frenzy hit the nation.

The line in Casey's wrapped around the inside of the store. Damaris waited in line and, at one moment, almost decided she would buy the milk later when the line died down. The clerk Loretta frantically kept up with regular sales as well as the lottery tickets, looking frazzled at the long line in front of her. She finally called her manager for help, too busy for gossip today. Reggie Hawkins, Damaris's postman, stood in line in front of her. He'd known the Kellys for years. After Mr. Kelly's tragic death, Reggie saw their daily incoming mail—late payment warnings, bank threats for past-due mortgage payments, and overdue utility bills. He often saw Damaris's mother dropped off by scruffy-looking meth heads like Charlie Hall, who made people call him Chief Red Cloud for some strange reason. He wasn't an Indian, and no Indians lived near Linn. Many mornings, Reggie saw Damaris open the front door for her mother with a combination of worry and anger on her troubled face.

He asked Damaris how she'd been doing; and Damaris gave the stock answer, "Okay, I guess," her eyes showing him she really wasn't doing well at all. She was embarrassed to tell anyone about her unhappy life. Reggie often thought she looked like a scared fawn standing in the middle of a highway, fearful and uncertain of danger. Reggie knew her family's predicament. He didn't have to ask how her mom was doing. The town's gossip ensured everyone knew.

"Damaris, could you do me a favor? I have two ten-dollar bills. I'm going to buy five tickets with one of them, and it would make me happy if you would take the other one and buy five tickets for yourself. Would you give me that blessing?" he asked sincerely.

"That's nice of you, Reggie, but—"

"No buts, young lady. Every day, I deliver your mail, and when you see me, you usually give me a nice smile. I haven't seen that smile too much lately, and I miss it. This is just a thanks for those smiles, okay? If you win the $960 million, you can buy me a brand-new Jeep, how's that?" He pressed the ten-dollar bill into her hand.

She reluctantly took the money, bought five tickets, and paid for her milk, which thankfully left her $6 for lunch tomorrow at college. She heard a customer say the odds of winning this jackpot were 1 in 390 million. She knew for certain she didn't have a chance, but she wanted to make Reggie happy. She folded the tickets and pushed them deep into her pocket. Weeks later, she would remember that day—the day she unknowingly walked out of Casey's with a winning $950 million lottery ticket in her back jeans pocket.

5

The Win

After putting the milk away in the refrigerator, she pulled off her jeans and threw them on top of her clothes hamper. Her mom was sleeping it off in her bedroom; and Bryan, as usual, was at practice. She sat down in front of her aging computer and studied for her architecture test the next day, forgetting about the ticket. She felt confident in the subject matter and knew she would ace the test.

At school, everyone talked about the lottery. Someone in Missouri had won the whole thing—$950 million! The winner hadn't come forth. The radio encouraged everyone to look at their ticket numbers carefully. If theirs was the winner, they advised the person to sign the ticket immediately, store it in a safe place, and make an appointment with the lottery commission to make the claim. Her mind was on how she was going to make the house payment this month, and she ignored all the lottery conversations buzzing around her.

When Damaris finished school the next day, she came home and made a sandwich, the radio once again announcing the winning numbers and no winner. Damaris wrote the numbers on a napkin, laid it on the kitchen table, and finished her food. On a whim, she decided she'd check her jeans pocket in the bedroom. Her pants weren't there! The dirty clothes were in the laundry basket but not her jeans! She looked in the washing machine. There were a load of wet clothes inside, and she pulled the wet pieces out one by one and threw them in the dryer. No jeans.

She went back into her mother's bedroom. "Mom, please wake up. This is important!"

"Lower your voice, Damaris. I have a terrible headache." Moaning loudly, smelling of whiskey and cigarette smoke, she lifted the pillow from her head, her hair a tangled rats' nest and her eyes smeared with mascara and eye shadow.

"Where are my jeans, Mom?" she asked in a disgusted voice.

Her mom threw the pillow back over her head.

"Mom, I'm serious." She yanked the pillow off her mom's face. "You came home this morning wearing these gray, foul-smelling sweatpants. Did you wear my jeans and then leave them somewhere? I mean it. Where are they?"

"I can't remember, honey. I was at BJ's for a while."

"Who were you with, Mom?"

"I was with a bunch of people. There was a band, and we were all dancing—"

"You didn't come home until this morning, Mom. Who did you go home with? What disgusting person brought you home this time? Whose foul-smelling sweatpants are these?" She picked them up with two fingers and waved them in her mother's face. She'd had it with her mother and was losing patience.

"You don't have to be so mean, Damaris," her mother said, angrily pushing the greasy sweatpants away from her.

"I wish Dad could see you now. He would be ashamed. You were beautiful then, Mom. Now you are an embarrassing alcoholic. You aren't even a mother anymore. Bryan and I are both fed up. I'm mean to you because you're making my life miserable. Now who did you go home with? Think!"

"Well, I think I was with Charlie. I did borrow your jeans. I didn't have anything else to wear, and they are so cute. Then I vomited. He took my pants, and he gave me his to wear home. I have a terrible headache now. Can you leave me alone, please?"

"Charlie who, Mom?" she said, her temper increasing.

"I think his last name is Hall."

"Where does he live?"

"Damaris, can you get me some aspirin and heat me up some coffee? I feel terrible."

Damaris left the bedroom and slammed the door as hard as she could. She jumped on her bike and rode to BJ's. She was breathing heavily from the bike ride but also because of her agitated spirit. Her hair was a mess. She asked Jonelle the bartender if she knew where Charlie Hall lived.

Jonelle came out from behind the bar and— with her loud, booming voice—yelled into the bar and the back restaurant, "Hey, people! Anyone here know where Charlie Hall lives?"

Sitting at one of the tables was Deputy Gardner, intently watching and listening to Damaris as he ate a sandwich in the bar. He wiped his mouth with a napkin and approached her.

"Hi, Damaris. I know where Charlie lives. Are you having a problem?'

"Hi, Deputy. I just need an address so I can get the jeans my mom thinks she left at his place. There's an important paper in one of the pockets. She doesn't remember his address or phone number. I just want my jeans back!"

"Would you like me to drive you over there? It's just down the street."

He was really hoping she would say yes. He had been attracted to her for some time. He was twenty-four now, just out of the police academy, and had been working up enough courage and looking for the right time to ask her on a date since the day he brought the bad news about her father.

"I rode my bike over here."

"Tell you what. You ride home. Park your bike. I'll follow you, then I'll take you in my car over to Charlie's, okay?"

On the way, he told her about Charlie. "He usually wears an old fishing hat with crow feathers sticking out of the top, a tie-dyed T-shirt, ripped jeans, dirty tennis shoes, and is missing two front teeth, probably from drug use. He wants people to call him Chief Red Cloud. Where he got that name, no one knows. He's a meth head and an alcoholic and has been in and out of jail for cooking and possession of meth. Not the greatest person for your mom to hang around with!"

"That's great," said Damaris as she looked out the window, embarrassed that her mother would be so desperate to hang out with someone like this.

This was a small town, and her mother was ruining hers and Bryan's reputations. Georgia was a laughingstock. The residents felt compassion for Damaris and Bryan, but people whispered about Georgia behind closed doors.

"Deputy Gardner, these jeans are a big deal to me because I bought them new with $20 I couldn't afford."

He could see the tears filling her eyes as she tried to hold them back. "Damaris, you don't have to apologize."

He could have taken her in his arms right then and there—so pretty, sweet, and vulnerable.

"Here's Charlie's place." He parked in front of a run-down apartment complex just off Main. Under the front window were two plastic trash cans overflowing with empty liquor bottles, McDonald's paper bags filled with garbage, four bald tires leaning against the wall, and a rusty metal chair with a dirty beach towel wadded up on the seat.

"Let's walk up there together and get this over with."

She was glad he was next to her. He led with his hand on her elbow and knocked on the door. No answer. He knocked again more forcefully.

"Tell him you're here, Damaris."

"Charlie, this is Damaris, Georgia Kelly's daughter. I came to get the jeans she left here last night!" she shouted.

Crazy Charlie opened the door a crack, saw the deputy, and slammed the door. "Go away! Both of you!"

"Charlie! Just get the jeans and hand them to Damaris."

"My name ain't Charlie, haven't ya heard? I changed it to Chief Red Cloud. I don't know what jeans you're talkin' about."

Damaris wondered if he found the tickets.

"Okay, Chief, just hand over the jeans, and we'll be on our way. The jeans belong to Georgia Kelly. You're on probation, and right now, you have stolen property in there," Corey warned.

"I ain't stole nothin'. That woman wore them jeans here, puked on 'em, and I let her wear a nice pair of my sweatpants home. That's all. And why juh bring a cop with you?"

"Deputy Gardner wouldn't let me come by myself, that's why," she shouted through the door. "Please, Charlie, just give me the jeans!"

"No more talk, Chief. Just hand her the jeans. You've got two minutes to get them, or I'll go get a search warrant, and no telling what I'll find in your place that just might violate your parole."

"I don't have them," he lied.

"Charlie, no more games. You know you do. Now I'm going to walk to my patrol car and call for backup, and if we're forced to kick the door in, we will."

"I dare you. What if I have a gun? The only good cop is a dead cop, and I'd be happy to make that happen."

"Charlie, you know having a gun will land you back in jail. Do you have a gun in there? If so, I need you to give me the gun and the jeans."

"Okay, okay, here." He opened the door and threw the vomit-covered jeans at the deputy and slammed the door.

Damaris yelled at him outside the door to leave her mom alone.

"Hey, your mom's a grown woman. She can make her own decisions. Girl, your mom is the biggest drunk in town, night or day, no matter who she's with!"

"That's enough, Charlie. Let's go, Damaris."

Charlie yelled, "My name's Chief Red Cloud, and don't you forget it! And don't forget I hate you cops!"

Later on, Corey would go back to Charlie's with a search warrant and get the gun, which would no doubt land Charlie back in jail.

As they drove back to her house, Damaris started sobbing uncontrollably in the front seat of the police car. He barely restrained himself from taking her in his arms but knew that professionally it was a bad idea.

"Damaris, Charlie's a jerk. I know your mom is a challenge, but you're doing great. So is Bryan. I know this is hard for you now. Maybe your mom will wake up soon and snap out of this. I could look around for a rehab for her if you'd like, if she would be willing to go."

"That's nice of you, Corey, but those cost a lot of money, and I hear the free county programs aren't that good. I'm not doing good. I feel lost and scared. I don't have anyone to turn to except my brother, and he's so busy all the time. Corey, is my life going to change? I look ahead, and it seems like I'm traveling down a long dark tunnel with no light at the other end. I wonder if this will be the rest of my life, and if it is, it doesn't seem like life is worth living anymore." She continued to cry.

Corey hated seeing her like this. If only he wasn't in uniform right now. He would take her in his arms and tell her it wouldn't be like this forever; but all he could say now was "Look, Damaris, just call me if you need help in any way. I'm a good listener. Here's my card with my personal phone number."

Taking the card, she smiled at him half-heartedly, thinking how she desperately need help these last three years and wondering how many more years this nightmare would last. She was losing hope. She dejectedly walked into her house, the jeans over her arm. Corey drove away feeling helpless. He wanted to fix her situation more than anything. He wanted her to feel safe and loved. If she gave him a chance, he could provide that safety and love for her.

When she walked into the house, her mom was watching a game show on television, wrapped in a warm blanket, holding some kind of alcoholic beverage. She asked if Damaris got her jeans from Charlie. Damaris ignored her. She was hungry but knew there wouldn't be dinner unless she made it herself. She took the jeans into her bedroom and hoped the tickets were in the back pocket. She would be sick if Charlie got those tickets and then won! She put her hand in one back pocket—no tickets. She put her hand in the other. They were there! She took the tickets into the kitchen, unfolded them, spread them out next to the napkin on which she had written the winning numbers, and began comparing the numbers.

No match on the first four tickets. But then on the fifth, one by one, each number was a match; and then the final sixth number, a match too. She compared them again, then a third time. It couldn't be! She couldn't believe it. Did she just win the $950 million lottery jackpot? She checked her ticket over and over again. She couldn't have the ticket! Her mother had gone to bed. Bryan was at band practice. Should she tell anyone? She jumped up and down in the kitchen, waving her ticket around in the air. She quickly got on her computer and read all the advice on what to do and how to get the money. She signed the ticket, made copies, ran into the bedroom, put the ticket in a decorative metal box, and hid it under some clothes on the top shelf of her closet where she knew her mother wouldn't look. She kept pinching herself, thinking she might be dreaming. She was going to have money! So was Bryan, and she could send her mom to a good rehab if she could get her to go! She didn't want to tell anyone just yet but felt like telling everyone! She danced around the living room to one of her dad's Irish music CDs.

"Oh, Dad! You don't have to worry anymore," she sang out loud in joyous abandon. "We're going to be okay!"

She could barely sleep that night, thinking how her life was going to change. She made lists in her head of all the things she could finally buy and all the fun she could have.

The next morning, she made an appointment with the lottery commission in Jefferson City two days from now. She would ask Pastor Dave if he could drive her over there. She'd tell Bryan tonight. When Reggie delivered the mail, she gave him a big hug and told him she was going to give him a nice thank-you gift soon. He wondered what she meant. Maybe bake him some cookies?

She called Pastor Dave and asked if she could come over and talk to him right away. She rode her bike quickly to his church. Breathlessly she knocked on his door, and he answered, concern on his face.

"Come in and sit down. Now tell me what's going on. Are you okay?"

"I am very okay. You are not going to believe this. Something truly wonderful has happened! You know the $950 million jackpot that got everyone buying tickets? Well, I checked my ticket last night. I had all the numbers. I won. The whole thing!" She paced around his living room, laughing and excited.

"The whole amount?"

"Yes! And guess what? I am going to buy the most beautiful steeple with the most beautiful bells in the world for this church!"

"What a miracle, child!"

"Day after tomorrow, I have an appointment with the lottery headquarters in Jefferson City. Could you drive me over there? Please? I have to fill out papers and forms, and I'd like you there beside me, okay?"

"I would be honored. Have you told your mother and brother yet?"

"I haven't told anyone but you, Pastor Dave. I'm going to break the news to Bryan tonight. Can you believe this? I'm rich! No more waitressing. No more looking at bills I can't pay. I can help Bryan with his music career. I can buy new clothes and get a nice car! I am so excited, Pastor Dave!"

"Well, there will be changes in your life, and I'll be nearby to help you make wise decisions, if that's all right with you."

She wasn't really listening, but he wasn't going to back down from giving her good advice.

He watched her jump onto her old Schwinn bike heading home. She couldn't wait to tell Bryan tonight when he came home from practice. Pastor Dave watched her ride away and knew this money could be a blessing or a curse for this naive and inexperienced young woman. He prayed she would consider his thoughts.

6

Surprise!

She spent all her money at Thriftway on two steaks, stuffed potatoes, garlic bread, and a bottle of sparkling cider since she was too young to buy champagne. She made sure Bryan would be home in time for dinner. As usual, her mother was out carousing around town. After dinner, they sat on the sofa listening to quiet music. Bryan knew she had something to tell him by her restless legs and hands and excited smile. She was like a shaken bottle of champagne ready to explode.

"Damaris, I have practice tonight. What's up?"

She could hardly contain her joy. She held both his hands and took a deep breath. "Do you remember a couple of days ago when everyone was buying tickets for the $960 million jackpot? Well, I bought five tickets at Casey's, thanks to Reggie our postman, and…and…and my ticket had the numbers, all six of them. I won that jackpot! The whole thing!"

"You won the jackpot? Are you kidding? Unbelievable, Damaris! You're kidding me!"

"No, Bryan. We are wealthy beyond belief. Pastor Dave said, after taxes, I'll get a check for about $422 million! Tomorrow I'm driving with him to Jefferson City to the lottery commission to validate my tickets and fill out some papers. It will take fourteen to twenty-one days before the money is deposited. We're rich, Bryan. We will never have to worry about making the mortgage payment again!"

Bryan jumped up, and they danced an Irish jig all over the living room to the Irish music in the CD player. The Kellys were on their way to freedom!

They sat on the sofa with a pad of lined paper and listed all the things they could buy when the money was deposited. They laughed together. Of course, Bryan's list was all things musical. He had notebooks filled with ideas for a state-of-the art recording studio. He had always wanted a Steinway piano and now he could buy one! The band could now buy a large Greyhound-sized tour bus that would sleep all of them and a good large used truck for hauling their music equipment to their various venues. He drove a dented Dodge around town now, bought with their father's car insurance money. He wanted a nice ten-passenger van for traveling with the Rogues with graphics on both front doors. He had researched recording studio equipment, not knowing his wish list would ever be realized.

He asked Damaris what his financial limit would be on a state-of-the-art recording studio; and she gleefully cried, "The sky's the limit, Bryan!"

He said a good recording studio could cost up to two million; and Damaris laughed and joyously offered, "Go for it, brother!"

This was unbelievable! His mind raced ahead to the future of his band and his music.

They decided their mother would not have access to the money. They would make sure of that. They worried she might do something irresponsible. Bryan wanted to know if he could tell the band about her win tonight. A recording studio, here in Linn! They would be as excited as Bryan! Bryan asked her what her dreams were for this money. She told him she always wanted a brand-new Corvette, a large new home, and to see the world outside of Linn. Pastor Dave had reminded her to think of her community first, so she told Bryan all the nice things she planned to do for Linn. He added some of his ideas too. This was their town, the town where they grew up. They both wanted to give back. They didn't know at the time how Linn would change because of Damaris's lottery win.

*****

The lottery headquarters looked like any government building—stark, with minimal landscaping, and a keypad on the entry door for entrance into the facility. Inside, metal chairs and countertops and lottery posters covered every wall. A service representative met them at the door and brought them into an office where she filled out the Missouri lottery claim form, the IRS W-9, and accounting paperwork. The employees applauded this attractive girl with her T-shirt and worn jeans. The officer asked her how many tickets she had bought and where she purchased them and if she would be willing to participate in a news conference at Casey's where she bought the ticket. The media would ask questions, and the conference would only last fifteen minutes or so. Eventually the world would learn about her win, but she could control the parameters by holding this press conference a few days after the ticket was validated. It would take fourteen to twenty-one days for the funds to be deposited into her bank account. She decided, with Dave's advice, to take the lump sum after federal and state taxes were deducted, as well as lottery commission fees. That amount would be around $422 million. They advised her to change her phone number and give it only to close friends and family. Damaris knew she could trust Bryan, but she would not give her mother her new phone number, not yet. Who knows who she would give it to after a few drinks? They suggested a financial adviser and a lawyer. Damaris would let Pastor Dave help her with that. As they left the building, the office workers applauded her again. Dave smiled, knowing full well the applause belonged to God.

On the way home, the pastor talked to her seriously. "Settle down, Damaris, and listen to me. I know you're excited, but what I am going to tell you will affect the rest of your life."

"Please don't get serious now, Pastor Dave."

"I will get serious, young lady, and you will listen. You have been given a tremendous blessing from God this week."

"Whoever it came from, I am going to be able to help my family and buy things I always wanted and go places I've always wanted to go. I don't know whether it's luck or God, but it sure feels good!" She giggled.

"Damaris, do you know there are more verses about money in the Bible than on prayer or even on heaven and hell? Some of the richest people in the world are the most miserable. There is no guarantee that money will last. It's His money, and He's going to let you manage it. He is entrusting this financial windfall to you, and He wants you to use it as He directs. Listen for His voice, Damaris. He will reward you with more blessings than money because of your obedience. This amount of money can be dangerous if it's not under His control and in His will and purpose. There will be great temptations. Trust only the people you know and respect. If you use this money wisely, great blessings will overflow into your life. Do you understand?"

"I understand that $422 million is a pretty big blessing, Pastor."

"Damaris, will you promise me you will consult with me on some of your big decisions?"

She stopped giggling, patted his hand, and assured him she would.

7

A Spending Frenzy

Damaris held a press conference in front of Casey's. Television, radio, and print media were there snapping pictures. Many people in Linn attended. She held up a four-foot-long cardboard facsimile check that said $960 million. The people of Linn were astounded at Damaris's good luck. Casey's was happy because they would get a huge check for selling the winning ticket and also it was great advertising for them. She was treated like a celebrity, which was embarrassing. Reporters overwhelmed her with questions.

"What are you going to with the money, Damaris?"

"Will you build a home in Linn?"

"Will you travel?"

On and on, they pummeled her with questions. She was glad Pastor Dave and Bryan were there because, a few times, she felt like fainting. She was grateful when it was over.

The day the $422,000,000 was deposited in her Legends Bank account, Legends Bank held a celebration with flowers and champagne as Damaris walked into the bank to look at the new balance in her checking account. Before the win, she had $122 in her account, and the house payment was due in a few weeks. Now she had $422,000,122. Once, Damaris worried how she would make the house payment. Now it didn't matter. She could buy ten houses in cash! She would stay in her small home on Benton Avenue for now. It belonged to her parents. In a year or so, she would build a luxurious large home.

In the next weeks, news media consumed her time until she finally had to say no to most interviews, except for their local newspaper, the *Osage County Unterrified Democrat*. She followed the lottery commission's recommendation and changed her phone number, but it didn't stop the harassment. People demanded her time. Damaris told her mother about the win, but in her alcoholic state, the enormity of the economic windfall didn't sink in. Damaris and Bryan finally had some serious talks with their mother and begged her to let them check her into an expensive, reputable rehab in St. Louis, the Harris House, where hopefully she would learn new coping skills, get counseling and therapeutic massages, eat a healthy diet, and develop healthy exercise habits. She promised she would stick with at least a five-month program, finally tired and ashamed of the lifestyle she had chosen the past three years. They drove her the hundred miles to St. Louis; and as she stood in the reception area, unkempt and looking forlorn, she resembled an eighty-year-old woman. Georgia held both her children in her arms and, through her tears, apologized for all the pain she had caused in their lives and asked them to forgive her. This began the healing they all needed. The counselors assured Damaris and Bryan they wouldn't recognize their mother in five months.

They decided, after getting their mom settled, they would go car shopping at a Chevy/Jeep dealership in St. Louis. Bryan's van, the one that had been replaced by the insurance company, had two hundred thousand miles on the odometer and some dents. But it ran good, and that's all Bryan ever cared about, getting from one point to another. Damaris's excitement was infectious, and he was happy he could please her by letting her buy him a new van. When they pulled in front of the dealership showroom in the worn-out van, the salesmen didn't know what to think about this handsome young man wearing a T-shirt with REO Speedwagon emblazoned across the front, one of Bryan's favorite '70s bands. He climbed out, and when Damaris stepped out of the van, they were surprised to see a beautiful young girl dressed in a baggy T-shirt and torn jeans.

Damaris went to the salesperson and told him they were there to buy three vehicles—a big new van for her brother; a new Jeep Gladiator for Reggie, the postman in Linn; and, for her, a two-door 650-horse-power silver C-7 Grand Sport Corvette, the car of her dreams, the exact one she saw displayed on the showroom floor. She asked to sit in the Corvette, and Bryan grinned as he remarked how gorgeous she looked in this amazing vehicle. The salesman thought he was wasting his time with these youngsters but played along. Damaris asked if she could test-drive it. He said she could test-drive another model. She told him again she wanted to test-drive this one. The salesman told her the cost, $100,000. Bryan found the van he wanted as well as the Jeep Gladiator for Reggie.

"We'll pay for them all in cash today, so how about letting her drive this one?" Bryan said forcefully.

Damaris was impressed with Bryan's confidence. She knew he led his band with the same decisiveness. She sat in the car, delighting in the smell of the leather. The car fit her like a glove. It made her feel like she was part of the machine. Sitting there with her hands on the steering wheel, she could feel the potential force under the hood. The dashboard looked like a jet's cockpit. It was an eight-speed automatic with all kinds of computer technology. The salesman showed her the button that lifted the convertible top into the hard cover so the top securely slid automatically into the trunk. He then pressed the same button to open it back up so the top lifted and secured itself for driving. She was told all this could be done with the button while driving less than thirty miles per hour. If she drove with the top down and it started to rain, a button would bring the top out of the trunk automatically without her even touching it! A feature to delight any woman! She pictured herself on the Interstate with the convertible top down, driving across Missouri or cruising around the Lake of the Ozarks. This car represented freedom, unlimited freedom, after so many years of responsibility. Damaris couldn't wait to finalize the purchases so she could get on the road.

The salesman hurried into the manager's office. The manager then came back to the floor with him as Damaris and Bryan looked over the car. The purchase price of all three cars would be around $300,000 with taxes and licensing fees. The manager had a hard time believing these two young people had money like that.

"Sir," Bryan explained politely, "this is my sister, Damaris Kelly. You might have heard her name. She just won the $960 million lottery jackpot. She has more than enough in her bank account. You can check with our bank in Linn, the Legends Bank. Call them if you don't believe me. I'm driving my new van back to Linn today, and you can give my old van to charity. We'd like you to deliver the Jeep to the Linn post office with a big red ribbon tied around it and a huge sign saying 'Thank you, Reggie.' Someone needs to drive with her now to show her the bells and whistles. Open up your showroom doors and get it ready for her to drive it out of here today. I'll call the bank. They'll make the money transfer. Let's get going, shall we?"

Damaris was impressed. Not only was he a talented musician, he had business sense.

Bryan drove off happily with his new van. He couldn't wait to show it to the band. He was going to put some really cool "Rogues" graphics on the doors. Damaris drove back to Linn on I-44, relishing her car's power. This car represented freedom, freedom from the past three painful years. The rumbling engine was a little scary at 650 horsepower. It was somewhat intimidating after years of driving her dad's van. She hoped she wouldn't speed because this machine wanted to go faster. As she drove through Linn, the engine rumbling with power, people waved or gave her a thumbs-up. How she loved this car!

She stopped at the bank and took out $50,000 for her shopping trip to Kansas City. She went home, packed a small bag, jumped back into her Corvette, and drove to Kansas City, a three-hour drive. She wished the weather was warmer so she could put the top down. As she drove on the Interstate and through Kansas City, truck drivers honked and waved, and even little kids riding with their parents gave her big smiles and thumbs-up. She stayed at the Raphael Hotel near the Country Club Plaza, an area known for its beautiful fountains similar to its sister city of Seville, Spain. She shopped in the best stores and bought quality clothes, 40 pairs of shoes, and designer sandals and handbags. The saleswomen put together stunning ensembles for her, some costing $1,000! She bought a thick blue fox jacket as soft as silk. After her dad died, she had to buy her clothes from thrift stores. This was a new world.

She went to a day spa and had her long blond hair colored and styled. She had a wonderful two-hour massage, and the accumulated tension of years seemed to dissipate as she relaxed on the massage table in a room lit only with candles and with soft music playing in the background. She needed this not only for her body but for her spirit too. After the massage, professional makeup artists highlighted her beauty with makeup, and she bought their expensive products. Her high school English teacher had worn Chanel No. 5 perfume; and she vowed, one day, she would have enough money to buy just one bottle. On this trip, she purchased five bottles and silk lingerie that felt like a new baby's skin. She relished her soothing pedicure and manicure.

All this cost thousands of dollars, and she didn't care. At first, she felt guilty, awkward, and unworthy to have all this, as if she were an imposter playing a part in some kind of surreal movie. She bought expensive Italian luggage, kept some of the new clothes and luggage with her, and asked the stores to ship the rest of her purchases to the Linn post office.

After shopping, she decided to visit Kansas City's Nelson-Atkins Art Gallery and spent the next day from opening to closing relishing the beauty of art in all its forms. She had never experienced the creative beauty of original oil paintings and sculptures except in books. She decided, one day, she would buy tasteful artwork for her new home. In fact, she would surround herself with beauty in every part of her life.

Even though it was a chilly December day, she decided to put the top down just for a few hours as she drove by the mansions along Ward Parkway and in nearby neighborhoods, relishing the exquisite architecture of each home. She snapped hundreds of pictures with her new Nikon camera, recording ideas for her future home. As she drove along the parkway, her hair blowing in the wind, dressed in her new wardrobe, wrapped in her warm fur coat and soft leather gloves, she cried a few times, remembering the threats to turn off their electricity and her worry about their home being foreclosed. Those days no longer existed, but the habit of worry and feeling insecure still lingered. When she looked at herself in the hotel room's mirror, she didn't appear to be the same person. With her gorgeous skin, long blond-streaked hair, and perfect figure, she looked like a supermodel; but inside she still felt like the plain Damaris who rode her old bike around town and worked at BJ's. This didn't feel real. She wasn't sure she could easily make the mental switch from an impoverished plain duckling to a wealthy, beautiful swan.

*****

Back in Linn, after five days of shopping and fun, she was mercilessly hounded. When she went to BJ's for a hamburger, the media followed her; and when she shopped at Thriftway for groceries, there they were, asking questions and snapping photos, not just because she won the lottery, but because she was gorgeous model material and looked great in photos. Bryan was busy with his band, so reporters didn't bother him much. Luckily her mother was tucked away safely in the rehab costing Damaris $15,000 per month, unable to be contacted by the media. Lottery headquarters warned this would happen, so Damaris decided to meet with a travel agent in Jefferson City who asked Damaris if she'd like to take a four-month round-the-world ocean voyage on the *Queen Mary 2* ocean liner leaving January 3 and returning to New York April 27. Usually these cruises were booked a year or two ahead, but a rare cancellation made the Queen's Grill Suite available. The agent quoted the price of $147,000 for the four-month voyage, and Damaris booked it without hesitation.

A year before her father died, he bought everyone in the family passports, promising one day they would visit the city of Galway, Ireland, where he was born. She had a passport and a round-the-world trip on a luxury ocean liner! Twenty-two ports of call! The agent assured her that traveling by herself was no problem and was a great way to meet new people. Because Damaris had always been somewhat of a loner, the thought of traveling alone didn't bother her. She had an adventuresome spirit and little fear of new situations. The crew would give her special attention and provide security, if needed, to ensure her safety. Day excursions met the *Queen Mary*'s standards for excellence and safety. She received the required inoculations for international travel.

As she returned from Jeff City, she sang Irish tunes in her loudest voice to her deceased father. "Dad, your daughter, son, and beloved wife are going to be okay! Don't worry, Dad. We love you!"

Damaris now held her head up high in Linn. The town was happy Georgia was in a rehab for Damaris and Bryan's sake. Damaris's best friend, Kris, had moved to California after high school; and they made plans over the telephone for Damaris to visit in the near future or for her to come back to Linn. She would have liked to bring Kris with her, but she had some major work commitments in California. Pastor Dave kept telling her God had a plan and purpose for her. Right now, her plan was a four-month dream vacation, and her purpose was to spend money as freely and extravagantly as possible.

Bryan found a piece of property next to Missouri Technical College—ninety-five acres of half forest and half meadow on Highway 50 east of town.

The asking price, $1 million. The bank assured them zoning would be no problem. Bryan and Damaris decided this would be a perfect spot to realize both their dreams, his recording studio and her new home. For now, neither wanted to leave Linn. It was where they grew up.

*****

This cool winter day, she drove her car through her property up the dirt road meant for tractors and parked in the meadow. In the spring it would bloom with purple lupines and black-eyed Susans, interspersed with delicate white Queen Anne's lace, but for now, the forest and meadow slept. She loved the outline of the trees in winter, each tree bearing its own personality and shape. The world opened up in the winter. As she stood next to her car, she looked up and heard the rolling bugle calls of twenty or thirty sandhill cranes above her in V formation between the white clouds and pieces of blue sky—their primeval, mystic, haunting sounds calling to one another. Red cardinals scoured the meadow for seeds or sat on tree branches, showing off their scarlet beauty. When the cranes disappeared to the south, she heard in the east the loud and persistent honking of a flock of white snow geese. She was free now, like the birds.

The sound of a motor behind startled her and interrupted her reverie. As a safety caution, she now carried a small can of Mace spray hidden in her pocket. She put her hand in the pocket as she turned around, and there was Deputy Gardner parking his sheriff's car behind hers. Her innocent sensuality mesmerized him as she stood there in her gray leather boots, wrapped in her fox jacket, her hair blowing in the slight breeze and her cornflower-blue eyes looking at him in surprise. He appreciated every line and detail of her body. He had never seen her look this beautiful. In the past, she dressed like a tomboy; but now her clothes, hair, and makeup accentuated her natural beauty and femininity.

"I hope I didn't scare you, Damaris," he said apologetically, nervously shifting from one foot to the other.

This was the first time she noticed Corey's looks. In the past, he was just the local sheriff who either brought her bad news or tried to protect her. That was his job. Today she saw a handsome man—muscled, broad shouldered, and fit under his uniform with curling brown hair and skin tanned from the winter sun, his intense dark-brown eyes and long eyelashes accentuating his clean-cut good looks. He was at least a head taller than she, and his virility surprised her.

"I heard you just bought this property. I saw the sold sign on the highway. Ninety-five acres, that's a lot of land!"

She pointed. "Bryan and I have big plans for it. Over there, on about five acres, will be his recording studio with a large parking lot in front. Behind it will be garages for the touring bus and small semi to carry the band equipment. Back down this road, close to the forest, will be the home of my dreams on twenty acres, far enough away so we will both have privacy and be far from any traffic noise on Highway 50. The last seventy acres? I'll wait and see."

"Sounds wonderful!"

What he really wanted to do was take her in his arms and kiss her perfect lips.

"Damaris, do you carry a gun for protection?"

This was Missouri, and most people carried guns.

"Can I advise you to buy a little pistol, take a gun safety course, and keep that gun with you at all times? This is a safe community, but there are a few people like Crazy Charlie. You are a beautiful target for some perverted weirdo."

"I promise I'll do that, Corey. Is it all right to call you by your first name instead of Deputy? I promise I'll purchase a pistol when I get back from my trip."

"Your trip? Where are you going?" *She was leaving?*

"Corey, I have been pestered and bugged by so many people. This money has given me a lot of headaches, and I've lost my privacy. I'm taking a four-month round-the-world cruise on the *Queen Mary 2* from January 3 to April 27. Bryan's driving me to St. Louis on January 1. I'll fly to New York and leave from the cruise port there, then a week's trip across the Atlantic to Southampton, England. From there, we'll stop at twenty-two ports of call. Four months! I'm so excited. Finally I'll get to see some of the world outside of Linn. No one on the ship will know I won that money unless I tell them. Privacy and adventure are what I crave right now."

"I'm going to miss seeing you every day," he said, afraid of saying too much.

He wanted, more than anything, to confess his love and tell her he couldn't see his future without her in it. Instead he asked if he could open the hood and look at the engine.

"Aren't you on duty right now?" she asked teasingly. "Well, I guess I could be having engine trouble and helping me would be part of your duty, right?"

They both laughed.

He opened the silver hood and bent over the engine. She noticed the muscles under his uniform, and for the first time in her life, she was stirred by the muscular body of a very masculine man. She knew he was a typical male fascinated with high-performance engines.

As he bent over, she again noticed the lines of his body as he declared, "Wow! This engine is a work of art!"

She couldn't take her eyes off his physique. *What is happening to me?* she wondered.

"They told me it will go two hundred miles per hour! And the speed limit is only seventy on the highways! I'll bet you'd like to sit in it, huh?"

Was she flirting with him? He hoped so.

He shut the hood; and with all his courage, sweat trickling down his face, he took a deep breath and bravely asked, "Damaris, I know you're leaving in a few weeks, but would you like to have dinner with me Friday? Anywhere you choose."

There, he said it. She was attractive beyond belief. Why would she even want anything to do with him? He felt like a beggar and wanted to jump in his car and back out down the road. He prepared himself for a no, but when she said, "Sure!" his heart rejoiced.

"I'll tell you what, Corey. I know you are probably dying to drive this car. It is really a race car, and I know how men feel about race cars. How about Friday you drive over to my house around four, park your car, and I'll let you drive us the seventy-five miles in this car to the Lake of the Ozarks. There's a restaurant called JB Hooks near the lake."

He would have to wait three days! He wanted to leave now before she changed her mind. He dreamed of having a whole evening with the most beautiful girl in the world!

"Okay! I'll see you Friday at four. My lunch break is over, so I'll head out. Can I ask you a personal question, Damaris? Please be honest." He looked at her intensely.

She wondered what he was going to say.

With eyes twinkling, he asked, "Are you going out on a date with me because of my money?"

They both laughed.

*****

The date with Corey was wonderful. He was a classy dresser with his soft brown leather jacket, nicely fitting blue jeans, and expensive leather shoes. He certainly didn't dress like a farm boy. She was proud to be seen with him as he was with her. Her car accelerated quickly, and the engine rumbled as he drove toward the Lake of the Ozarks. Corey couldn't believe he was driving a vehicle with such power, a true race car. Corey was a competent driver and didn't exceed the speed limit, but he knew the car could go two hundred miles per hour. Driving at seventy was like pulling the reins of a thoroughbred racehorse as it sped down a racetrack. He asked her what the use was of having a car that will go so fast when highway speed limits were never over seventy. She told him she liked the sound of the engine, the way it handled, and the way it looked. It represented freedom and beauty. Corey had to agree.

The scent of her Chanel filled the car, intoxicating him. He reminded her of Josh Lucas in the romantic movie *Sweet Home Alabama*. He was a cop, but there was a tender side to him that made her feel comfortable. She told him she didn't date in high school, and that surprised him because she was so beautiful. He reminded her of her dad, full of life and love.

At the end of the evening, they pulled up in front of her house on Benton Avenue. He opened the car door for her and took her arm as they walked up to the small porch. They both agreed the night was wonderful. Corey said he would never forget this time with her and bravely asked if he could kiss her good night. He tilted her chin up, his kiss sweet and tender. He wanted to wrap his arms around her and never let her go but held back.

He whispered in her ear, "I have loved you for quite some time, Damaris."

She unlocked the door as she let herself in and whispered, "See you later, Corey."

The intensity of his feelings scared her, and she knew she wasn't ready for this kind of love right now. She didn't know she would find a new kind of love in the months ahead.

8

Ready, Set, Go!

She spent the rest of the week packing for all kinds of weather during her world voyage. She had a security system and cameras installed in her house, mainly to protect her car parked in the garage. She covered the Corvette with a custom-made tarp. She sent Corey a text asking if he would drive by her house every day and check the doors. She reminded him she would be back around April 27. He asked if he could come over on Christmas Day to give her a gift before she left. Against her better judgment, she agreed but told him she had so much to do before she left. She didn't want to lead him on or give him false hopes. She made arrangements with her investment adviser, Jim Maxwell, at Legends Bank for money transfers as needed; and she applied for and was granted a Chase Bank Sapphire Preferred card with a $500,000 credit limit. She called her mother's counselors at

Harris House in St. Louis, and they assured her she was doing well. Damaris made a hefty donation to ensure her mother could stay there for at least five months, her mother happily agreeing. The car dealership delivered Reggie's Jeep with a big red ribbon and a huge sign with "Thanks, Reggie" in bold letters. Reggie was so proud of his new Jeep! As people drove by the post office, they honked in appreciation or with a thumbs-up.

Before she left, she met with the city council, asking for permission to donate the items on the wish list she handed them—new sidewalks the length of Main Street, thirty antique green lampposts along Main with flower planters wrapped around them, and the same number of wrought iron benches next to them where people could sit and visit. She said she would pay for placing all the street utilities underground, tearing out the present pool and building an Olympic-size pool in McGuire Park with four lifeguard stations, a large snack bar next to it, and picnic benches and shade arbors. The old pool would be filled in, the old snack bar torn down, and a huge white gazebo surrounded by grass built in its place where regional musicians could perform at any time and with lots of seating for people to enjoy the new park. If the school needed a new bus or the ambulance district needed new equipment, Damaris would buy them with the council's and school district's inputs. There was so much she wanted to do for her small town, and donating these things gave her joy.

Pastor Dave had advised her to give to her community first, and she listened. She acknowledged that most of these gifts were the pastor's idea. He wanted her to think of other people's needs first. He prayed for her to make good decisions, and she readily agreed she would talk with him first before making large decisions. She consulted with the administration at Missouri Technical College and contributed to the college trust fund for those who needed financial assistance for their schooling. She wanted to do more for her town but had only days before her trip. Christmas came and went. The town of Linn knew how to beautifully decorate their town for Christmas, but Damaris didn't even put up a tree or decorate this year. She was too busy. Damaris was homesick for the preparations her family used to make years ago before her father's death. Her father always made Christmas fun. If it snowed, he played in the snow with them like a child. He liked stringing popcorn while they watched the George C. Scott version of *A Christmas Carol*. He made the whole family walk around their neighborhood singing Christmas carols, which the neighbors enjoyed because of Phillip's bold tenor voice. Damaris hoped, one day, her family tradition would continue when she had children of her own.

When Corey came for his visit, he brought her a nicely wrapped small box and lovingly watched her open it. He was happy to see her. They had both been busy. Corey was busy issuing DUI tickets for the holiday revelers, and Damaris was getting ready for her trip and buying everything she needed for such a long journey. In the box was a beautiful silver necklace with two hearts entwined, each with a diamond in the center. As he hooked the necklace around her neck, he asked if she would wear it on her trip sometimes to remember him. She looked in the mirror and smiled. He asked if he could take a picture of her with his phone and then a picture of both of them together. She smiled. It was a sweet gesture coming from his loving heart. She hadn't thought about getting him a gift and apologized in embarrassment.

"Corey, I want to be honest with you. You've shared your feelings for me, and I'm grateful. I hope we'll speak on the phone while I'm gone, but I don't want you to have any expectations right now. I'm just not ready for a serious relationship."

She knew her honesty hurt his feelings, and she felt guilty for making him sad. He stood up and asked if he could give her a Christmas hug. As they held one another, his arms felt good. She knew she was safe with Corey. He kissed her lips lightly, wished her a Merry Christmas, and walked out the door. It would be months before she saw him again; and in those months, her world travel would change her in many ways, from a naive small-town girl into a confident and worldly young woman.

9

The Queen Mary 2

On January 1, Bryan drove her to St. Louis. They had a wonderful lunch together in a restaurant overlooking the Mississippi River. Together they agreed on a two-million-dollar budget for his new recording studio. He told her that the sound equipment was very expensive, plus all the mikes and the acoustics built into the building itself. He wanted a three-bedroom apartment built on the back, which would sleep at least ten, equipped with a full kitchen so musicians didn't have to leave during recording sessions; and men's and women's bathrooms with showers available for both genders. His meetings with sound engineers and contractors made it more difficult meeting his own practice and performance commitments with the Rogues. He was dedicated to the band, and the band came first. He was hoping the recording studio would be finished by the time she came home so he could surprise her. As they said goodbye at the airport, he gave her some advice.

"Damaris, don't let this money change who you are. Pastor Dave has been giving you good advice. You could very easily start thinking you're better than everyone else. Our band is receiving some notoriety. We are on the verge of a huge breakthrough, and I believe national fame lies ahead, but we will never be truly successful if we cave in to people who want to change us. My musical vision is strong. I have a band with the same vision, and I will not compromise that vision. Be true to yourself, Damaris. I know who you are. Do you? I have a feeling this trip is going to change your way of thinking in many ways. It will broaden your horizons and enlarge your view of the world. Again, stay true to yourself and be open to these new experiences without changing who you are. Promise me this."

*****

She flew to New York nonstop in first class, luxuriating in the large leather seats and excellent service. First class! This was her first time in an airplane. She loved seeing the huge city of New York below her and was overwhelmed by its size, comparing Linn's fifteen hundred people with New York's eight million! She wondered how people lived in huge cities, like ants! She spent the first night in the Marriott, and the next day, she and all her luggage were transported to the

Brooklyn Cruise port. There she stood in awe in front of the last of the great transatlantic ocean liners still in service. Parked among huge cruise ships, the *Queen Mary 2* stood out like a solitary perfect diamond in the midst of costume jewelry, her pointed bow and lower half painted black and the bright-red strip painted around the circumference of the entire ship at the water line. The retired *Queen Mary*, now a hotel in Long Beach, California, had three stacks. This ship had only one, and next to it was the famous huge red air horn, which blasted three times to announce the *Queen Mary*'s arrivals and departures which could be heard for ten miles. Standing next to this ship, she felt like a miniature doll and had to bend her head back to see the top of the ship. She had done the research on this ultimate cruise liner, but no words could really describe its sleek beauty. Damaris started crying, and a nice older gentleman asked if he could help her in any way as he handed her a Kleenex. She told him she was crying because the ship was incredibly beautiful. He nodded in agreement.

Porters loaded baggage as the 2,600 passengers checked in for this sold-out seven-day voyage to Southampton, England. Damaris took as many exterior pictures as she could. After boarding, she finally settled into her large Queen's Grill Suite with its living area with sofa and coffee table, a large queen bedroom suite with a Jacuzzi tub and walk-in closet, and a balcony running the length of the suite. Soft white towels hung in the bathroom with "Cunard" embroidered on each one. The butler knocked. He introduced himself as Gerard, her own personal butler for the entire voyage. He asked if he could assist her in any way. He smiled because he would be this beautiful girl's butler for the next four months. He hoped she would be polite and not rude or arrogant like some passengers. He also brought a bottle of iced champagne in a silver bucket and asked if he could pour her a glass. Of course! He showed her the phone button she pressed to call for service, night or day. She sat on the balcony sipping champagne while observing the busy wharf as they prepared the ship to sail. Her own butler! For three years, she had been her mom's butler. Now it was her turn to be waited on! She called Pastor Dave and Bryan and told them she was on the ship and would be leaving in a few hours. Pastor Dave prayed for her safety. Bryan told her he loved her, and Damaris was grateful she had such a caring older brother and a good friend like Dave. Corey didn't call, and she knew why—he was waiting for her to call first.

After drinking two glasses of champagne on an empty stomach, she felt dizzy, and she was told she could eat in the King's Buffett now, then explore the ship until 5:00 p.m. when the ship departed. The buffet was amazing, and so was the complete view of New York and its harbor through the large floor-to-ceiling windows. The Statue of Liberty! Ellis Island! The Empire State Building! In the center of the ship was the Grand Lobby with its six-story-high silver-

and-gold atrium and a wide winding staircase curving up to the next floor. There was a British pub, a wine bar, a smoking room, a huge shopping area with designer clothes and expensive perfumes, five swimming pools, fifteen restaurants, a cinema, computer school, and a well-equipped gymnasium and elegant spa. She looked through the carved wooden doors into the richly decorated dining rooms with their crystal wine glasses and crisp white linens, ready for tomorrow night's first gourmet dining experience.

The showroom! She had seen pictures of European opera houses with their gold balconies and velvet seats. This showroom could equal that! And the library—deep leather chairs, glass-covered bookcases, carved wooden coffee tables, brass lamps, and eight thousand books to choose from! It had been so long since she could sit in a library with no time pressures or responsibilities dragging her away from reading. She swore, one day, she would build a huge library in her new home and fill it with the best books in the world by the best authors. She would buy expensive leather easy chairs and bronze lamps and pipe in soothing classical music for relaxation. There was so much to see.

*****

She realized she would have four months to explore it, but now she was like a little kindergartener on her first day of school—everything was new and fresh!

The famous air horn gave its three loud blasts announcing their departure. The people in all parts of this busy city of New York heard the blasts and knew this elegant ship was underway. Spectators lined the sidewalks along the harbor pier, excited by the grand ship as she sailed past the Statue of Liberty. Cameras flashed. Passengers on the decks watched the skyline of the great city slowly disappear and waved to those left behind.

"Goodbye, America. See you in four months!" she shouted as she waved, and those around her did the same. She didn't know then that an unexpected encounter would push her to leave the cruise early before the four-month trip was officially over.

10

Anthony Armstrong

As on most ships, you chose your time to dine in the finest dining rooms on the ship. This first night, as the new passengers got settled, passengers had to eat something light in the King's Court Buffet or in one of the other twelve restaurants. It was crowded, and she asked if she could join a table with an extra place to sit. The friendly family from Lancaster, Pennsylvania, was getting off the ship in England to begin their two-week vacation touring the British Isles. She enjoyed talking with them. They were surprised such a beautiful young girl was brave enough to travel alone. She told them this trip was a gift and that the crew was looking after her. After dinner, she stood on the deck watching the stars. She went to the showroom for the "Welcome Aboard" show. She had never been in a lovely theater like this one! It would take a week to get to England. She would have a whole week on the ocean! It didn't seem real. After all the stress of the past months, she slowly walked to her suite, took a relaxing bath, and curled up in her comfortable balcony chair recording the observations she would share in a slide show at the high school when she returned. She made her first entry:

> January 3
> I am on the *Queen Mary 2*,
> and here my adventure begins.

Later she luxuriated on her queen-size bed's silken sheets and fell into a deep sleep until noon the next day.

A new day! The first day! She enjoyed a wonderful massage, swam laps in the pool, jogged a few miles on the top deck, perused the library, and visited the planetarium for a star show. She would never get bored. Just traveling on the ocean was exciting! Pods of dolphins leapt for joy as they raced next to the ship, looking almost like they were smiling. She felt like the dolphins leaping freely through the water.

Because she stayed in one of the Queen's Grill Suites, she could eat in their best dining room, the Queen's Grill. Very prestigious, she was told. Her table was reserved, the same table every night with the same people, and she didn't like that. She wanted to meet all kinds of people and not be stuck with the same people the entire cruise. She sat at a large table with six other people, and it felt awkward to her. A table of strangers and the small talk was mind numbing. They were interested in why she was traveling by herself, and that seemed to get the conversation going. She told them the trip was a gift and that seemed to satisfy their curiosity. The food, however, was definitely not BJ's food, where a great hamburger and sweet potato fries sprinkled with cinnamon and sugar was considered a gourmet meal. Each course here looked like a piece of art, and the tastes and textures were unlike she had ever experienced. She was served by tuxedoed smart waiters with utmost skill and precision, the whole dinner experience a gourmet's delight.

The first night, she ordered a tender filet mignon with a fresh-caught lobster, neither of which she had ever eaten. The steak was as tender as butter, and the fresh lobster with garlic butter a taste of heaven. The waiter suggested wine with every course, enhancing the flavor of each. She didn't know that certain wines should be ordered with certain foods, and the waiter taught her patiently. She learned that fine dining was the epitome of the culinary arts. Across from her table, sitting by himself, was an attractive older gentleman with snow-white hair. He lifted his wine glass in a toast to her. The second night, he did the same. He reminded her of Pastor Dave. She walked by him on the way to the 8:30 p.m. show and approached his small table.

"Hi! I've noticed you've been staring at me. Do we know each other?"

"You might say that. My name is Anthony Armstrong, and you are Damaris Kelly." He beamed.

"How do you know that?" she asked, surprised.

He answered, "It's a ship, and word gets around. Would you like to sit down and join me for dessert and coffee?" He stood up and pulled out a chair, politely offering her to sit opposite him. "Actually, Damaris, I have some connections."

"Did Pastor Dave or Bryan or Corey send you?" she asked, but she knew that couldn't be possible.

"Look, Damaris. I've been sent to show you around as a combination tour guide and friend."

"Did somebody pay you?"

"Not exactly. I'm on this wonderful ocean liner with great food, beautiful accommodations, sitting next to the loveliest young woman on the ship. I'd say that's pretty good pay!" He grinned.

"How do you know me?"

"I know two good friends of yours, Pastor Dave and, yes, Corey Gardner."

"Are you a cop? Do you work for the bank? Are you a private detective? Are you one of those awful media people who keep following me around?" she asked in frustration.

He laughed. "None of the above! I'll tell you at the end of the voyage as a departing gift, okay? Right now, eat that blackberry cobbler. It's not as good as BJ's, but it's not bad."

"How do you know about BJ's?"

"I told you. I have connections. Finish your dessert, then let's walk around the deck before we see the fabulous show. All right with you?"

That night began a four-month odyssey exploring new and strange places and changing her old ways of thinking. Not only would she start seeing the world with larger eyes, she would also see it with a new heart. It was Mr. Armstrong's assignment to make sure of that.

From that night on, she ate her meals with Mr. Armstrong, and he was her constant companion. He insisted she call him Mr. A. He introduced her to several people who also knew him, and these people became her shipboard friends. He told her nothing about himself. He thoroughly enjoyed good food, music, art, and books. He loved to dance! They took ballroom dancing classes. He knew the dance steps, and Damaris was a quick learner. She and Mr. A were asked to demonstrate for the class. The passengers applauded them in appreciation. Some wondered if he was her real daddy or her sugar daddy. After the dance class, they sat on the upper deck at the end of the evening, enveloped in the blackness of the night which highlighted the brilliant stars. Mr. A taught her the names of star constellations and the stories behind their naming. A few whales breeched near the ship. The vastness of the Atlantic, the second largest ocean in the world, exhilarated her. If large waves rocked the boat, she felt safe, knowing Mr. A was nearby. She was happy she had met him and that he wanted to be her traveling companion. He filled a void her father left after his death.

She called America. Bryan was excited that his recording studio was under construction. Pastor Dave said the steeple had arrived and was installed. The electronic bell blessed the city of Linn three times a day and twice on Sundays. She didn't know that Corey learned of her travel experiences from Pastor Dave. He was disappointed Damaris wasn't calling him.

11

Barcelona, Spain

After arriving in Southampton, England, and unloading passengers and boarding new ones, the *Queen Mary* sailed for Barcelona via the Strait of Gibraltar on the southern coast of Spain, connecting the Atlantic Ocean and Mediterranean Sea. As they journeyed north off the east coast of Spain, she began her travel journal.

> Our first stop is Barcelona, Spain. Isn't that a lovely name? I think of Queen Isabella and pirates when I hear that name. Mr. A told me not to sign up for any shore excursions because he wanted to show me the city personally. It's time to meet him in the atrium. I'll write later!

As they left the ship, at the end of the dock, there was very handsome man standing next to a white limousine. He looked like a Spaniard, with black hair and deep-brown eyes, dressed in a black suit and dark tie. He had a small black automatic military weapon that the Israelis might use strapped across his shoulder and looked formidable. Mr. A introduced him as Raphael, a bodyguard and friend. Mr. A guaranteed her the gun was necessary, especially in Barcelona, where a beautiful blond, blue-eyed American woman traveling through a large Spanish town might encourage boldness in the local male behavior.

Mr. A also convinced her he could give her a better tour of Barcelona than any prearranged shore excursion. The port itself was one of the few good harbors in the country and an important seaport for thousands of years. Crowded city roads and parkways and horrendous traffic jams notwithstanding, no doubt Barcelona was truly a magnificent city. Damaris slid back and forth on the leather seats, not wanting to miss any aesthetically pleasing architectural feature in any direction. Mr. A laughed at her excitement. He knew the history of the buildings and taught her patiently. High on the hill stood the Gothic cathedral of Barcelona, begun in the 1200s, with original Roman walls still standing nearby. They stopped at a café for coffee and a history lesson. Damaris took pictures at a frantic rate.

"People often confuse the Barcelona Cathedral with Gaudi's Sagrada Familia, the amazing Spanish

Gothic revival structure begun in 1882, the number-one attraction in Barcelona. The twelve spires represent the twelve apostles. It is considered one of the most original and ambitious modern buildings and is still being completed. They estimate it will take another twenty-five years to finish," continued Mr. A.

Damaris cried out in joy. "Mr. A, it's fantastic structure! I am overwhelmed!"

They drove on to the University of Barcelona with its ninety thousand students. Its exquisite architecture dated back to the year 1450. They drove through the campus, and the abundance of historical architecture awed her.

She learned the Romans founded Barcelona in the first century and built a defensive wall which still stands in the old part of town. Barcelona is known not only for its stunning world-class restaurants and nightlife but, of course, for its once-strategic location on the Mediterranean Sea.

"Mr. A, I wish we had more than one day here! What are those fountains over there?"

"Those are the Magic Fountains of Montjuïc, built in 1929. They are even more beautiful at night with colored lights similar to the fountains at the Bellagio in Las Vegas. We are now driving by the National Museum of Art. It is one of the most visited places in Barcelona. It looks like a castle, doesn't it? It was refurbished in 1992 for the Olympic Games. We don't have time to tour the inside, but you can see pictures on your computer back on the ship. I want to show you the Olympic Stadium built by Barcelona for the 1992 Olympic Games. It was once a fantastic stadium but now abandoned and in ruins, weeds and grass growing wild, trash littering the interior."

Mr. A explained this happens to many of the Olympic venues. Barcelona spent billions of dollars, as do other cities who host the Olympics, then lose interest in the expensive structures they built, then allowed them to deteriorate.

Mr. A suggested they stop in the outdoor Plaza Catalunya area close by with its fantastic food and live music. Damaris told him she thought Barcelona the most beautiful city in the world with its ancient architecture, flowers, and fountains. He laughed, reminding her this was the first of many great cities she would see and that she would have many favorites. They sat in a lovely outdoor café, and Mr. A and Raphael ordered in Spanish.

"You both know Spanish?"

Raphael dined with them but only conversed with Mr. A in Spanish, both delighting in the food and thanking the waiter for "*la comida deliciosa y el servicio excelente!*" The good food and excellent service.

Mr. A told her he spoke many languages. He was a world traveler and wanted to converse with as many people as possible in their language. He assured her that, if she spoke Spanish, he would also. As they dined and drank a delicious Spanish sweet wine, Mr. A had more to say. He told her about what she wouldn't see or hear as a tourist on a cruise liner.

"Areas of poverty emerged during the corrupt communist leadership of Francisco Franco, but worse than physical poverty is the spiritual poverty of Spain. Once religious, Spain is now nominally Catholic and rapidly becoming secular. Many show suspicion of any expression of Christianity that is not Catholic, yet few people attend worship services, especially the younger generation."

After lunch, he asked Raphael to drive them through a poor area called Raval.

"It is not safe to walk the streets here. There is graffiti in the stores. Homes are cardboard shacks with sheets of aluminum for walls. Old tires are used for chairs. There are homosexual nightclubs and pornographic graffiti everywhere, degradations of humanity that proliferate because Spain is trending secular, much like the United States and most of Western Europe. It is an urban paradox of beauty and darkness," he explained.

Damaris took some disturbing pictures, sickened and appalled by what she saw in Raval.

Mr. A shared that Christian missionaries in Spain make connections through sports and by developing relationships in home settings other than in churches. They also use the arts, especially music.

"Spiritual poverty is what is destroying not only Spain but the entire secular world," Mr. A told Damaris with a sad look in his eyes.

As they approached the ship, Damaris thought deeply about what Mr. A shared. He talked like Pastor Dave, and he made sense. She thought about herself. She didn't love God. She didn't even know who He was! If He was real and good, why did He let her dad be killed and her mother become an alcoholic? She didn't attend church or read the Bible Pastor Dave had given her. She didn't pray for herself or anyone else. She had done some good things with the money she won. She cared about her brother and her mother and the people in her town. Wasn't that good enough? She didn't steal. She was still a virgin. It was true, at one time, she was jealous of what other girls had—intact families, enough money, mothers who weren't alcoholics, and fathers who weren't killed. But who wouldn't be jealous? Did that mean she was she spiritually impoverished?

12

Athens, Greece

Damaris loved traveling on the Mediterranean Sea, with its almost-crystal-clear azure-blue water. Growing up surrounded by forests and meadows, she was delightfully surprised by the ocean in its vast beauty. The Port of Piraeus, eight miles from Athens, bustled with cruise ships, yachts, and fishing boats. Mr. A pointed out the Parthenon at the highest elevation in Athens, a wonder of the ancient world and one of its highest achievements, now crumbling.

After docking, Raphael again waited at the dock in his white limousine. Damaris asked Mr. A if that was Raphael with the same limousine he drove in Barcelona.

He gave the answer he would give her throughout the rest of the voyage. "I told you, Damaris. I have connections."

They began their tour of Athens. He and Raphael spoke another language. She asked him if they were speaking Greek.

"Yes, we are. It's a beautiful language, isn't it? One day, you'll know more about the Greek language. Athens, here we come!" he announced happily and enthusiastically.

The day was a delight. She saw ancient temples, cemeteries, secret gardens, many small churches, and Greek sculpture, the smell of barbecued lamb permeating the air. Outdoor cafés bulged with people socializing and drinking ouzo, the Greek national drink made from anise. Mr. A ordered them each a glass. Damaris loved the taste and the smoothness of this sweet beverage. The Athenians smoked heavily and joyfully danced to live music on the pavements in front of the cafés. After lunch, Mr. A pointed out the roads and paths where the apostle Paul, who wrote most of the New Testament, walked and preached in the synagogues and churches in AD 51.

"See that building over there, Damaris? No fancy architecture or gardens, but it houses AMG ministries. They model Christian principles and values and run a children's center, providing medical care, food, and clothing. They present the Gospel as did the apostle Paul and try to meet the needs of their community with limited resources. Fifty dollars a month supports one missionary. Ministries like this depend on charitable donations. Decades of a poorly run Greek government, high taxes, and lucrative pensions have nearly bankrupted the country. There are ten million people in Greece, and a third live in poverty. That's over three million people, Damaris. Many can't make their house payments or pay their utilities. There is very little disposable income. The public sector bureaucracy is fraught with corruption. Hosting the 2004 Olympics cost Greece $12 billion. Greece still hasn't recovered from that loss of money. See that former Olympic stadium? Just like the Barcelona stadium, crumbling, with dead brown grass, broken fences, smashed bottles, and cans littering the inner field? This was once a beautiful stadium. All those billions spent on it, and a third of the nation living in poverty? This is a shame beyond shame, don't you think, Damaris? When you write in your journal tonight, remember AMG ministries and the children, will you? Now let's eat at the Agora and spend time in the National Archaeological Museum, which does a fabulous job of showing the vast history of this most ancient of cities."

Damaris loved history class in high school, but nothing compared with learning the history of Athens in the Acropolis Museum, where they spent three hours. Such a short time and so much to learn! She didn't want the day to end. She wished they could have visited the Greek islands of Santorini, Mykonos, Crete, Corfu, and Rhodes, whose spoken names rolled around in your mouth like honey. She vowed one day she would return and spend time experiencing their beauty.

At the Piraeus dock, Mr. A shook hands with Raphael and said, "See you in Egypt, dear friend!" as he drove off.

Of course, they had spoken Greek most of that day.

13

Egypt

Damaris was having fun on the ship. She became proficient in ballroom dancing. She had purchased ten lovely evenings gown in Kansas City, and on formal attire nights, she was a stunning Cinderella from the fairy tale. Many of the passengers were older, and this astonishingly attractive young girl turned many heads. Rumors spread, and finally someone snooped around on the Internet and learned she was a huge lottery jackpot winner in America. News spread like wildfire on the ship, much to Damaris's horror. She wanted people to like her for herself and not have their perceptions tainted by her money. Of course, nearly everyone wanted to ask her questions. To get away from that, she spent time lounging in an upper deck chair watching the ocean. Her thoughts changed daily. She wondered if Linn would satisfy her now. Would she get bored or restless? Her money meant freedom from fear and worry and gave her more choices about what she could do with her life. Would it make her happy? She felt more comfortable around people now, emerging from her former constricting cocoon and becoming a confident, free-spirited butterfly.

Three days after leaving Greece for Egypt, they would transit the Suez Canal and spend two days in Egypt. Before the stops in Sokhna and Safaga, Mr. A told Damaris he wanted to talk to her about an issue of concern. She ordered lunch and lovely sweet tea from room service and sat cross-legged on her sofa waiting to hear him, the sliding balcony door open to the warm desert breeze.

He began, "Damaris, you are learning about the world outside of Linn now. In a day, we will be in Egypt. You will see millennial-old treasures from the times of the pharaohs, the Pyramids of Giza and Cheops, Cephron, Luxor, the Valley of the Kings, the great Sphinx. They truly are inspiring structures built thousands of years ago, costing the lives of millions of slaves. What the Egyptian government doesn't want the tourists to see is Cairo, a city of fifteen million. We won't be going to Cairo, but I am going to tell you about it.

"Even though the Cairo Museum houses mummies and King Tut's tomb artifacts, this city is a dangerous place to visit. It is called the City of the Dead. There is a chronic housing shortage. Five million live in cemeteries with cockroaches, mosquitoes, flies, and vermin. There is an overwhelming smell of garbage. Sewage leaks out of undrained tanks. Children play on the gravestones, which people use for tables. Kitchens and bedrooms are in the aboveground tombs. Living among the dead is a source of anxiety and nightmares. People live on $30 a month in these slums. There are 171 slums in Cairo with no access to clean water. There is inadequate nourishment, terrible public schools, low-paying jobs, no way to learn a trade. A few lucky ones stay in school and are able to receive an education.

"The overcrowded conditions lead to poor health. Public health care is overused and underfunded. There are few doctors, sparse medical equipment, and unsanitary hospitals. Nurses and medications are rare. The children have no safe spaces to play, no way to develop or pursue hobbies or spend leisure time. There is no space for sports or access to computers. The streets are dusty with no trees or parks. Sometimes three families live in a small house with as many as fifteen people with no kitchen and only one bathroom. It's as if these human beings are being buried alive."

"Mr. A! Stop this. I can't stand hearing these things!" She walked onto the balcony and leaned over the railing, trying to erase the pictures he drew of these horrible conditions. "Please don't tell me anymore!" she cried.

"You need to hear it. There are Christian organizations who minister to these people and offer joy in the midst of poverty. These organizations help to change lives with the love of Christ. One I know about is the Stephen's Children ministry in Cairo. Their goal is to release children from pain and the hopelessness of poverty. The workers give care, love, and smiles to children who have no basis for spiritual values but who crave love and acceptance. This ministry has 1,400 staff members, all supported by charitable organizations."

She turned around and asked him sincerely, "Mr. A, you said millions live in poverty. No one person, no one organization can meet the needs of so many. It's an impossible task!"

What was he asking her to do?

"Let me go further, Damaris."

"No! I'm having a lovely trip. Please don't spoil it with all these sad stories. I've had enough pain in my life already." She was angry.

"Have you had the kind of pain I have just described to you?"

She was silent.

"Many of these children grow up in garbage dumps, suffer sexual abuse, live on food scraps and moldy bread from dumps, not listened to, not loved, not valued. The goal of Stephen's Children ministry is to equip children spiritually, morally, and educationally. They fund ten kindergarten schools and equip vocational training centers. They do home visits, staff sports camps, run literary camps, provide medical care. I am on their advisory board. A very great lady founded this ministry and is a close personal friend of mine. Her name is Mama Maggie Gobran. People call her the Mother Teresa of Cairo. She said this, Damaris. I want you to remember her words. 'When one has nothing, then God becomes everything,' and 'When I touch a poor child, I touch Jesus.' She also said, 'When you are obedient to God and do His will, you become a hero.'"

Damaris's answer revealed the battle going on in her spirit. "I don't want to be a hero, Mr. A."

Folding his hands on the table in front of him, he looked at Damaris with knowing eyes but didn't speak. She hated his knowing silence.

"Mr. A, who are you? Why are you with me? Why is Raphael with me? I heard you both speaking what I assumed was Egyptian today. When we stop in Singapore, will you speak Chinese? The Thai language in Bangkok? Vietnamese in Vietnam? I don't understand."

"You will one day. Just know we both have the gift of picking up languages as we travel around the world as I have done many times. I will tell you this. You have been given a great financial gift, and I predict, one day, you will be a hero like Mama Maggie if you use this gift wisely."

"You talk just like Pastor Dave."

"He and I have been friends for many years. Also I want you to know I've been talking with Corey and your brother, Bryan, and one day, they will know me well too. So will your mother."

"You've got to be kidding! I'm tired of these riddles!" She paced back and forth in her room, agitated by Mr. A's words. "I'm on this trip to see the world, spend money as I like, and have a good time. Are you implying I'm selfish or that I don't care about people who are suffering?" She turned toward the ocean, leaning on the railing.

"I'm not implying anything," he said calmly. "Is your conscience bothering you?"

"Why should it bother me? Look, Mr. A. I need some space. Can I not see you for a few days?"

"Of course. I never force myself on anyone. You have free will. But if you need something, just call on me."

Perplexed, she asked, "How do I get in contact with you?"

"Well, I'll be around the ship introducing myself to as many lovely people as I can. Tonight, however, I am going to soak in the Jacuzzi. Good night, precious child. Know that I love you." He smiled as he patted her cheek gently.

Damaris sat glumly on her sofa, looking at their half-finished food. He was frustrating! Why did he get so serious after all their fun times? She was sorry she spoke to him so harshly. She was nineteen. She wanted to do what young people do. How could an old man understand?

She picked up her cell phone and dialed Corey's number. He answered immediately.

"Damaris! Thanks for calling. It's so good to hear your voice. How are you doing? I thought you had forgotten me! Are you okay?"

She snapped at him, "Why shouldn't I be okay?" irritated by his question.

"Gosh, I'm sorry."

Did he say something wrong?

"I didn't mean to speak so harshly to you, Corey. This nice, strange old man befriended me. Tonight he irritated me. He talks about God and the poor all the time."

"That makes him strange?" asked Corey, perplexed.

"He knows people in Linn. He knows about my mom and Bryan. And you! At first, I thought he was some kind of private detective, that you or Bryan sent him to spy on me. He said he'll tell me more when the time is right."

"He says he knows me? That's pretty mysterious." He wanted to ask her if she missed him.

"Tomorrow I'm going to ride a camel in over one-hundred-degree heat! And see the Sphinx and the pyramids."

"How cool!"

"Well, I'm going to get dressed for dinner and then go to the show afterward in one of my new dresses."

"I wish I could you see you wearing one of your dresses, Damaris. Could you take some pictures and send them to me?"

"Sure, Corey. Well, I've got to go now. I just wanted to hear your voice. I'll talk to you soon, okay?"

She didn't understand why talking to Corey made her feel so uncomfortable, but at the same time, his voice was comforting to her.

"Goodbye, Damaris, and good night. Sleep well." *I love you, and I hope one day you'll love me*, he said to himself.

The next day, neither Mr. A nor Raphael were there at the gangplank. She was disappointed, but she had made the choice. She traveled to Luxor and the Valley of the Kings on a guided tour. She rode a dirty, smelly camel in over one-hundred-degree heat. Her guide was knowledgeable and interesting, but she missed Mr. A's insights and his laughter. Her depression hung over her like a dark cloud. At the end of the day, after she reboarded, she luxuriated in a cold shower and sat on the balcony as the ship left the port. She didn't feel like being around people and making small talk, so she ordered a room-service meal and champagne. She wasn't a drinker, but she craved relief from her depression. The half-moon light covered the ocean like a blanket of diamonds. She was lonely. She should have brought a girlfriend, but who? Her only close friend, Kris, lived in California. She had no one to share this with except by a long-distance phone call and no one to share her laughter or delight in the new sights, smells, or sounds like she could with Mr. A. She curled up on her comfortable balcony chair, looking out on the Red Sea, and started crying, then sobbing uncontrollably. She was rich now. She was supposed to be happy, but she wasn't. Lonelier than she had ever been, she missed Bryan, Pastor Dave, and her mom; and yes, she even missed Corey and her familiar small town of Linn, Missouri. She felt like life had left her as the ship rolled on through the dark night.

The Red Sea is a seawater inlet of the Indian Ocean 1,800 miles long and 190 miles wide. It would take the *Queen Mary* six days to sail to Dubai, with no port stops in between. There were too many activities on the ship to be bored. She attended afternoon tea, enjoyed theater productions, learned to cook, participated in enjoyable game shows, played slot machines in the Empire Casino, listened to live music nightly, jogged, used the luxurious gym and spa, took a fencing class at which she excelled, played darts, and loved Big Band Night in the Queen's Ballroom. She dressed for the Harlequin Masked Ball and relished time in the library. All these activities would be available for the entire cruise at one time or another. One of her favorite classes was an etiquette class where she learned how to walk, sit, and stand in a graceful manner; how to get in and out of chairs and cars gracefully; phone etiquette; what good grooming looks like; and how to set tables correctly with silverware and napkins. Why didn't parents teach their girls these things? The etiquette classes truly changed her by giving her confidence in social situations. For the rest of the cruise, she remembered these rules which would one day serve her well as a public speaker, hostess, and mother. Each night, before she went to bed after showering or soaking in her spacious bathtub, she wrote in her journal. For the first time, she picked up the Living Bible Pastor Dave had given her and read some Psalms, which relieved her depression and helped her sleep. Reading them made her feel less alone.

14

Dubai, United Arab Emirates

The *Queen Mary* entered the Persian Gulf after traveling six days from Egypt. The docking activity outside her room woke her. She slid from her silken sheets and walked onto her balcony in her silk nightgown. Before her, in the middle of a barren desert, was an astounding magical city of glass and mirrors inundated with tall skyscrapers—some the tallest in the world—built on man-made islands, some islands shaped like palm trees. The towering Burj Khalifa, one of the tallest buildings in the world, was half a mile high and shimmered like gold in the intense sun. This city was an over-the-top Las Vegas on steroids. Damaris was told she had to be careful what she wore as she planned a tour of the city. It was Muslim with semi-strict

Sharia law. Women were not allowed to wear revealing clothes, no short shorts or spaghetti straps. Luckily her clothes were expensive and already in good taste. She wished Mr. A could show her the city.

She heard a knock on the door, thinking it was her butler, and heard a voice announce, "Room service." After unlocking the door, in walked Mr. Armstrong with a silver plate of fruit and pastries and a decanter of hot coffee. He sat down comfortably, acting like it hadn't been over a week since he saw her.

"Did you miss me?" He smiled.

"You know I did. It isn't much fun without you." She sat down next to him and patted his leg. "Where have you been?" she asked, knowing she wouldn't get a straight answer.

"Well, I've been here and there, like you, keeping busy all over the place. I've been staying in the shadows, letting you do your own thing. If you had really looked for me, you would have found me. Now eat your breakfast and get dressed. We have two days of sightseeing and lessons to learn."

"What makes you think I want to see the sights with you?" She was still mad at him.

"When you were in Egypt, you kept wishing I was there with you because you knew life was more fun and interesting in my company, right?"

"How do you know that?"

Was he some kind of mind reader?

As usual, he took charge of her day. "We have two days in this amazing city, a testament to man's architectural ingenuity. Eat, get dressed in something Sharia appropriate, and meet Raphael and I on the dock in an hour. It's going to be very hot! We've hired a personal guide for the day."

Yakub, the private driver for the limousine company Mr. A hired, informed them his name was the Arab equivalent of the Hebrew name Jacob, meaning "God will protect." Mr. A looked at Raphael, and they both laughed. Yakub spoke flawless English and had a wealth of knowledge about this fantastic city in the middle of the Arabian desert.

"Dubai is a tolerant society that welcomes foreigners and tourism. Surprisingly the basis of the economy is not oil in this oil-rich area. Its tax-free imports and exports and no corporate taxes for up to thirty years, unlike the other Gulf states, make it profitable for companies to do business here. It is ruled by Sheikh Mohammed ben Rashid Al Moktoun, the architect of Dubai's economic success."

Yakub drove skillfully through traffic. Service trucks mingled with an abundance of Bentleys, Ferraris, and Maseratis. He told them the average income in Dubai is $60,000 per year, compared to America's $30,000 per year. Damaris waited for one of Mr. A's lectures on "the poor."

Yakub pointed out the Burj Khalifa, the tallest building in the world, built in 2010 for $1.5 billion, designed by American architects, 160 stories tall built with concrete, aluminum, and structural steel—with residential housing, commercial space, a hotel, office space, and exorbitantly expensive leasing agreements—and built to withstand the hot summers. It has fifty-seven elevators and eight escalators. There is a 360-foot tall atrium in the Armani Hotel housed within the building with dancing fountains and touches of gold everywhere as well as a fleet of Rolls-Royces for their guests' use. Damaris asked how expensive it was to stay in the Armani Hotel, and Yakub said she could rent a suite on the twenty-fifth floor at the small price of $24,000 per night!

Another well-known hotel was the Burj al Arab—shaped like a sail, built on its own island, sixty-six floors with only luxury suites, very ostentatious, and containing the famed Al Arab restaurant with the most expensive food and cocktails in Dubai. He told them about the island shaped like a palm tree, the Palm Jumeirah, built at a cost of $12 billion. On this island, there are hotels and malls, the Al Fahidi Fort, and the Dubai Museum. The Grand Mosque was open only in the morning, so Mr. A decided they would catch a tour the next day. Damaris couldn't wait to explore the architecture of this mosque and planned on taking her sketch pad, charcoal pencils, and camera.

They ate lunch at a favorite restaurant named Mahareb, which served traditional Yemeni food. Patrons sat on the floor in a room filled with many other Arabs from the Gulf states. The three men spoke in Arabic most of the time and occasionally in English for Damaris's sake. Mr. A apologized, but he said he needed to refresh his Arabic skills because of the great need here for Arabians to hear what he had to say. Damaris loved the food. Eating while sitting cross-legged or lying sideways on the floor was a new but very pleasant experience. In that room of dark-skinned Arabs, Damaris caused a stir with her angelic blond looks and shapely body as she reclined on abundant pillows. One group of men sent each of them a glass of Arak, a popular Arabian drink made from grapes and anise seed, very potent, with a milky-white anise flavor. Damaris loved the taste and thanked the group of men with her dimpled smile. Mr. A warned her not to greet anyone with a left-handed wave, a social taboo. He also warned her to stick close to them because beautiful White women like her were worth high dollars in the sex trafficking trade, and these traffickers were ruthless criminals.

Mr. A decided they should do something touristy, so they drove out of the great city to the Camel Desert Safari's location. Damaris enjoyed a camel ride, cultural entertainment, and the evening in a Bedouin camp. Her senses were assailed by the smell of camels, the softness of the sand, the soft desert breeze, the rhythm of the Tanoura belly dancers, and an Arabic gourmet lamb and hummus meal under a tent, with torches lighting the darkness as they watched a falcon trainer. Mr. A contently smoked a pipe as the three men conversed quietly in Arabic. This experience was one of Damaris's richest memories. She was glad she had taken this trip because she was learning a great deal about different cultures.

They drove an hour back to the ship, and he told them he would meet them tomorrow at the same time for a further tour. Mr. A and Damaris sat on her balcony for an hour, watching the stars as he taught her more names of constellations and reviewed the others.

"Damaris, I want to tell you more about the stars, and then I'll let you get some sleep. In Psalm 147, it says God Himself determines the number of the stars. God also gives them their names. Psalm 8 and Isaiah 40 declare the stars are works of His hands. Job 40 says that the stars sing together. I love that image, don't you? Look at them now. Can you hear them singing together? First Corinthians 15 says that the stars are His glory. In Genesis 1, it says they are all good. The stars proclaim His handiwork. In the book of Revelation, Jesus himself tells us He is the bright and morning star. I guess the stars are like a love gift to us, don't you think, Damaris?" He looked at her as she focused her gaze on the sky thinking about what he said. He stood and gently said, "I'll say good night, dear child. See you tomorrow for the rest of the Dubai tour."

Mr. A watched her constantly out of the corner of his eye. What was he hoping to see? What was he looking for? Did he expect certain actions? Was he hoping she would express words he wanted her to say? She sensed he was waiting, but waiting for what?

She wrote Mr. A's words in her journal before she went to bed and turned off the lights, and as she lay there, she thought about the stars and who made them. Thanks to Mr. A, the stars were now more than twinkling lights in the sky. They were made for her enjoyment, and they sang her their lullaby as she fell asleep on this clear, starry night on the beautiful Persian Gulf.

*****

The next day, Yakub was again their driver and had been instructed by Mr. A to show Damaris other parts of Dubai. Yakub continued his narration from yesterday.

"Dubai is the richest city in the world with a population of 2.5 million people. Five hundred thousand are Indians, Pakistanis, and Bangladeshis who come as migrant workers. They work twelve hours a day, six days a week, in extremely hot temperatures. They live in camps often with eight or more men sharing a room. Many only make $175 a month, but to them, a low-paying job is better than no job at all in their native countries. The Dubai economy is booming, yet there is no minimum wage! These men help build these fantastic high-rises, luxury hotels, and huge shopping centers, yet two months of migrant pay is held back when they first arrive, and their passports are held for security, ensuring they can't leave. Their debt is great, so they have little freedom. Recruiter fees and visa fees add to that debt. They live in fear and anxiety. These people need medical care and more inspectors to monitor the camps for safety and sanitation. It is January now, and the heat is not bad, but workers die from heatstroke in the hotter months. Don't be deceived by the beauty of these glass-and-steel skyscrapers. Even though there is Sharia law here, there is also the drug trade, money laundering, and human trafficking. Although prostitution is illegal, it is a thriving industry, and prosecutions are rare."

Mr. A added, "Have you heard the expression 'All that glitters is not gold,' Damaris? Dubai may be the richest city in the world, but underneath it lies corruption, greed, and inhumanity. What do you think, Damaris?"

"I think what you are trying to tell me is that it truly is a magnificent city and looks good, all sparkly and shiny on the outside, but that doesn't mean it's pure gold because, maybe on the inside, it has little worth at all. You made me think of some of the popular girls in my high school who dressed perfectly, had stylish hair, perfect makeup, and who were part of the in crowd, but what I saw in many of them was meanness, stupidity, lack of concern for other's feelings, backbiting and arrogance. They looked pretty on the outside, but on the inside, they were ugly."

"Exactly, very astutely put," he said approvingly. "Now think about yourself. You have beauty and money. You can choose the kind of woman you want to be or not want to be. First Peter says what matters most is not your outward appearance, the styling of your hair, the jewelry you wear, the cut of your clothes, but your inner disposition. Cultivate your inner beauty, the gentle, gracious kind that God delights in, Damaris."

Yakub and Raphael listened intently because Mr. A's words were always the very breath of God.

Mr. A went on. "Let's look at this city. No doubt there are amazing pieces of architecture and beauty in their modern, shiny structures. These man-made islands, the expensive cars and homes, crowded tourist attractions, gigantic malls—the biggest in the world, filled with expensive products most people can't afford—all are temporary like the pyramids. People rush around in their Bentleys and Jaguars, going who knows where, staying in $25,000-a-night hotel rooms, while many of the workers live on $130 a month with little money left to send to their families. Yakub, let's drive to northern Dubai where the main population lives. Hotel workers, taxi and limousine drivers, mechanics, food service workers, repairmen, this is their area. They have jobs. They feed and educate their families and drink clean water. Do you remember cities in Spain, Greece, and Egypt where fathers and mothers are unable to experience any of these things?"

"I remember," she said sadly.

Later they stopped at a pristine flat white-sand public beach, the Jumeirah Beach Park, on the warm aqua-blue Persian Gulf. Mr. A had prepared for a possible beach trip if there was enough time before dark. They changed in public changing rooms; and when Damaris emerged from the room, all eyes were on her shapely body, especially Yakub, who stayed close to her most of the time. Tourists felt safe in Dubai; and the police constantly drove through the park in their Rolls-Royce, Bugatti, and Lamborghini police cars, monitoring all activity. Lifeguards walked the beach. Mr. A brought snorkeling equipment in the trunk, and Yakub was especially interested in this beautiful girl in her alluring flowered bikini. Raphael was always close by. Even Mr. A snorkeled! They had a lovely day on the beach, the magical Dubai skyscrapers in the distance shimmering with light. She gave Yakub a generous tip, and he asked if he could kiss her cheek. As he did, he murmured something sensual in her ear in Arabic, which Mr. A felt was inappropriate to translate. After all, Yakub had the Arabs' fascination for beautiful blond-haired, blue-eyed American women.

That night after an elegant dinner with Mr. A in the Queen's Grill restaurant, Damaris took a menu to her suite and, in her journal, wrote down what she had eaten. She knew people in Linn had never heard food names like this. This was one meal, one dinner. Every night was different. The *Queen Mary* had the finest chefs in the world and the finest service. She was lucky she exercised daily. She hadn't gained weight and was eating healthier ever.

Appetizer—salmon gravlax with poached quail eggs, mini capers, and lemon puree

Entrée—pan-seared salmon scallopini with roasted almond and haricot vert orzo, roasted shiitake mushrooms, and cherry tomato etude

Dessert—mango panna cotta with passion fruit granita

Cheese trolley—a selection of international cheeses with fine biscuits, fruits, and artisan breads

She texted the dinner menu to Bryan, Corey, and Pastor Dave. She knew they were probably eating either spaghetti or hamburgers! They texted back saying she needed a translator to translate the food names into the American language! She laughed. She decided she would ask for copies of every dinner menu in the dining room for the entire cruise. The idea of opening a five-star restaurant was a plan percolating stronger in her mind each day. She would share her ideas with Bryan and Pastor Dave on returning.

After the nightly entertainment, she and Mr. A drank coffee on her balcony as the ship prepared to leave Dubai.

"Damaris, I want to continue the conversation we had in the limousine today about true beauty. When we were swimming at the beach, every eye was on you. You are truly lovely, which can be a blessing in attracting a mate and opening doors of opportunity, but it can be a curse in other ways. You get irritated with me when I talk about God, but there is nothing on earth that is good apart from Him. If you don't have a firm handle on who you are and who you are truly meant to be, temptations will come your way, and you will have no way to resist them. Listen to me carefully. A woman's commitment to the Lord is what truly matters in life. Charm is deceitful, and beauty is vain, but a woman who fears the Lord is to be praised. The true beauty of a woman is reflected in her soul, and this beauty grows with the years from a life of giving of herself. A beautiful woman is clothed with strength and dignity. She speaks with wisdom, and she is not idle. I pray it will be in your heart to develop a quiet and gentle spirit, a spirit that can pause, meditate, and reflect on the glory of God."

After he left, she sat on the balcony, the light from the living room illuminating the darkness, lost in the echo of his words. She thought to herself that people kept telling her how beautiful she was, but did she have a beautiful soul and spirit? Was her beauty merely on the surface? Did she have a quiet and gentle spirit? She knew she wasn't committed to the Lord. She didn't even know Him! Maybe she wasn't beautiful on the inside, where it really counted. She would think about these things as her travel continued.

15

Abu Dhabi, United Emirates

The next day, they docked on an island in the Persian Gulf with a modern skyline, a city focused on oil exports and commerce. Raphael and Mr. A waited for her as usual with the white limousine. They took her on a tour to the amazing Zayed Grand Mosque, the largest mosque in the country, holding forty-one thousand worshippers with the world's longest carpet—sixty thousand square feet of wool, weighing thirty-five tons! In the center of this huge mosque were two German chandeliers thirty-five feet in diameter and fifty feet high, made with millions of Swarovski crystals. The pools along the arcades reflected the mosque's columns. At night, the entire mosque was illuminated. The massive prayer hall floor was inlaid with mother-of-pearl, and Damaris snapped many pictures of exquisite examples of Middle Eastern art and architecture. She brought her sketch pad and pencils, and as the three of them sat in the still hall, she captured the beauty as well as she could. Mr. A was impressed with her artistic ability and decided they should take a quick tour of the Louvre Abu Dhabi, which showcased artwork from around the world with the purpose of bridging the gap between Western and Eastern art. It was built in conjunction with the Louvre in Paris, France, and they shared collections. Damaris loved the art museum. Her sensitive and artistic nature embraced the beauty of the artwork, and she could have wandered the galleries for days.

Time was getting short, so Mr. A asked Raphael to drive into one of the poor sections of Abu Dhabi. Damaris protested to him that, after seeing all the beautiful places, she didn't want pictures of ugliness in her mind.

All he could say was "This has to be, Damaris. Twenty percent of these people live below the poverty line. The government is very secretive. It controls the information, and reporters are discouraged from writing about it. The government subtly squashes dissension. However, the government is working to improve the conditions of the migrant workers, but there is little public outcry against the abuses of the workers, 88 percent of whom are foreign and lack citizenship. These are beautiful cities, especially Dubai.

Tourists like you don't usually see the poorer areas and the slums because the governments try to create an image of perfection. Their crime rates appear to be low, but there is deep corruption, mostly hidden, like drugs, sex trafficking, and prostitution. All that glitters is not gold, true?

"We have many countries to see in the next months and weeks. You'll see the best of each country, and you'll see the worst. I want you to know the truth, Damaris, for a reason. I won't always be 'lecturing' you, as you call it. You are a perceptive, intelligent young woman, no longer a child. By the end of April, you will be wiser, and you will be sure of the next steps that should be taken. There will come a time in April when you will rarely see us, but until then, I promise we will always be by your side. There are consequential people and places I still have to show you."

"You are going to leave me at times like you did before?" She felt the tears gathering in her eyes.

"Yes, Damaris, but I promise you will never be alone."

16

Cochin, India

The next few months, Damaris, Raphael, and Mr. A were constant companions. In most of the ports, they used the limousine. Damaris stopped asking how this was accomplished because Mr. A always said the limo traveled with them in the hold of the ship. During the five-day journey at sea from Abu Dhabi, Damaris enjoyed the shows, the lectures, the history classes, researching information in the exquisite library, the live music, the dancers, and the costume parties, which the travel agent prepared her for. Damaris, at times, felt like a college student or like a child who was told she could enter a candy store and eat all the candy she liked. Mr. A also knew how to have fun. He was filled with life and joy. He loved to laugh, and the sound of his infectious laugh carried through the entire ship. He swam. He ate with gusto. He loved to sing at the karaoke bar with his clear and booming voice, always the star of the night, excelling in Irish tunes like her dad. He liked ballroom dancing and was debonair in his turns and dips. He said he was sixty, but he appeared ageless, as if the aging process had stopped and he lived in the world as a delighted child. Later she realized he was eternally young. Maybe because she needed a father figure after losing her dad, she stopped resisting the healing his presence provided for her wounded spirit of the last three years.

Mr. A told her about the next stop, Cochin, India, on the Arabian Peninsula with 1.5 million people, a world-class port since 1341. The top three religions there are Hinduism, Islam, and Christianity. Christians are 35 percent of the population. Cochin was once the head of the world spice trade. Now it is a busy port, but sadly there is high unemployment and poor sanitation. Lifestyle diseases like hypertension, diabetes, and cancer are on the rise, pushing people below the poverty line. Thankfully the state is improving health care. The people are warm and welcoming. There is a high literacy rate. It is an artistic culture; and the people are very clean, kind, and hospitable. People of divergent religions live together in harmony. There are divine beaches and transparent waters in this area of the south Arabian Sea. It is one of the most visited tourist places in India. She researched the town and decided to stay on the ship. She was exhausted and needed sleep. Mr. A understood. She called Bryan and told him she was having fun and asked him to say hello to Pastor Dave and Corey. She wrote in her journal and on post cards, read some chapters in *Gone with the Wind*, and slept deeply.

17

Langkawi, Malaysia

Growing up in a small Midwestern town, predominantly White and Christian, Damaris had never been exposed to such a diversity of cultures and religions. Langkawi is a district of ninety-nine islands, only four inhabited, off the coast of northwestern Malaysia covered with rice paddies, fields, jungle, swaying coconut trees, and white-sand beaches. It has a small population of eighty-five thousand, Islam and Christianity the main religions. The major cruise lines dock here because of its ecological beauty. Mr. A took a raincheck, and just she and Raphael took an afternoon four-hour Jet Ski tour. It was a day filled with laughter . Even serious Raphael smiled a few times and several times surprised Damaris by laughing out loud! They swam in the crystal blue waters of the Dayang Bunting Lake, the largest fresh-water lake in Malaysia. Damaris loved the rural feel and the ecological beauty, and they ended the day snorkeling, Raphael always by her side. She was surprised it was such a satisfying and enjoyable day. No big cities today, thank heavens, a day to relax and think about all she had seen and experienced.

18

Kuala Lumpur, Malaysia

Damaris faithfully wrote in her journal each night. Not only did she research each port stop the night before, but she recorded her thoughts and impressions of each place at the end of each day. She wanted to remember everything! She learned that this city is close to Singapore. It is the capital of Malaysia with 6.5 million people, 55 percent of the population Chinese. The most recognizable landmark is the Petronas Twin Towers, the tallest twin towers in the world. There is a diversity of races, religions, and cultures and little violent crime. Mr. A and Raphael showed her around in horrendous traffic, Damaris clinging to the above-the-door handle, her feet planted firmly in front of her as Raphael capably wove in and out of lines of cars, amazingly avoiding colli-sions. They stopped at an indoor restaurant and ate a traditional spicy Malaysian dish called Nasi Lemak, which was rice cooked in coconut milk, eggs, pea-nuts, vegetables, seafood, and samboi, a chili-based sauce so hot she could barely swallow it but tasted wonderful! The city was an overcrowded metropolis, and amazingly they arrived back at the ship without an accident.

That night, after a wonderful dinner in the Queen's Grill, Mr. A taught her more about Malaysia. It is a country working on reducing pov-erty. Industrialization and urbanization have lured the rural populations into the cities. Only 9 percent are Christian. Private Christian schools are part of the government's education system, unlike the United States. There is freedom to practice Christianity, but if you advertise or pass out religious literature, it has to say "For non-Muslims only." Some practicing Christians even disguise themselves as legal Muslims, but luckily the government doesn't interfere with Christian schools. There are many Christian song-writers in the country (Damaris would tell Bryan to check them out). There is an interesting juxtaposi-tion of faiths.

Mr. A said with authority, "Damaris, in spite of many different religions in many countries, there can be only one truth, one God, and not many. I am telling you this truth. Do not doubt me."

That's all he said to her about this, and he spoke with such authority there was no doubt he stood firm for the absolute truth. That night, they watched amazing Chinese acrobats in the showroom, but Damaris also thought deeply about what Mr. A told her. She wondered how there could be only one God when there were so many different kinds of people, cultures, and religions. She wanted to ask him why all religions weren't the same and if the Christian faith was the only truth. Mr. A would soon reveal to her the reasoning.

19

Singapore

Singapore is called an oasis in Southeast Asia. It is a city, a nation, a state, and an island with the world's busiest seaport, which is clean and well located. It was a British protectorate until 1963. Supposedly crime is rare because of extremely harsh penalties for offenders who commit crimes which may seem petty to the rest of the world. Damaris learned from Mr. A that Singapore hides the truth about the actual prevalence of crime. There is poverty and rampant prostitution and sex trafficking. How can someone say there is no crime? The slums are hidden. In them, there is a shortage of food, clothing, shelter, and safe drinking water. Elderly people eat scraps and are not taken care of. Most of the poor are the elderly. Every three seconds a person dies of poverty. Most Singaporeans and Western visitors think poverty is not an issue in this prosperous, globally admired city; but migrant workers live in cages or are housed in storage containers with bug-infested beds, water drawn from sinks lined with scum, broken and clogged toilets, humid and damp basements in tenement homes with no ventilation or refrigeration, bedbugs, mosquitoes, and cockroaches. There are thousands of profitable companies yet no decent housing. The poor work twelve hours a day, seven days a week, building luxury homes and condominiums worth millions. Damaris could barely listen to Mr. A. Her heart was so full of what she had seen and heard. There was so much wealth in this world yet so much poverty, suffering, and hopelessness!

She booked a Heritage Singapore sightseeing tour with their own private driver. Raphael came too, taking a break from driving. The traffic was horrendous. Six million people live in this one city. The whole state of Missouri had only six million! Their guide made it interesting, but this city was not an oasis to her. She couldn't wait to get back to the *Queen Mary*. She spent the rest of the day walking around the ship, watching huge cranes load and unload shipping containers from a parade of semis arriving and departing. Watching port activities was far more interesting than driving around the crowded streets of Singapore.

20

Ko Samui, Thailand

Damaris knew nothing about this city. She researched it the night before and learned it was an island in the Gulf of Thailand known for its palm-tree-fringed beaches, coconut groves, and dense rainforests. Its landmark was a fifty-foot-tall golden Buddha statue. It's a touristy town, the streets lined with massage parlors. There is tension with the migrant workers. Islam and Buddhism are the main religions. There are several Buddhists temples, dangerous roads, and many people trying to scam the tourists. Insects and reptiles abound, so huge amounts of bug repellent are needed. She could take an elephant ride, but the reviews were bad. The place did not sound appealing, so she stayed on the ship and enjoyed a much-needed massage. She was homesick. She missed her mom and hoped her rehab was doing her good. She started thinking about Corey and wondered if he was interested in her because of her money, or was she mistrusting people's motivations for befriending her now? She wondered about Mr. A too. Why was he so secretive? She listened to live music in the atrium that night but was depressed and went to bed early, glad she had *Gone with the Wind* for an escape from these thoughts. There was no escape though. She thought of Scarlett O'Hara, who was starving after the Civil War was over. She had worked her fingers to the bone just to keep her family from starving and to protect her home from the carpetbaggers. All she could think of was getting money and more money because it was the most important thing in the world. Damaris asked herself if she could turn out like that. Would she be another Scarlett? Would money become the most important thing in the world to her?

21

Ho Chi Minh City, formerly Saigon, Vietnam

Mr. A informed Damaris that tomorrow would be a very important port of call. She would meet some very influential people who were changing the world for the better. Even though Damaris wasn't alive during the Vietnam War, she learned about it in school. When America pulled out its troops, Vietnam became a Communist nation very hostile to Christian churches. Only 2 percent of the population now are Protestant, and 7 percent Catholic out of a population of ninety-eight million. Even though there aren't many churches comparatively speaking, the churches do much good in Vietnam.

They are helping get people off drugs as they open up the Gospel to them. The atheist regimes cannot deny God's work in restored lives. Vietnam does allow Christian concerts, and these concerts are resulting in conversions. The city of Saigon itself is overcrowded, smoggy, and crime ridden. Mr. A and Raphael met her at the pier, ready and smiling.

The first place Mr. A wanted her to visit was the Phu My Orphanage, a passionate ministry which preaches among the poor and marginalized. There are three hundred children here with disabilities like cerebral palsy, autism, and Down syndrome. These children have been either abandoned or taken there by their parents. The orphanage needs many volunteers so each child can have individual attention. They enjoy playing games and having volunteers reading and singing to them. Three hundred children and only twenty staff members! Well-meaning Western tourists sometimes stay at the orphanage to help and often make donations. Many Australians volunteer and offer financial support. Australians believe it is their national responsibility even though the orphanage is not in their country. Some of the children's disabilities are linked to the residues of dioxin-laced Agent Orange sprayed during the Vietnam War. Several worldwide organizations send volunteers here, along with college students, for their work-study programs. There are enough doctor volunteers who visit daily, but volunteers are needed for loving acts—pushing children in wheelchairs and on swings and reading them books.

As they walked through the orphanage, she felt shame at how she complained after her father was killed. She was raised in a loving home. Most of these children were abandoned by their families. They reach out for any tiny scrap of love or attention. The head nun, Sister Mary, guided them to a family room with bookcases full of picture books in Vietnamese, French, and English. Mr. A, Raphael, and Damaris were each led to a comfortable sofa with a large stack of books; and one by one, the disabled children were brought to them. Raphael read the French books. Mr. A read in Vietnamese; and Damaris, of course, read in English, enjoying each child. The children delighted in touching and smoothing Damaris's long silken hair as they nestled close to her as she read. They were sweet disabled children who needed attention, love, and to feel valued. The two hours flew by quickly. Damaris had $1,000 cash in her handbag, folded up the bills, and pressed them lovingly into Sister Mary's hands, promising she would send more. She saw the tears in the sister's eyes as they said goodbye.

As they drove through Saigon, Damaris's thoughts and emotions overwhelmed her. Mr. A explained that the Vietnam War left many children not knowing their parents. Children were found in buses, and police brought them to orphanages. Many

Westerners have adopted Vietnamese children, who were the lucky few. The next orphanage they visited was the Annunciation Orphanage with fifty children and two nuns. The nuns woke at four thirty each morning and didn't get to sleep until late in the evening. The older children helped care for the younger children. They had no family support. Each child was treated with tenderness and compassion. They were clean, healthy, and full of smiles. Again the three of them took time to interact with the children. The nuns needed donations, but the most important thing they needed were Band-Aids! Even a small contribution made a huge difference. A simple toy could make a child's day.

Back to the ship, the pictures of these children lingered in Damaris's thoughts. She was ashamed she spent the last years complaining and whining about her life. Nothing compared to the suffering many children experience. She thought of all the uneaten food on this ship alone, leftovers to the travelers but life and death to children, a banquet of uneaten food which could mean the difference between living and dying to millions. She slept fitfully that night. She had seen so many needs on this trip, and she guessed she was being led in a direction where she could make a difference in the lives of at least a few.

22

Hong Kong, China

Damaris knew nothing about Hong Kong, but she knew Mr. A was joining her for breakfast in her suite and would give her the background and history of this city of eight million. She always thought most American products came from China but was surprised to learn only 5 percent of their production comes to the US. Hong Kong is a financial superpower with the seventh largest port in the world. There is even a Hong Kong Disneyland! It has an abundant labor supply and low taxes, and the Communists increasingly control more and more of the city's capitalistic system. Two million people live in poverty, a fourth of the population. Affordable housing is a big issue. It was once a British colony. It is freer than mainland China, with a limited democracy. The poor live on $700 a month. A nine-hundred-square-foot apartment rents for $4,000 per month. Many of the youth must cohabitate with their parents because rent is 70 percent of the average income. Many homes have no kitchens and have exposed electrical wires. Bathrooms and a tiny kitchen were all in one space. There is pressure on the government to improve conditions for these people. Public housing is being built, but one hundred thousand are on the waiting list. Because of little political will for change, there are gangs, organized crime, extortion, illegal gambling, drug and sex trafficking, and racketeering. China has the world's greatest irreligious population. The Communist party is officially atheist. China bans the sale of Bibles online, and there is increased religious persecution. Only 7 percent of the population is Christian. Missionaries are officially forbidden to share the Gospel.

Mr. A told her about the House of Hope in the Henan Province founded by an American high school teacher and supported by Catholic nuns, a Baptist Sunday school class in Missouri (Damaris wondered if it was Pastor Dave's church), and a Christian church in Kansas City which gives $10,000 a year. It is estimated that five hundred thousand have been baptized here since the 1970s. God's work has not been stopped in spite of repression and persecution. It was a ministry that needed donations.

"Pastor Dave, I can see Hong Kong from the ship, but what I'd really like to do is spend the day in the library. You have given me so much to think and learn about. I know the lights of Hong Kong at night are fantastic. I'll watch them from the deck tonight.

I'd like to enjoy some cruise entertainment tonight, then look at the lights from a distance."

Mr. A understood.

Thoughts had been percolating in her brain, and she said to Mr. A, "There are so many people who don't know about God. The atheists outnumber the Christians ninety to one. The government is too big, too strong, too powerful, isn't it?"

Mr. A crossed his leg and asked her a question, "Damaris, when Jesus walked this earth, do you know how many men walked with Him when He started His ministry at age thirty-three? You might not know because you haven't been taught. Twelve men, ordinary men, who came along beside Him, learned from Him and heard Him speak and teach about God. Presently there are 8 billion people in the world, and 2.5 billion are considered Christians. In Africa in 1900, there were 9 million Christian adherents, and now there are 390 million. It is predicted, in 2025, there will be 600 million—from 9 million to 600 million—all beginning with Jesus and His twelve disciples sharing the love of God and the forgiveness of sins. Here in China, the odds are overwhelmingly against the followers of Christ and His church. These odds do not stop God's work. Tomorrow we will be in Shanghai, our last stop in China. Keep your mind and heart open. You have seen these megacities and learned that spiritual poverty is their close companion. However, the work of God is moving through this world slowly but surely, just as the sun rises daily in the eastern sky and the seasons change."

23

Shanghai, China

After Mr. A left, Damaris cuddled up in her bed, and she used her phone to do some research on Shanghai. It was a British protectorate until 1997 and the largest city in the world with twenty-seven million people. The whole state of Missouri has six million, and New York City alone has eight million! It has more skyscrapers than New York City. More people live in this one city than the entire country of New Zealand! Located on the Yangtze River, it is very polluted with vehicle and factory emissions and dust destroying the air quality. It is the world's largest cargo port. The drinking water is unsafe. It has spectacular architecture but the worst slums in China. Rural populations move into Shanghai looking for work, and these migrants suffer the most. It has the world's largest public transportation system and a fairly good educational system. There are thirty universities and colleges; but the society itself suffers from growing materialism, rampant corruption, and high suicide rates. Twenty-three million abortions are performed each year because of birth restrictions. There are not a high number of Christian leaders, only one for every seven thousand people. There are few Bibles available.

Damaris decided she didn't want to leave the ship. She wasn't too interested in Chinese art and architecture. She didn't want to be out in the polluted air and insanely busy traffic. She decided to watch the port activities from the safety of the *Queen Mary*. Cunard Lines chose the ports because they were once British protectorates. She thought Shanghai should be taken off the list, just for the safety of the passengers. Three large cruise ships docked near the *Queen Mary*, and watching the port activity was interesting enough for her. Of course, tonight was another night of great dining and onboard ship activities. She was excited about finally leaving China. She didn't have a good feeling about the country and never wanted to see it again. She hated the huge cities. She looked forward to seeing New Zealand and Australia.

24

Cairns, Australia

It would take nine days to voyage from Shanghai to Cairns; and the *Queen Mary* crew did its best to provide supreme entertainment, impeccable service, and the best in fine dining. Damaris laughed that it would be hard to settle for a hamburger at BJ's after this trip. This ship was spoiling her! The entire three months was a plethora of black-tie soirees where she could wear her beautiful evening gowns, attend balls, and hear the finest classical string quartets and jazz groups, the Rhythm of the Night Orchestra, and the musical Broadway Rocks and Big Band Night in the Queen's Ballroom, reliving the golden age of ocean travel. Damaris's travel agent luckily prepared her for these specialty nights, and Damaris brought country Western clothes as well as flapper clothes from the 1920s. The British National Symphony was onboard for part of the cruise.

One of her favorite memories was the tour of the kitchen, which was vast and meticulously organized. Each of the twelve specialty restaurants has their own kitchen. There were two hundred kitchen workers preparing 3,500 meals three times a day. They used 600 pounds of butter a day, made their own ice cream daily, and used 250,000 eggs a week. They bought local ingredients whenever they could at port stops, including fresh herbs and spices. Trucks arrived at each stop bringing thousands of pounds of meat and beverages. There was a butcher shop and gigantic storage lockers for beef, chicken, lamb, seafood, and pork. Lobster was the most popular seafood, and thousands of pounds were served each day. A hundred types of pastries and forty types of bread are baked daily. They were able to look into the deep freezer, which burgeoned with whole carcasses of beef, sheep, and lamb and crates of chicken.

The kitchen tour overwhelmed her, its organization and the quality of the food prepared carefully and presented beautifully. She had made a decision that, with her newfound wealth, she would build a five-star restaurant in her little country town. She would hire reputable chefs and present a plan to Missouri Tech to use the restaurant as part of a proposed culinary program at the college. If well-trained, the students would learn a trade that could provide them with chef's jobs possibly on a cruise ship like the *Queen Mary*. She wrote down all her ideas in her journal and couldn't wait to talk about them with

Bryan, Pastor Dave, and the president and board of trustees at the college.

The lifeguards by the pool flirted with her brazenly, like moths drawn to a light source. Waiters tried to bring her drinks and plates of food, grateful for one of her bright smiles. When she dove in the pool, then emerged from the water, all eyes were on her. The crew knew she was traveling alone and were bold in their attention to her. The bank faxed her papers to sign, and Bryan's recording studio would be finished when she returned. They had budgeted $2 million, and the final cost would be about $1.5 million. It was only the first of March. She wouldn't be home until the end of April. Two more months. She wondered if her homesickness would get the best of her and if she could shorten the cruise. There were still so many stops. She wanted to experience them, but she missed the familiarity of Linn. She had seen so much and was eating constantly, hoping she wouldn't gain any weight. She decided to call Corey. It had been a while since she talked to him.

"Hi, Corey!" she said, trying to sound upbeat.

Corey wasn't fooled. "What's the matter, Damaris?"

Why did he ask her that?

"Come on, you sound a little unhappy."

How did he know?

"I'm not really unhappy. I'm just homesick, and I wanted to hear a familiar voice."

"You've been gone a month. That's a long time, and you have a ways to go. Are you seeing interesting things and socializing with people?"

"I think China depressed me, and I'm looking forward to being in Australia in a few days. That should perk me up. How are you?"

"I'm doing fine. Work is the same old thing. No major crimes going on. My dad is getting ready for spring planting, and I help him when I can." He wanted to hold her in his arms.

"My friend Mr. A has been talking to me about the 'poor' and teaching me about God, so I guess that's good." She sighed.

"I've been talking to Pastor Dave, and he has been visiting Bryan at the recording studio. I think they're becoming friends."

"He's a good friend to have," she acknowledged.

Corey wanted to tell her he loved and needed her and that each day not hearing from her was like a hundred years, but he controlled himself and just listened. He knew that was what she needed now. She looked through her journal and shared some of her observations and experiences. He told her that he had talked to Reggie, that he loved his new Jeep Gladiator, and that every day she had so much mail he had to store it at the post office in huge boxes.

"It looks like you are getting tons of requests for money from every place possible."

"Great." She sighed. "That's what was happening before I left. That's why I'm on this ship, to get away from that pressure. I've learned I hate big cities, Corey, with their millions of people, traffic, crime, poverty, and pollution. I get so nervous. I really am a small-town girl."

"I'm glad to hear that, Damaris, because I'm a small-town boy."

"I've got to say goodbye, Corey. We're docking now. Thanks for listening to me. Keep an eye on my car!"

"Stay in touch!" He wanted her to tell him she loved him, but she heard a knock on the door, quickly said good-bye and hung up.

"It's me!"

She hadn't seen Mr. A for nine days since as they left the East China Sea and moved into the Pacific Ocean.

She happily opened the door. "I missed you so much!"

"No, you didn't. You were having the time of your life. I watched you." He sat comfortably on her sofa. "You're glad those two big cities are off your bucket list, huh?"

"I hated them. They were like big, impersonal, monstrous machines."

"Good descriptions. You'll find Cairns, Australia, a small village comparatively speaking, with only 150,000 people. Have you looked over some of the shore excursions?" he asked as he sipped his strong cup of coffee with clotted cream.

"I've been reading about the Great Barrier Reef. It's so large it can be seen from outer space. Some call it one of the seven natural wonders of the world. It's the most pristine coral reef on the planet. I signed up for a snorkeling and diving cruise for eight hours. I can't wait to experience it. The boat named *Evolution* leaves at 8:00 a.m. and takes ninety minutes to get to the first snorkeling location, then on to another, and we'll return around 5:30 p.m."

Mr. A said he wouldn't be coming along but Raphael would go with her. She really appreciated Raphael's company because of what happened later in the day.

*****

After snorkeling in the Saxon and Norman reefs in the morning, the Hastings Reef was next, about a ninety-minute boat ride. She took some seasick pills because of the choppy reef waters. The crew went through the safety procedures. The snorkelers were warned not to touch the coral. Reef cuts quickly became infected and caused pain and inflammation. The crew assured them they were equipped with all the materials needed for treatment but to heed their warning. Several people were concerned about sharks. They were told reef sharks were harmless. Dangerous sharks like tiger sharks stayed in deep water outside the reefs and were unheard of in this area. Damaris whispered to one of the crew members she had started her menstrual period and wondered about any leakage of blood into the water. She was told not to worry.

They continued their instruction on snorkeling techniques. Damaris loved their Australian accents but often had a hard time understanding them because their accents were so heavy. They spoke English, but sometimes their English sounded like another language. The experienced crew took turns instructing this beautiful American girl, and then she was ready to enter into the water. She delighted in looking at the colorful marine life in the clear, clean blue waters of the Coral Sea. Raphael faithfully kept his eyes on her as she swam farther and farther from the main group. The snorkelers wondered who Raphael was to Damaris—a husband, a brother, a boyfriend, or perhaps a bodyguard? Raphael stood apart from the people on the boat, carefully watching Damaris. The crew assured everyone they were keeping a close eye on the swimmers and admonished them to stay together and not snorkel far from the others.

Damaris was amazed at the diverse wildlife below the crystal-clear surface and astonished by the plethora of shapes and color, a foreign environment teeming with life. The other snorkelers kept within shouting distance of the boat, but Damaris ventured farther out into the reef, totally absorbed in this underwater spectacle. One of the guests on the boat, drinking her beverage, saw a large dark shadow about a hundred feet from the boat. She looked at her husband, pointed to the shadow, and asked him what it could be. His eyes narrowed as he followed her pointing finger. The shadow alarmed him, and he called to the captain to look where he was pointing. The captain saw the ominous shadow as it turned toward Damaris. No other snorkelers or crew members were aware of this, nor was Damaris. As the shadow moved closer, the captain and Raphael were on high alert. The shadow slowly submerged, and Damaris felt a rough texture and a bump against her thigh. It surprised her.

"What was that?" she cried out. Seeing no aggressive action on her part, the shadow emerged, and the crew saw the gray dorsal fin and striped body of a fourteen-foot tiger shark checking out Damaris's vulnerability and quickly approaching her through the water. The captain used his megaphone to call people into the boat, telling them to move slowly without kicking or splashing their arms. The crew looked on in horror as the shark circled Damaris.

"Turn your back to the boat!" the captain shouted.

"Damaris!" shouted Raphael. "Move slowly toward the boat with your back toward it!"

Instantly Raphael pulled out a diver's knife from a belt under his shirt and dove into the water. To get the shark's attention away from Damaris, Raphael started splashing violently. As the shark turned toward Raphael, Damaris moved slowly, kicking with her flippers, encouraged by the crew who then pulled her out of the water. The shark took a swipe at Raphael, trying to bite him, ready for the kill. Raphael moved aside and grabbed the dorsal fin with his left hand as the killer moved past him. With the razor-sharp blade in his right hand, he reached down and made a deep sweeping arch in the shark's soft underbelly. As the intestines spilled out, great billows of blood gushed into the clear sea. As the body drifted toward the bottom, Raphael raised his knife triumphantly as the passengers clapped and shouted appreciatively. Damaris cried as Raphael swam toward the boat, grateful her protector was safe. Back on the boat, the crew shook Raphael's hands vigorously and patted him on the back. Raphael smiled and said he was just doing his job.

The buzz for the rest of the day and evening was the encounter with the tiger shark. The *Evolution*'s owners flew over the large sea in a helicopter close to the surface, looking for any other tiger sharks. A second shark was seen swimming out into deeper water. They told tourists tiger sharks were unheard of in this reef. This encounter shook the owners of the *Evolution*. They were worried it would drastically hurt their business.

Evening at dinner, with Mr. A in the Queen's Grill, Damaris relived the day and told him how thankful she was that Raphael was there to guard her.

Mr. A smiled and simply agreed with Raphael. "That's his job!"

25

Brisbane, Australia

Damaris didn't see Mr. A for two days on their trip to Brisbane, the capital of Queensland. She learned about the youthful, vibrant city of 1.5 million. The new cruise port could handle the super-max cruise ships as well as the *Queen Mary*. Brisbane was popular because of its 265 days of sun, which drew beachgoers year-round, making it feeling more like a small town than a large city. The Brisbane River flows through the town into the Moreton Bay and finally into the Coral Sea. It is a hilly city in the shadow of the 2,700-foot Mount Coot. Eucalyptus, banyan, and jacaranda trees line the avenues and parkways. October is called the jacaranda season, when the trees bloom in riotous purple and the sound of kookaburras fill the air. Damaris remembered as a child standing outside the kookaburra cages in the Springfield Zoo, listening to their silly laughing, crackling birdcalls. She thought of those happy times with her father. Mr. A had joined her once again for breakfast and patted her hand sympathetically as she remembered her childhood years.

Australia and Antarctica are the only two countries completely within the Southern Hemisphere. The seasons were opposite to America's! In Brisbane in March, summer was ending, and winter beginning. In Missouri, winter was ending, and spring and summer were on their way. Maybe there was snow in Linn now, and it was beach weather here!

The Australians were working hard on social issues—lack of jobs, affordable health care, and education, in that order. The aboriginal and asylum seekers, migrants from non-English-speaking backgrounds, were poor. The disabled were subject to human rights abuses.

Nevertheless, Damaris felt that all of Australia was a fascinating country with a fairly religious population, heavily influenced by both Catholic and Protestant churches. It was very similar to America but not as diverse. America with its 330 million people had additional issues compared to Australia's 25 million.

Damaris couldn't wait to see Brisbane. Mr. A and Raphael drove them in the limousine along the river and visited a koala sanctuary. Such cute furry little creatures, sitting in eucalyptus trees and chewing happily on their leaves! They saw wild kangaroos, which she loved, but her favorite part was the self-guided Brisbane architecture tour. Each exquisite building represented different styles or types— colonial, Gothic, and neoclassical. She took notes and many pictures of the All Hallows' School and Convent, St. Andrew's Church, the Brisbane City Hall, and the parliament house. Amazing architecture; but the most impressive was St. John's Cathedral, begun in 1901 and not finished for a hundred years, a Romanesque and Gothic Revival structure in the manner of French cathedrals dedicated to St. John the evangelist. Awe inspiring in itself, it is a major center for art and music with its own orchestra and well-known boys' choir and famous for housing the largest cathedral organ in Australia.

Damaris asked if they could tour the inside. The lofty ceilings, the tall and delicately proportioned columns and low-level lighting, and the masking of exterior walls with long sequences of colonnades resembling the great abbey churches of twelfth- and thirteenth-century Europe were impressive. Damaris had studied this church in her architecture class! Then the golden altar, cross, candlesticks, pulpit, canopy, clergy stalls and pendant lights, and a carved organ case added to the beauty. Sadly the pews had been replaced by freestanding chairs, which Damaris thought took away from the grandeur of this beautiful cathedral. Mr. A and Raphael smiled as Damaris explored the interior awed by the stained glass and its rich colors, each pane telling a biblical story. She promised herself that one day her home would have beautiful stained glass created by the best artists no matter the cost. Her newly acquired fortune would enable her to buy many beautiful works of art her sensitive nature craved. Her gratitude showed in the tears that welled up in her eyes and there was more beauty to enjoy ahead.

26

Sydney, Australia

Two days of cruising to Sydney, the capitol of New South Wales, meant more good food, great entertainment, and much-needed exercise in the spa facilities and pools. Damaris spent time in the library researching Sydney, an attractive city of five million, housing 66 percent of Australia's population. She learned that it was founded in the 1700s with about 1,500 people; 800 of those were convicts from England. It's a very multicultural city. Two hundred and fifty languages are spoken here. It is a 212-year-old colonial town, now with many beautiful skyscrapers but also elegant buildings with intricate colonial architecture. Even though it is a cosmopolitan city, there are, within the city limits, 2.5 million acres of nature preserves. Twenty-six percent of the city is covered in trees. Damaris compared it to Shanghai and Hong Kong—Sydney the overwhelming winner in beauty.

Most Australians own their own homes. There are few rentals. The city is expensive. It is estimated 3.5 million residents live in poverty, but there are no slums! There is a push for increasing public housing and rent assistance. Australia itself is an extremely literate country, and newspapers abound. The government funds artistic endeavors, and the arts thrive. There is no media censorship.

No words could explain the breathtaking entry into the Sydney harbor. The iconic and architectural wonder, the Sydney Opera House, stood like a welcoming sentinel, a masterpiece of human creativity, with its gleaming white sail-shaped shells as its roof structure, one of the most photographed buildings in the world visited by more than ten million people a year. All the passengers were on deck as the *Queen Mary* entered the harbor, and the ship's air horn could be heard ten miles in every direction. The cruise port lies directly across the harbor from the opera house, and Damaris had a full view from her balcony. Mr. A knocked on the door and told her there was much to see during the day and evening, so she needed to get ready quickly. Raphael would drive them. He liked driving in Sydney because it was less dangerous than Hong Kong or Shanghai. With Mr. A's help, she arranged for a private tour of the opera house, promising a substantial donation. She was enthralled. It is a multipurpose performing arts facility. The largest venue is the 2,679-seat Concert Hall, which hosts symphonies, choir performances, and popular music concerts. The Forecourt is used for outdoor musical performances. Thirty shows a week and two thousand per year enrich the public with excellent performing arts experiences. The facility is kept at a constant 72°F, the optimum temperature for the orchestral instruments. The building is cooled by seawater running through the extensive pipe systems. It also houses excellent restaurants and a professional recording studio. She hoped, one day, she could bring Bryan to see the facility. It has been designated a UNESCO World Heritage site. Damaris's private tour also included backstage, where sets are stored and costume and makeup areas prepare performers. The dressing rooms have televisions and intercoms. There are twenty pianos in the facility, many of which are Steinways. All this on only four and a half acres!

Damaris took hundreds of pictures of every part of this performing arts facility. Ideas percolated in her mind about possibly building a performing arts facility in Linn which would rival those in Kansas City and St. Louis. She and Bryan could use design ideas from the Sydney Opera House. How the people in Linn and surrounding cities would benefit! She couldn't wait to tell him about it!

She thanked her guides and made a generous donation to the Sydney Opera House Trust with her credit card. They ate at a lovely restaurant called the Portside near the opera house. Damaris could not stop talking about it. Mr. A listened and then told her they were now driving to a place called the Exodus Foundation, a short distance from the cruise port.

Mr. A introduced Damaris to Reverend Bill Crews. His office was in the back of a church where they provided 1,800 meals a day to the needy, 40 percent of whom were homeless. The high cost of electricity was one reason people were pushed into poverty in Sydney. Many lived in boarding houses, hostels, crisis centers, or on the street, unemployed and with alcohol and drug addictions. Some were victims of domestic abuse, mental illness, and gambling addictions. Many of their appliances didn't work. There were no security provisions, and unhygienic conditions in rentals were more harmful than alcohol or cigarettes. Many of their clients suffered from diabetes and stomach and liver problems. Seventy percent had dropped out of high school at age sixteen. Exodus's many volunteers and employees at night went to the King's Cross area to serve hot meals; offer blankets, clothing, and sleeping bags; and give counseling and hugs. Most of the clients were male with mental issues, victims of family breakdowns and incarceration. They staffed a health-and-well-being clinic and offered free services by health professionals who volunteered their time for dental, optometric, orthopedic, and chiropractic needs. They ran a literary program and taught basic reading skills. Damaris could not believe how many needs there were in this affluent town. Mr. A told her about the Exodus Youth program for at-risk kids age fifteen to nineteen who need help due to family breakdowns, drug and alcohol trauma, and disrupted education. Their goal for these youths was to provide an education program; teach skills for living; and address their mind, body, and spiritual issues.

"We change lives one person at a time. We serve rather than ask to be served. We wash the feet of those in need as servants, as did our Lord. I was an electrical engineer and volunteered at the Wayside Chapel here in Sydney, helping the needy, and after much prayer, I started he Exodus Foundation. When you get back to the ship, look it up. I became an ordained minister, and now God is using me to share God's love. This ministry, with its many volunteers, has given hope to so many, and for that, I am grateful."

Mr. Crews was friendly and warm.

"Mr. A told me about you. He told me about all the good you are doing in your town in America. Our goal here is to demonstrate roll-up-your-sleeves Christianity, meaning less talk and more action, as I tell our volunteers. We share the Gospel message, but our actions are what show our love."

He spent the next thirty minutes sharing ministry stories, the successes as well as the failures. They have a radio show that gives hope and encouragement. She asked questions. He gave her a business card and told her to call him sometime. He asked her how she liked the *Queen Mary*, and he shared how he loved seeing the ship entering and leaving the harbor and hearing the air horn blasts resounding throughout Sydney.

Driving back to the ship, Mr. A asked her what she thought. She had many thoughts! Damaris asked him what it cost to run a busy ministry like this, and he told her $5 million a year. Damaris was flabbergasted at the amount, and she asked him how they received that much money. He told her it was through many people around the world donating sacrificially to help the least of those who are in need. Again she wrote down her observations before she went to bed that night. She thought about the money she had won. At first, she had only considered making Linn a nicer place to live and buying nice things for herself, Bryan, and her mom. But outside of Linn, the needs of the world were greater, and she now knew why Mr. A showed her these places.

The next three days, they would travel to the Bay of Islands, New Zealand. With no port stops, she had more time to think about all she had been shown. She knew she was at some kind of crossroads in her life. She felt like she was riding a huge wave moving slowly and inexorably toward the shore, and when it hit, she knew her previous priorities would be shattered and her old ways of thinking would be engulfed by this gigantic wave of change.

27

Frustration

With two uninterrupted cruise days, she decided to call Bryan and Corey. Bryan was ecstatic! Exodus Studios was nearing completion. He hired a sound engineer to do final sound checks, answer the phones, and book reservations for studio time. She had never seen him this excited. The Rogues could now practice in the studio instead of a garage. With Damaris's permission, he ordered the touring bus for the Rogues, which slept ten, and a huge semi for carrying all their equipment. The Rogues were performing at the JQH Arena in Springfield, a sold-out concert one month from now. This would be their breakthrough concert!

He told Damaris that Corey stopped by the studio frequently and asked about her. "He said you don't call much. He has a huge crush on you, Damaris."

"Of course, he does. I'm wealthy now."

"Corey is not that kind of man, Damaris! You know that! He's honest and decent. He is not the kind of man who would date a girl for her money. He is a good man, and people trust him."

Damaris knew Bryan told the truth. She was sorry she blurted out something uncomplimentary about him without thinking. She remembered he told her he loved her before she won the lottery.

She next called Corey because she was homesick and felt guilty about accusing Corey of liking her because of her money, which she knew wasn't true. He had just finished his shift and jokingly shared his "exciting" day—issuing three speeding tickets and a ticket for not wearing a seatbelt; arresting a couple of people driving while intoxicated, failing to register their vehicle, and not stopping at a stop sign; and a couple of marijuana possession citations. He was working at his family's ranch on his days off. She told him all about the Sydney Opera House. He listened as usual and said he was glad she was having a good time.

"Corey, I never asked you where you live. Do you live in an apartment in Linn?"

Silence on the other end.

"Are you there, Corey? Did I say something wrong?" she asked.

"No, Damaris. I guess I'm sensitive because I'm twenty-four years old and still live on my parents' property in a small house behind theirs, and I'm embarrassed."

"I live in my mom's house too! Don't feel so bad! You're helping your parents! That's a good thing!"

"You won't be living in your mom's house for long, will you?"

"No, I won't! The recording studio is almost finished, and when I get home, I meet with the architect to design my home on twenty of those ninety-five acres. This trip has given me so many good ideas!"

He perked up and asked hesitantly, "Damaris, you really will be staying in Linn? You've got the money to live anywhere."

"Linn is my home, Corey. But when my mom's better? I don't know. This is a huge world, and there are many beautiful places. If I could live anywhere else, I think I would live on the Greek Islands, or maybe Brisbane, Australia. I don't know. I'm just thinking out loud."

Corey shared that his parents were in Destin, Florida, right now enjoying the sunshine in their condo. "I'm running the operation here. It's still winter, but there's lots to do. We have several thousand head of cattle which need to be fed."

"You shouldn't apologize for living on their property and running the place too."

"Can we change the subject, Damaris? May 5, when you return, is a long way off. I miss you. I'll be glad when you're back."

She smiled into the phone. "I'll be glad, too, Corey, but I'm having a great time. I have fallen in love with this ship. It's never boring, and the people are all so nice. I have experienced so many different kinds of people, cities, and architecture I've seen only in books. Corey, I am seriously thinking about building a smaller version of the Sydney Opera House. I'll tell you about my plans when I get home. I've been sketching and taking pictures, designing the building in my mind. I want to use my money to create things of beauty which will lift human spirits out of the ordinary into the extraordinary. I'm having a hard time expressing my thoughts, but do you kind of understand, Corey?"

"I think I do, Damaris. You are a thing of beauty, and when you walk into a room, you fill it with light. When you stand near me, the world around me reflects your beauty. Your beauty makes everything beautiful." He knew he probably said too much.

"Gosh, Corey. That's so nice of you. I know that all the beauty I have seen on this trip has filled some empty spaces in me." She wanted to get off the subject of his love for her.

Corey said he needed to hang up—ranch business called. He hoped, one day, he would be the one who filled her emptiness.

28

Bay of Islands, New Zealand

Damaris had never heard of this area. She liked the sound of it. It is nicknamed "the birthplace of New Zealand." Captain Cook named the islands in 1769, one of the first Europeans to visit there. In its early history, Christian missionaries civilized the native Maoris, introduced them to the written word, and helped them develop a Maori language. The Maoris were the indigenous Polynesian people of the area. The missionaries made a lasting impact on the Maoris, many of whom today are Christians. There are about 775,000 Maoris in this area. They face significant economic and social obstacles, have lower life expectancies, more health problems, and lack a good education. In the early colonial society, there was great intolerance toward these indigenous people.

Damaris decided to hire a private parasailing charter boat in the morning. Raphael came along too. Mr. A said she wouldn't see him for a few days. The handsome crew members took turns joining her on the parasail. She loved sailing high in the air and seeing the lovely islands as well as whales, dolphins, and seals and the majestic *Queen Mary* below her. It was quiet above the ocean, just the sound of a light wind filling the sail, and she thought how happy the birds must be as they soared and caught the thermal breezes. She paid for additional time. In the afternoon, she took a four-and-a-half-hour private jeep tour, visiting the small whaling port of Russell, looking now as it did in the colonial days. The harbor wasn't deep enough for the *Queen Mary*, so the passengers had to be tendered to and from the shore, which Damaris enjoyed. She was exhausted at the end of the day. She ate from the buffet, took a long hot bath in her suite, and fell asleep on the soft, comfortable balcony recliner as the ship cruised toward Auckland. She was falling in love with New Zealand.

29

Auckland, New Zealand

Damaris had been on this ship since January 3, and it was now March 11—over two months! She was pampered, waited upon, and spoiled. She felt like a queen, but she was getting restless. A mysterious force was pushing her forward to an unknown destiny. She didn't know what was causing this feeling. Was it homesickness? Was it boredom? How could she be bored when every second was filled with activity?

Auckland, a large town of 1.6 million people, is built around two lovely large deepwater sheltered ports. When the *Queen Mary 2* arrives, it causes excitement. People line the sidewalks near the cruise port to see it dock. As always, its loud air horn blasts announce its arrival throughout the city. In 2003, it was the tallest, longest, and widest cruise liner in the world, and people traveled long distances to see it enter the harbor. Damaris loved this part of the cruise, the entering and exiting of the ports.

Later in the day, she put on a colorful flowered Polynesian wrap and joined a group from the ship attending the Rotorua Maori Hangi Dinner and Performance several miles from the ship. The food was cooked over volcanic rock as the audience watched the tattooed Maori dancers. The Maoris were indigenous natives to New Zealand, proud of their heritage and traditions. There was prejudice against them held by White New Zealanders. The Maoris were lovely and gracious. She didn't understand the prejudice. Damaris enjoyed the evening and the group she was with as torches provided light in the darkness and rhythmic drums and chanting filled the night air. They volunteered Damaris to teach her their dance. Her body moved with the music, and unknowingly she captivated even the Maoris. She wasn't social in high school, and she was learning to be comfortable with people and actually enjoy their company. Her natural shyness began to fade. She felt like a rosebud opening up into its fullness; and she was learning to accept who she was, the good and the not so good, and who she was meant to be.

30

Wellington, New Zealand

Two days and then in Wellington, the political center of New Zealand and the southernmost capital city in the world. With a high quality of living, many international film companies come here to film movies, like *The Hobbit*, *King Kong*, *The Lord of the Rings*, and *Avatar*. Strong winds blow through the Cook Straits, so the city is named Windy Wellington, with one of the world's finest deepwater ports. The city is built on dramatic hills and is considered one of the best places to live in the world with its tiered suburbs and funicular railways which work by pulleys—one is pulled up as the other goes down. The rugged mountain ranges surrounding the town added drama to the landscape.

She missed her bike, so she decided to spend three hours on a guided Wellington electric-bike tour through the harbor area. The bikes took them up some very sharp inclines where she experienced the magnificent view from Mount Victoria. She learned a great deal from the female tour guide. She worked up an appetite and was ready to dine later in the Queen's Grill, sitting with some new people who were curious about her. This night was the Western Theme Night; and Damaris had come prepared with Levi's, white embroidered cowboy boots, a form-fitting rhinestone-embroidered snap-up shirt, and a white cowgirl hat. Her outfit definitely drew appreciative stares from men and women alike. The dance instructor taught the crowd the group dances—the Tush Push, Cotton-Eyed Joe, the Cowboy Cha-Cha, and the Electric Slide. Damaris picked them up quickly because, in community events and Missouri fairs, that's what they danced, so she was chosen as the instructor's helper. Damaris laughed because he was a Czechoslovakian!

She wrote down an observation in her journal that night that she made up on her own:

> Here I am traveling on a luxury British ocean liner at the southern tip of New Zealand in the southwestern Pacific Ocean, learning American Country music line dancing taught by a

Czechoslovakian dance instructor, traveling close to Antarctica in the middle of the Southern Hemisphere in summer, which is really winter in Missouri, when it's ten at night on this ship and eleven in the morning in Linn. What a world!

Tired but happy after a busy day, her legs ached from riding the bike up steep hills and dancing for several hours until midnight on the ship. She called Corey again as she sat on the balcony, smelling the pungent sea breezes, and told him about her day.

"I'll bet you looked cute in those cowgirl clothes!"

"I'll send you some pictures tonight. What's going on in Linn?"

Your brother's studio has become a local attraction, not only for people in town, but for tourists, even though it's not quite finished He made some signs limiting visitors. You are both the talk of the town."

"Be sure to tell people I'm going to have a slide show about the trip when I get back."

"Media people are skulking around town trying to get gossip on both of you. Our local businesses seem to like it!"

"How's Crazy Charlie? Is he causing any trouble?"

"Of course he is. He got arrested again for possession, and he is back in our jail now. He just doesn't get it. He thinks us cops are stupid."

"Is my car still safe and sound? I wish I could have it around here on these lovely roads next to the ocean."

"We have picturesque roads here in Missouri, Damaris."

"Of course we do, Corey!"

She knew he was worried that she was losing interest in Linn.

"I am painfully tired now, Corey. My legs ache. Tomorrow we'll be in the city of Christchurch, which, they say, looks just like England. I'll call again soon, okay?"

Corey hated their phone conversations. He wanted to tell her how much he cared about her, but he knew his strong feelings caused her to distance herself from him. She was on this fabulous trip, and there he was in Linn living a boring life. It sounded like she just wanted to be friends. He knew that would never be enough. He wanted more than friendship.

31

Christchurch, New Zealand

There is a rhythm on a long voyage like this. Every hour and every day is scheduled, planned, and predictable. The predictability gave her a sense of security. She was grateful her mom was in good hands getting whole again and putting the pieces of her broken life back together. Damaris didn't worry about bills anymore, which had been an obsession the past three years. Slowly but surely, she was healing from her deep grief. The gifts her father passed on to her—the gifts of enthusiasm and love of adventure—were reemerging from ashes, which had been locked tightly in her heart. Slowly the box was opening, and the ashes were blowing away in the wind. Her love of life was rekindled. She tried writing these feelings in her journal, but her words seemed inadequate. She guessed what she was simply trying to express was that she once again had hope. She didn't know that, in a few weeks, she would meet someone who would tempt her in a way she had never been tempted.

Christchurch, a city of five hundred thousand, is the oldest established city in New Zealand, founded in 1856. It has several nicknames, the Garden City or the Gateway to the Antarctic, with the purest, cleanest water in the world and a temperate oceanic climate. It is the most British of cities outside of England and the wine capital of New Zealand. The economy is based on tourism, agriculture, many sheep farms, seed developers, dairies, wool and meat processing, olive production, and deer farms. New Zealand lies on a major earthquake fault zone, and in 2011, Christchurch experienced the strongest earthquake ever recorded in an urban area. One hundred and eighty-five people were killed, and it cost the city $30 billion to rebuild. With burst water mains, damage from flooding and liquefaction, a damaged port, cracked roads, and broken sewer pipes which caused contamination, businesses closed. Now 67 percent of the residents felt tired, and half were not sleeping well. Damaris learned from her research that it takes five to ten years to emotionally recover from a disaster. Damaris hoped that she was on the road to recovery from the loss of her father.

There is a 43 percent more of a likelihood of a 5.0 to 6.0 magnitude to hit Christchurch again. Since that terrible day, the city has rebuilt with more earthquake-resistant structures.

Christchurch is not a wealthy city. Half the people live on less than $30,000 a year. A third of the households are renters and rents run from $1,200 to $2,400 per month. It is a lovely city in spite of the earthquake tragedy, not a wealthy city by any means, but filled with strong New Zealanders with resilient spirits.

The cruise ship docked in Littleton, and tenders transported passengers to the mainland. Then it was a thirty-minute shuttle drive to Christchurch. Damaris was nervous because of potential earthquakes. She decided she would charter a helicopter from a facility near the airport. She told the woman at the desk she wanted to hire a private helicopter with a pilot. The employee said she had to be part of a group. Damaris looked around the office. Two parents and their young son stood looking at the displayed brochures. Damaris guessed they would like to charter a helicopter, but it was too expensive. Damaris asked the clerk how much it would be for three adults and a child. She quoted $2,400 for an hour. She walked over to the family, introduced herself, and asked if they would like to go with her on a helicopter ride, no charge. They looked at her in disbelief, thinking it was a joke.

Damaris walked back to the counter and said, "I'll tell you what. I want to treat this family to a two-hour ride with me. I want us to see more things than in the one-hour flight, and I will pay $4,500 for these two hours."

The clerk walked back into the manager's office and came back smiling. "It's a deal!"

Damaris and the family filled out the paperwork, and she told them they were going to have the flight of a lifetime. They flew over the picturesque city and stunning bays, the spectacular coastline, Mount Cook and the skyscraping mountains, ancient glaciers, wide-open plains, and coastlines where mountains plunged straight into the sea and saw landing spots untouched by human beings. The pilot was a great tour guide, a native New Zealander, a skier, and a bike rider; and he couldn't believe he had this gorgeous girl sitting beside him delighted as a child. They landed on a glacier and had snowball fights and built snowmen. When the phenomenal trip was over and they landed back at the hangar, Damaris gave their pilot a $500 tip. The family vigorously shook her hand in thanks; and their son, Archie, hugged her legs. Damaris was happy she could give them this experience, realizing that it truly is more blessed to give than receive. This is what Pastor Dave talked to her about. She hoped her Nikon took great pictures that captured the beauty of the mountains, glaciers, the sea and little redheaded Archie hugging her legs in thanks.

32

Milford Sound, New Zealand

The night before the trip through Milford Sound, Damaris's table in the Queen's Grill buzzed with excitement. Experienced travelers knew that the thundering waterfalls, sky-high mountains, and lush rainforests would be awe inspiring. Damaris did not know anything about fjords. One of the more knowledgeable men explained to her that a fjord was a long, narrow, deep inlet of the sea between high cliffs formed by a glacial valley. Rudyard Kipling called the Milford Sound fjord, which is not actually a sound, the eighth wonder of the world. It is New Zealand's most famous tourist attraction and part of the Fjordland National Park on an inlet of the Tasman Sea. It rained 182 days a year there, so forget styling your hair!

Damaris was assured that bad weather made the inlet even more beautiful. It would be an early morning passage; so people woke early, dressed warmly, put on rain gear, and waited on deck for the *Queen Mary* to enter the fjord. Damaris was not disappointed. Towering peaks with waterfalls falling along their face plummeted down the sheer sides of the mountains. Gusts of wind changed the direction of the waterfalls at time, making them looked like they flowed upward into the sky. Fur seal colonies perched on rock shelves above the water or swam alongside the boat, as did schools of dolphins and penguins. The top layer of the inlet held fresh water from the waterfalls. At the bottom was seawater from the Tasman Sea, and the water sparkled. Sharks, pilot whales, and orcas swam close to the entry. Sea anemones, sea stars, eels, and octopus could be seen from the ship. The pristine loveliness of Milford Sound silenced conversation. This place of profound beauty in the early-morning chill. There was a reverential feel to it, a holy feel, and Damaris felt the presence of God as she stood at the rails. The shipcruised at a leisurely pace for ten miles. At the end of the fjord, the ship's azimuth thrusters rotated the ship 360 degrees, turning the ship around so it could travel in the opposite direction back to the entrance of the fjord, the passengers having complete views of the waterfalls and steep mountains on both sides. She wondered how someone could not believe in the Creator after seeing a place like this. As they left the fjord, she wished Corey could experience this eighth wonder of the world. Corey? Why did he come to her mind at this moment? After all, he was just a friend.

33

Sydney Again!

In two days, they would be in Sydney again. They had circumnavigated the island country of New Zealand. Of all the places she had been, New Zealand was the most beautiful and least crowded. She wondered if she would be a different person when she returned. Would she be smarter and worldlier? She worried at the thought she might turn into a snob. There were many wonderful people on the boat, but there were some English and American snobs too. Some subtly bragged about their homes, their jobs, their money, their education, or the universities their children attended.

One stuffy Englishman asked her one night at dinner, "Tell me, my dear"—he pronounced it *de-ah*—"what university do you attend there, they-ah, in America?"

Damaris answered politely, but his arrogant words and tone irritated her.

"Well, I attend the Missouri State Technical College in Linn, Missouri, where I live. Residents call it StateTech. It is one of the best trade schools in the nation."

"Oh, really?" He pronounced it rally.

"There are about fifteen hundred students, and I am working on two-year degrees in architecture and interior design."

His wife drolly sneered in her condescending English voice. "Do you mean you attend a *trade* school?" She emphasized the words *trade school* as if it was a leprosy colony.

Damaris laughed at the way some English people spoke with their lips and teeth practically glued together. Damaris sensed the nice people at the table felt uncomfortable.

"I love my teachers, and I love my classes, and I am proud to be a student there," she answered.

She wanted to say, "And I have $400 million in the bank, lady." Instead she excused herself from the table and vowed she would never eat a meal with that couple again. She promised herself she would never act like those condescending people. Pastor Dave and Mr. A warned about staying true to herself. She had money now, but she knew she wasn't any better than anyone else. She was just luckier.

Back in Sydney, she finally realized she'd had it with the big cities. She laughed to herself and practiced her best English accent impersonation.

"Lodge seeties ah *note* moy cup ov tea!" Large cities are not my cup of tea.

She, of course, was in love with the Sydney harbor and the opera house but decided she would take a taxi to the Exodus Ministry building and ask if she could volunteer in the mission for the day helping serve lunches at the Fishes and Loaves restaurant for the homeless. She wanted to feel useful and be involved with people who needed her smiles and maybe a listening ear. After lunch, she read or play with the kids. Spending time serving the neediest in the lunchroom was more fulfilling than eating at a table of self-congratulating snobs. She missed her time with Mr. A. She missed his wisdom and laughter. He promised Raphael was nearby, but she missed him standing by the white limousine ready to handle anyone who might try to harm her. She didn't like this unsettled feeling, this feeling of emptiness and lack of purpose. Reverend Crews thanked her for helping, and she gave him the $1,000 she had gotten from an ATM machine for this reason. He gave her a thankful smile. Her time at his ministry was another highlight of her trip because she was helpful and doing good for people.

34

Melbourne, Australia

Melbourne is a city of five million people with the largest container port in Australia. Station Pier is the berth for the cruise chips. Damaris remembered Melbourne from her high school English class when the teacher required they read the book *On the Beach*, published in 1957. The author Neville Shute had immigrated to Australia and wrote the novel about people as they await the arrival of deadly radiation spreading toward them from the Northern Hemisphere following a nuclear war the year previously. The book scared Damaris, and now she would be in that exact town that was the setting of this novel! After much research, she decided she would take a taxi and spend the whole day at the National

Gallery of Victoria, one of the premier galleries in the world. She was awed by its architectural beauty and its extensive collection of art. Founded in 1861, it was Australia's most visited museum, filled with Asian, Australian, aboriginal, and international art—paintings, fashions, textiles, decorative art, sculptures, the old masters, Greek and Egyptian artifacts, ceramics, and famous paintings she had studied in high school. She rented headsets which narrated her own private tour. Prints, drawings, watercolors, and fantastic sculptures—so much to see! She ate at an elegant restaurant in the National Gallery next to the Water Wall where she had high tea—jam scones, egg and watercress sandwiches, and a variety of tea to choose from drunk in specialty cups representing each kind of tea you chose. She loved the deep bucket seats and gilt-edged mirrors. It was high tea at its finest. She wasn't a tea drinker before the cruise. Good ol' coffee from Caspar's 66 was good enough for her, but she recognized the beauty and tradition that made high tea so unique and pleasurable.

After a day at the National Gallery, she fully appreciated the creative and spirit-enlarging powers of people which could only come from a creative God.

35

Adelaide, Australia

Adelaide is known as a premium wine-producing region with its incredible food and myriad festivals, a not-so religious city of 1.5 million with well-preserved nineteenth-century pubs and hotels and a huge collection of colonial buildings built in the 1800s. Half of the population identifies as Christians. A nice elderly couple traveling back to America overheard she was looking for a private driver and vehicle, and they gave her the phone number of a private security company who provided cars and armed drivers for VIPs with an armed driver. She was tired of organized shore excursions because she was more independent and spontaneous. After breakfast, wearing her smartest and most attractive casual wear, her driver, Oliver, waited at the pier in a Chrysler 300 limousine. She wanted to sit in front, but he told her it was against their policy, assuring her he had a sound system that would enable them to hear each other. She was told by the company that Oliver was a college history student and knowledgeable about Adelaide's history and had a perfect driving record. When he saw the attractive Damaris, he knew it would be a satisfying day. She told him she was an architecture student from America and was interested in seeing colonial architecture from the 1800s. She wanted to see as many old churches as possible, and they had until 5:00 p.m.

Oliver told her that Adelaide was known as the City of Churches. Near the Morphett Street Bridge, he would show her eight churches. The first was the Holy Trinity, built in 1838, the first Anglican Church in South Australia, an evangelical church and not Catholic. Next was the St. Peter's Cathedral with its Gothic Revival architecture, built in 1869. Oliver asked if she would like to take a short self-guided tour of the interior—breathtaking with tapestries, flags, and intricate tiles on the floors, awing Damaris with its majestic beauty. Next was Christ Church, built in 1848, part-English Norman and part-Neo Romanesque styles built with limestone and red brick. Inside the ceiling was painted blue, studded with gold stars with side inscriptions of the Lord's Prayer and the Ten Commandments. They moved on to St. Mary's Catholic Church built in the nineteenth-century in the Greek Revival style, constructed with Sydney sandstone, marble, gleaming alabaster, and granite. It had the greatest length of any church in Australia and was such an imposing structure you could see its spires from all parts of Adelaide. The pope visited the church in 2008. During the tour, they were able to visit the interior of four cathedrals, richly dressed with magnificent stained-glass windows and huge pipe organs. Damaris made sketches and took many pictures. It was a whirlwind of architectural delight. She would have liked more time to study them in detail.

She told Oliver about the small churches in her town, very humble compared to these European-style cathedrals but alive and well attended and who did much good for Linn. The new alabaster statue of Jesus in front of the Catholic church in Linn was a blessing to all who drove by. She hoped to buy some large bronze statues for the public places in Linn, perhaps commemorating its early history. She made a pledge to herself she would offer assistance to all the churches if there was a pressing need, not just Pastor Dave's. She believed the churches were the heart of Osage County and probably all of America. She remembered reading a quote in one of high school history books by Alexis de Tocqueville, a French philosopher who visited America in the early 1800s, who said America was great because America was good; and he attributed the goodness of America to its churches. Damaris saw the churches in action in Linn and knew this to be true.

Oliver drove her through luxurious residential areas so Damaris could get ideas for her new home and its landscaping. She asked Oliver to take her through some poorer neighborhoods, an unusual request for Oliver. She saw neighborhoods with few trees, trash-laden streets, and cracked and crumbling sidewalks and remembered the squalor, the abandoned children, the diseased, and the forgotten and abandoned people in other neighborhoods she had seen. She was reminded of the organizations and volunteers addressing the issues of poverty begging for donations, sacrificing their time, their finances and loving unconditionally. She knew she had to help. She couldn't give to all those she was shown, but she could make a difference.

The last few hours, Oliver drove her through the downtown area with its colonial architecture and centuries-old buildings, many now turned into offices and bars. The parliament house, with its abundant marble columns, rivaled the Missouri State Capitol in Jefferson City. She loved the architectural traditions blending in with the modern. Her mind filled with ideas she could incorporate into her own home and in the city of Linn itself. At the cruise port, she profusely thanked Oliver for his knowledge and good driving and left him a very generous tip. In the evening, she looked through her camera pictures reminding her of all the exquisite historical buildings she had seen.

She wanted to talk to Bryan, but she knew he was extremely busy, so she called Corey. Her feelings, thoughts, and ideas exploded from her. She told him how much she was learning about history and architecture. She also saw so many similarities between America and Australia, their economic challenges, immigration problems, social challenges, and governmental issues. People weren't much different in each country. Her travel so far made her more broad minded and accepting of cultural differences.

"You are finding new worlds, Damaris, and noticing that there are more things that unite us than divide us, aren't you?"

"Exactly, Corey. You're being philosophical now."

"Do you mean I normally talk like a dumb cop?"

"I didn't mean that at all," she said, surprised that Corey was so touchy tonight.

"You really don't know much about me, Damaris, about who and what I am. You never ask, obviously because you don't really care. I'm just a small-town cop, boring and dull to you, especially after the fabulous experiences you're having."

"Corey, stop this!" Her feminine instincts told her that self-pity was driving this emotional outburst.

"Damaris, do you find me at all interesting?"

"Corey, you are a sweet, kind, smart, thoughtful man—"

"But not interesting, right?"

"Corey, it sounds like you've had a bad day, and you're discouraged—"

"Why wouldn't I be? I can't offer you anything, Damaris, not now. I don't have anything to lose by telling you my true feelings, which I've failed to share for fear you'll run away from me. What I really want to hear is that you admire me, miss me, and that you love me as much as I love you. There! I've laid it on the line. I can see now my hopes are futile. I'm going to hang up now. Please don't call me again. I hope you stay safe. I'll pray for that. Goodbye, Damaris."

He hung up on her! Why did he have to complicate her life now? She was free, economically independent, and on the trip of a lifetime. She hoped he wouldn't call her back. She just wanted to have a good time without problems or demanding entanglements. She didn't know that soon her life would have complications which had nothing to do with Corey.

36

Perth, Australia

Perth—1,300 miles from Adelaide—would be her last day in Australia. Known for its beautiful beaches, low pollution, and fine dining, this large city of two million on the Swan River, founded in 1829 with many government buildings, is considered Australia's sunniest capital. It was a naval shipyard in World War II. Most residents here were born in Australia, England, New Zealand, India, or South Africa. Thirty-two percent aren't religious. Catholic and Anglican churches predominate. There are four public universities and two technical schools. For some reason, Damaris wasn't interested in the shore excursions. She decided to eat in the King's Grill buffet, which was packed with passengers eating before their time onshore.

She couldn't find a seat until an attractive, well-dressed older couple invited her to sit at their table and introduced themselves as Amelia and James Hoffman. They graciously told her they had lived in Perth for sixteen years. They left Cape Town, South Africa, their home in 1997. Mr. Hoffman asked her if she knew South African politics, and Damaris admitted she didn't. Damaris told them about herself, her brother, and her town but not about her lottery win. They shared their observations of New Zealand and Australia. It was a pleasant breakfast.

Mrs. Hoffman whispered something to her husband. He smiled and nodded his head. She asked Damaris if she had made reservations for a shore excursion and, if not, if she would she like to spend the day with them. They were disembarking after a twenty-four-day cruise from Cairns to Perth. She hadn't met the Hoffmans on the ship yet, which was unusual. By this time, many friendships were made on a long cruise like this. They lived in Perth and told her they could show her the city better than a paid guide. Damaris was flattered and excited, instantly agreeing to spend the day with them. She loved serendipity moments like this when good things happened unexpectedly!

Mr. Hoffman's limousine waited at the pier, and after loading their bags, he took them on a drive through this very clean city with its glittering beaches and lush green parklands. They told her about the cruise port, which was Australia's busiest general cargo port. The Outer Harbor Port is a bulk cargo port ten miles south used for grains, petroleum, liquid gas, fertilizer, and iron ore deliveries. They liked living in Perth with its five world-class universities. They told her their son, Patrick, graduated from medical school two years ago from the Notre Dame University in Fremantle, about eighteen miles from Perth. It was a youthful town with a thriving art and music community like the city of Perth. They showed her the oldest buildings in Perth—the Old Court House, built in 1836, and the Round House, a prison built in 1788. Eleven British ships came with the first convicts and housed them in this building. Originally the English first sent their convicts to America, but when the Revolutionary War started, their convicts were sent to Australia.

Amelia was involved in charities and the Garden Club. Mr. Hoffman played golf and fished, and both loved to travel. They asked if she would like to see their home in a gated community with a security guard on duty twenty-four hours a day, their unsettling experiences in Cape Town leaving a lasting impression. Later Damaris learned this neighborhood of Dalkeith was not only wealthy, but the median price of a home was around $2,815,000! Located on a peninsula surrounded by the Swan River, the Indian Ocean could be seen in the distance. Their home was modern in architecture and surrounded by rich vegetation with a three-tiered living room facing the ocean. They offered Damaris wine as they sat and visited. The Hoffmans were eager to tell Damaris about their son, Patrick, a dedicated physician working with Doctors Without Borders in Cape Town. They showed her his graduation pictures from medical school, and Damaris admitted he was strikingly handsome. They brought out his childhood albums from under their coffee table, with photos showing him playing in the ocean as a child, boating on the river as a family, and playing golf and tennis with his father. They were obviously proud and told Damaris they missed not having him close by. Perth was 5,400 miles across the Indian Ocean from Cape Town, South Africa! No weekend visits for sure, thought Damaris! She realized she wasn't much different from Amelia. She had the same pride in her brother's success as this mother did in her son's.

As they sipped their wine, Mr. Hoffman explained South Africa after apartheid officially ended in 1994.

"In the early 1900s, 10 percent of the country was White, and 90 percent Black. The Black population was marginalized before Nelson Mandela became the first Black president. The White Afrikaners were of Dutch descent, taking control of the country in 1910. The parliament at the time began enacting laws and policies with a devastating impact on Africans. In 1948, a rash of legislation upheld segregationist policies against non-White citizens of South Africa. Their history sounds very similar to the past segregationist policies in America, doesn't it, Damaris? This segregation was very inhuman. From 1961 to 1994, almost four million Blacks were forcibly removed from their homes and deposited into another part of the country where they plunged into poverty and hopelessness. Many groups opposed apartheid. There was violence. Nelson Mandela, who led these protests, was imprisoned from 1963 to 1990.

"This violence got the world's attention, and when Mandela was freed from prison in 1990, a new constitution gave Blacks the right to vote, and Mandela was elected president in May of 1994. He discouraged Blacks from retaliating against their former oppressors. He was much like Martin Luther King in your country and received the Nobel Peace Prize for his persuasive nonviolent activism.

"So there we were. Apartheid had ended. I was a CEO of a multinational company. Because of so much civil unrest, I decided to resign and move our family to Perth, where I became a CEO of a large mining company. It was very unsafe for Whites in Cape Town then. It has gotten better since, but we still wouldn't live there. The slums began encroaching into the beautiful city. Inexperienced, corrupt people took over the reins of government. White residents feared for their lives and property. We didn't want to raise Patrick in a corrupt and dangerous society. Since then, over a million Whites have left South Africa. Sixteen years later, beautiful homes are surrounded by high walls lined with barbed wire. I do miss the unparalleled beauty with the imposing six-thousand-foot flat Table Mountain, the Twelve Apostles mountain range rising above the city, and the white sand beaches; but my family's safety was more important.

"After Patrick graduated from medical school, he worked here in Perth for several years, then, one day, surprised us by telling us he signed a contract with Doctors Without Borders, an organization which provides medical care all over the world, relying on charity to fund the salaries of doctors and nurses. The French name for the organization is *Médicins Sans Frontières*. We refer to it as DWB. They do not receive any government compensation, so they can stay politically neutral. It is a top-rated, reputable charity. The organization does provide abortions, but Patrick refuses. He understands the proabortion arguments, but he is a doctor who wants to save lives, not destroy them. Other doctors in the organization volunteer for that procedure. He works to educate women and men about effective birth control. He chose to volunteer in a medical clinic outside of Cape Town, in a poor area called Khayelitsha, where the medium income is $1,872 a year. Ninety-nine percent of the residents are Black Africans, and their main language is Zulu. Five of the largest slums in the world are near there. There is a high crime rate in Cape Town with massive government corruption, including the police. Seventy percent of the residents live in shacks. Some have to walk a half a mile just to get water. Only 53 percent are employed, and 89 percent are hungry.

"This is the area he chose to practice. He signed a two-year contract. He is very interested in finding cures for HIV and tuberculosis. They just built a new hospital in Khayelitsha with three hundred beds, providing support to the surrounding primary health-care facilities similar to where Patrick works. The hospital is understaffed and undersupplied with no MRI or CAT scan machines. It mans a twenty-four-hour emergency-care facility, which handles mostly victims of car accidents and gunshot wounds. It has medical, surgical, gynecological, and pediatric wards and a nursery. The clinics like Patrick's provide a variety of health-care services to men, women, and children, including HIV testing and treatment for sexually transmitted diseases. He also travels to medical clinics outside the Cape Town area to check on medical procedures and caseloads. He has access to a small lab in the hospital to do research but is so busy healing the sick he has little time for research, which he usually has to do in the evenings. Sadly it's very dangerous there at night. He works hard, doesn't sleep much, and we worry about his health. He is paid $2,000 a month for his services from DWB. He can live on that because a friend of ours in Cape Town provides him a new apartment for nominal rent."

Amelia told Damaris she recently spent a few weeks in Cape Town helping him furnish and decorate the apartment so he could have a restful, beautiful place to relax at the end of physically and mentally challenging days.

After sharing all this, they eventually asked Damaris about herself and her life in America. She told them about her father's death, their financial issues afterward, and her mother's struggles with alcohol.

She, of course, told them about her brother's musical gifts and the offer for him to attend Julliard. She shared her desire to become an architect one day and that this cruise was teaching her so much about the elements of architectural design. They asked how she ended up on this very expensive ocean liner, and she told them about winning a large amount of money in the Missouri lottery. They were happy for her good luck. She told them the whole story and how it was suggested she leave town until the media frenzy died down. Mr. Hoffman agreed it was an amazing story. They were happy they met her and hoped she could meet their son in Cape Town.

When it was time to return to the ship, they exchanged addresses and phone numbers, called for the chauffeur, and vowed they would stay in touch. Damaris believed in her heart she would never hear from them again, but she couldn't know the future or that the Hoffman's would be a strong presence in her life several years from now.

37

The Long Journey

The next eleven days, they would travel across the Indian Ocean, the third largest ocean in the world, 3,659 miles to Mauritius, an island country off the eastern coast of Africa, the distance like driving across the United States from New York to California. Damaris did a great deal of research on this part of the trip. This area of the world is susceptible to monsoons, cyclones, strong winds, and tsunamis. The sea-lanes are strategic as 80 percent of the world's oil is transported on the Indian Ocean. Its history dates back seven thousand years. It is estimated that seven hundred thousand slaves between 1500 and 1850 were transported on the Indian Ocean to the Americas, a small number compared to the twelve million slaves transported across the Atlantic to America.

In December of 2004, fourteen countries around the Indian Ocean were hit by a wave of tsunamis caused by an Indian Ocean earthquake. The waves radiated across the ocean at speeds exceeding three hundred miles per hour. Waves reached up to sixty-six feet and killed 236,000. In the early 2000s, the ocean became a hub of pirate activity. Somali pirates began terrorism when international fishing vessels illegally fished in Somali territorial waters, depleting their local fishing stocks, so Somali fishing communities formed armed groups to deter these invaders. The Somalis held these vessels for ransom, and it became a lucrative operation. Then they started hijacking commercial vessels. Because of poverty and their government's corruption, Somali youth began seeing it as a means to support their families. International organizations began forming security patrols to protect seagoing vessels from pirates.

In May of 2010, a Somali ship seized a US flagship, the *Maersk Alabama* (dramatized by the movie *Captain Phillips* in 2013), and kidnapped the captain; and the perpetrators were caught and sentenced to thirty-three years in prison. By the year 2013, only nine vessels had been attacked by pirates with no successful hijackings, a 90 percent drop from the year before. Passengers who had seen the movie wondered about a possible hijacking of the *Queen Mary*. The captain assured them the *Queen Mary* was prepared, but any attack was highly unlikely. The ship could do zigzag maneuvers and outrun any pirate. Nevertheless, he advised them to listen to the loudspeakers and go to a lockdown area in case of an emergency. Blackout conditions would be imposed on outside cabins and outside decks readied with water cannons. These young pirates arm themselves with AK-47s and generally target cargo ships. Damaris was surprised when she read that every cruise ship employs two snipers. Ships also have LRADs, long-range acoustic devices, which send sonic waves to a target, the resulting din causing eardrums to pop and bleed which stuns the criminals. Sadly some hijackers pose as tourists as in the case of the *Achille Lauro* when PLO terrorists easily hijacked the Italian cruise ship in 1985 because there was no security. They shot an American wheelchair-bound tourist in the head, then threw his body overboard, causing panic, fear, and terror in the passengers. Damaris had heard about this brutal hijacking. Many at the evening dinner talked about the *Achille Lauro*. After sailing for so many months, it gave the passengers something new to discuss.

The captain assured them the *Queen Mary* had security which they couldn't see, so they should relax and continue having an enjoyable Indian Ocean crossing.

Damaris thought to herself, *Yeah, sure, remember the* Maersk Alabama *and the* Achille Lauro, *which were now heavily on everyone's mind?*

Damaris made phone calls to America. Pastor Dave was full of questions. He was happy she was reading the Bible he gave her. She told him about the mysterious Mr. Armstrong and Raphael and their adventures together.

She heard him silently whisper, "Wow!" and then "Hey, your brother's studio is finished. It's amazing. Media people are still fishing around town trying to learn more about you and your brother. Many people in town still don't know where you are."

"Good! I've called my mom several times. She says she's 'met someone' and wants to surprise me when I return. She sounds like the happy mom I used to know. Another burden lifted from my shoulders."

"By the way, I saw Corey Gardner the other day, and he said you and he had stopped communicating. He told me he's had a few dates with a girl he met in college and that she was pretty and really nice. He was tired of the town gossip that hinted he was dating you because of your money and that he was glad he could move on."

Damaris was stunned. He just told her a week ago how much he loved her! Yet she was the one who spurned his advances. Oh, well. What did she care? Now she could be free from guilt and worry about making him feel bad.

"Good riddance," she said to herself as she sat on her balcony after she and Pastor Dave hung up. "I don't care if Corey has another girlfriend…do I?"

38

Mauritius
OFF THE SOUTHEAST COAST OF AFRICA

Damaris was very interested in this island country because she had never heard of it before the cruise. It was 1,300 miles from Madagascar, another island country, both off the east coast of South Africa. It was a plantation-based colony of the UK when it became an independent country in 1968. Mauritius is known for its beaches, lagoons and reefs, beautiful mountains, rainforests, hiking trails, and waterfalls. The residents are of Indian descent, mostly Hindu and Muslim with a small percentage of Christians. Creole, French, and English are the main languages spoken. It is the richest country in Africa with a population of 1,350,000—as large as Maui, Hawaii—and famous for the now-extinct dodo bird. It has the highest per capita income in Africa and is a wealthy, very cosmopolitan, stable democracy known for its French, Chinese, and Indian food. Horse racing at the beautiful Champs de Mars track has been popular since 1812. Four hundred and fifty thoroughbred racehorses and their jockeys are imported from South Africa for the season from late March to early December. The spectator areas are filled to capacity during the entire racing season. Damaris really wanted to see the horse races, but the ship wouldn't be in that port in March.

Since horses were so popular in Mauritius, she hired a limousine to drive her to the Centre Equestre de Riambel, where she could ride a retired thoroughbred racehorse along a two-mile stretch of white-sand beach relatively free from people or hotels with the mountains close by. Both she and her black thoroughbred horse cooled off in the ocean as they rode along the two-mile stretch. Armina, the owner of the equestrian center, asked if she could take pictures of Damaris as she rode. Damaris was lovely, and Armina wanted to use the pictures for her advertising brochures. Damaris agreed as long as she was sent copies of the pictures to her home in America. After returning her horse, she walked along the beach, enjoying the quiet and solitude. A light breeze blew her hair as a guide snapped pictures and promised her copies of those also. Damaris returned to the ship in time for dinner. By the end of the evening, her legs were sore from riding, but her happy memories of the day helped her forget the pain. She didn't know at the next stop—Durban, South Africa—she would meet a man who could possibly change the course of her life.

39

Durban, South Africa: A New Beginning

In the evening, a gentleman introduced himself to her in the library, introducing himself as Robert Stanley, a British pastor who lived in Durban. He asked if he could sit with her and if she knew much about Durban. He told her the Durban climate was great, with sun 325 days a year and a temperate climate averaging seventy degrees, a sunny place but also with much spiritual darkness. Sadly South Africa has a high level of crime. Violent crimes including rape and murder, muggings, armed assaults, and theft occur even with tourists. Durban is a city of four million people. There are many shantytowns, which pose danger to those who live or visit there. After apartheid collapsed, many people moved into the cities from rural areas. There is 40 percent unemployment, and Americans complain when unemployment rises above 6 percent! In the shantytowns, the walls are lined with newspapers. Houses are built with dirt for floors and often have only one door and no windows. There are many fire and cholera breakouts from people bathing, drinking, and defecating in the same water. Piles of litter and waste cover the streets, attracting rats. Rape is prevalent, even of ten-year-old girls. Violence and fights of all kinds run rampant, terrorizing innocent people. The government and police have turned their backs and lost interest in these shantytowns.

One million out of five million Whites have left the country since 1995. There are many attacks against Whites and White farmers in particular. The highly educated have relocated, leaving government and education with unskilled workers. The transition from apartheid to democracy visited on the residents, especially the Afrikaners, all manner of evil. More people are murdered in one week under the Black majority than were murdered under the White majority. Poverty is worse now than under apartheid. South Africa has one of the largest welfare systems in the world. Half the Blacks are below the poverty level. Many who rule South Africa now are corrupt and inept.

"I was a new pastor in Durban, and the Christian churches spoke out against apartheid and treating other human beings worse than animals. Now it's worse. South Africa is reaping what was sown in the apartheid years. Many churches are doing what they can to bring hope into this hopeless, desperate area. Churches provide food, shelter, medical care, but the numbers are overwhelming. Our churches teach people about God, about His love and forgiveness. We teach them to hope and that each person is valuable to God. We are a drop in a large ocean of despair. We spend much time in prayer. We encourage people to give their testimonies during worship services, which encourage others. The church I am involved with is called the Durban Christian Center. Some call it the Jesus Dome. In fact, when I leave the ship, I am headed over there. We're having a special Sunday service tomorrow morning, a special time of prayer and worship. Do you have plans for the day? If not, I'd like to invite you to come with me. You'll get back in time for dinner. Again I'm Robert Stanley. I'm British, as you can tell. You're Damaris, right? Let's meet at the bottom of the gangplank at eight tomorrow morning. How does that sound?"

Damaris had no idea what was ahead, but tomorrow, something would happen that would change her life more dramatically than her lottery win.

In the morning, Damaris dressed in a beautiful flowing dress. Mr. Stanley was waiting at the dock, and standing next to him were Mr. A and Raphael! She ran to them with huge hugs, totally surprised they were there.

Mr. Stanley said to Damaris, "I believe you know these gentlemen, Mr. Armstrong and Raphael." He smiled.

"You know each other?" She was dumfounded.

Mr. A suggested they all get into the limousine and drive to the worship center.

"We are all going over there together? Mr. A, did you plan this meeting?" asked Damaris.

"We are all here for a reason, Damaris. By the end of the service, you will know the reason."

The huge Jesus Dome was packed with three thousand worshippers of all races and colors. Mr. A and his group walked toward the front of the church, and the four of them sat in chairs with their names on printed cards attached to the backs.

How did they do that? she wondered.

There was her name—Damaris Kelly. How did anyone in this church know she would be there? The lights dimmed, and the service opened with a powerful prayer. All heads bowed as soft music began to play. Something warm and invisible covered her like a soft cloud of love. The prayer was not the type she had heard before. She felt its warmth, its fire. All the accomplished musicians were Black, their voices blending in perfect harmony. In the congregation, Black and White sang together in unrestrained joy, in the presence of the Father, Son, and Holy Spirit.

Worshippers raised their hands, including Mr. A, Raphael, and Mr. Stanley. The red letters, the words of Jesus she had read this morning, filled her brain. She felt God was talking to her. The worship began slowly and sweetly.

"The light shone in the darkness, but the darkness has not understood it."

She knew in her heart these three wonderful people next to her led her here for this moment.

"The true light that gives light to every man came into the world."

Something was happening to her. She felt as if she were on a boat adrift on a huge ocean with no control over the boat or where it was headed.

"Yet to all who received Him, to those who believed His name, He gave them the right to be called children of God, born not of natural descent or of human decision or a husband's will but born of God."

Where were these words coming from? Was the band singing these words?

"The Word became flesh and made God His dwelling among us."

Is that what He's doing now? Is He making His dwelling in me?

"It is He who will baptize you with the Holy Spirit."

No, cried her flesh.

Yes, cried her heart.

The music, the flashing colored lights, and the glimmering cross elevated and hovering above the band.

"I tell you the truth. No one can see the kingdom of God unless he is born again."

She had been mad at God and didn't want to know about Him.

"I have food to eat that you know nothing about."

She had so much now, yet she wasn't satisfied. Her empty stomach grumbled.

"He who comes to me will never go hungry, and he who believes in me will never be thirsty. The Spirit gives life, and the flesh counts for nothing."

She was looking at the words on the screen behind the band. In a moment of light, she cried out, "Jesus, are you calling me?" her tears gushing out uncontrollably.

"Whoever believes in me, streams of living water will flow from within him."

She heard Mr. A's voice, "This is a place where miracles happen, Damaris. Do not despise small beginnings, for the Lord rejoices to see the work begin."

She thought she heard Pastor Stanley whisper, "God is the only good thing inside our hearts, and we inhabit the earth for a purpose."

The music was more heavenly than earthly, the band responding to the spirit as it touched minds and hearts. She wished her brother could be here.

"Lord, I honor and worship you…Lord, you are holy and righteous. Let me walk beside you…"

The words of the worship songs blended together in one song and one voice.

"You are the lamp unto my feet. Lord, you are worthy. Let me walk beside you. Holy is your name. By His stripes, I am healed. By His nail-scarred hands, by His blood, the power of sin is broken. Jesus has won my freedom. Dry bones rotting and now coming to life again, my God is able to save, deliver, and heal. Open the grave. I am coming out. I am going to live again!"

The music and the words continued, a gigantic outpouring of God's grace and love swelling in her spirit, lifting her into spiritual heights she had never known.

"Save me, Lord. Forgive me. I surrender to you."

In that moment, she fell to her knees, her hands raised up high and her head bowed. Her friends gathered around her, laying their hands on her shaking body and praying joyfully.

"This child belongs to you now, Lord. We give you thanks!"

The music played on and on as she wept tears of repentance. At the end of the service, she stood up, spent and broken. The men gathered around her, enveloping her in their love as they laid hands on her in benediction.

She looked up at the golden cross for what seemed like an eternity and simply said, "Here I am, Lord. It's me, Damaris, your daughter."

40

Port Elizabeth, South Africa

On the way back to the ship, the men had satisfied smiles on their faces. Damaris leaned her head against the back seat and closed her eyes. It seemed words weren't adequate for the powerful roller coaster that had just driven her into this emotional and spiritual state of grace. They knew. They understood. She laughed an exuberant laugh. The walls she had raised against God had crumbled. Her friends opened the door for her. As she boarded the ship, Pastor Stanley disappeared, and Mr. A and Raphael drove off into the darkness of Durban.

Damaris went back to her suite, bathed, and sat on the balcony with her Bible. She read again the words in the book of John. She knew the truth now.

There was no longer doubt or ambiguity. She knew the truth, and the truth had truly set her free. She stood and looked up at the twinkling bright stars in the clear night sky, fixed in their positions for millions of years, unchanging and eternal; and each one had a name.

She thought, *How wonderful it is that He knows their names and He knows mine. He made them, and He made me. He loves me. I am His daughter, a child of God, and I am valuable to Him.*

The next stop, Port Elizabeth, was a vacation destination with pleasant year-round weather. More importantly, it was a gateway for the African Big Five game safari tourism. Damaris decided to go on a full-day nine-hour safari. It promised close proximities to elephants, lions, zebras, warthogs, giraffes, zebras, and buffalo. The safari didn't disappoint. These animals were in the wild, and this wasn't a zoo. It wasn't a hunting safari. They drove in an enclosed bus and ate a great barbecue lunch with wine and beer under a roof that kept them cool. They saw a lion stalk, chase, and kill a zebra, disturbing to some and exciting to others. Damaris had grown up where hunting was the norm. The guides were armed, but there were no close calls. She remembered a song she heard last night about the Lion of Judah, and she praised His name on this momentous morning. She was changed, a new person. The old had passed away.

41

Cape Town, South Africa

Damaris had no hint on this day Cape Town would be the end of her cruise even though there were officially four more stops before arriving in Southampton. This was a two-night stop. She woke up early as the ship entered the harbor. She was awed as white clouds spread over the top of the flat Table Mountain and the Twelve Apostles Mountain Range, just as Mr. Hoffman described. He shared that Cape Town ranks among the most beautiful cities in the world. The three air horn blasts announced the *Queen Mary*'s arrival into the breathtaking harbor. Damaris had already been told about the politics in Cape Town and about apartheid by two different men.

In 1944, the racial composition was 47 percent White, 46 percent colored (mixed races), and 6 percent Black. Now, after apartheid, it is 77 percent Black and 10 percent White. Twenty percent of 3.5 million are unemployed, 60 percent of whom are Black. Seventy-seven percent are Christians. Only 38 percent have graduated high school. There are eleven languages spoken in South Africa. Crime is pushing out more and more Whites, who still hold most of the wealth and are the best trained but make up only 10 percent of the population. There are many gold and diamond mines but not enough skilled workers. Twenty-five thousand teachers leave a year, and only seven thousand come in. White Africans question the rule of law. There are high levels of corruption, nepotism, racketeering, and incompetence and many unskilled people. Criminals feel they are entitled to take from those who have more. Afrikaners are leaving by the droves. On a positive note, seventeen years after apartheid, there is a growing Black middle class and hope that perhaps, one day, Cape Town will be a better place to live. Mr. Hoffman shared in that hope.

Damaris wasn't sure what to expect when she left the ship, but when she saw Mr. A and Raphael, she ran to them with joy, her camera and beach bag bouncing along with her.

"Well, my dear, you seem especially buoyant this morning."

"Of course!" She smiled radiantly.

"I know you are anxious to see Cape Town. It's lovely, isn't it? But first we are going to visit a clinic in Khayelitsha. I believe the Hoffmans told you about it when you were in Perth."

"How do you know that? You weren't even there!"

"Did you forget I have connections?"

"How could I forget? That's the answer you give every time!"

"I've always told you the truth, Damaris. I have never led you astray, have I? Continue to believe me, okay?"

As they drove to the clinic, about fifteen miles from the town's center, Damaris shared how she felt about her newfound relationship with God. She hadn't been taught as a child, and after her father's death, she thoroughly distanced herself from even the thought of a loving God. She had blamed Him for allowing her father to be killed and for her mother's slip into alcoholism and her stolen teen years lost because of her effort to support her family. Last night, the wall between her and God crumbled, and she was set free from the bitterness she had held on to for so long. She thanked him for taking her to the Durban Christian Center and told him how the whole experience changed her.

Mr. A smiled approvingly and said simply, "I knew it would. It was your destiny, Damaris."

The clinic was close to the new hospital, which she could see in the distance. It wasn't located in a green part of town; the building was surrounded by dirt. The clinic had many posters taped to the outside walls describing the services offered there, mostly HIV and tuberculosis testing. When they walked inside, Damaris couldn't believe the huge crowd in the waiting room, every chair filled and people sitting on the floor, many coughing violently without covering their mouths. Children cried. Mothers sat as if in a stupor. The heat was oppressive. Apparently there was no air-conditioning, except for a few floor fans. The receptionist operated an old computer, a landline, and a loud, busy printer. Beat-up file cabinets lined the walls, piled with hundreds of file folders. Nurses and doctors ran in and out of the office area looking stressed and pressed for time. Mr. A asked the receptionist to let Dr. Hoffman know they were there.

After a short interval, a tall dark-haired doctor with piercing brown eyes hurried into the office holding a clipboard, wearing a starched white coat with his name "Dr. Patrick Hoffman" and the French words *Médicins Sans Frontières* embroidered on the pocket, a stethoscope hanging around his neck. Time stopped for Damaris as his intense dark-brown eyes met hers. He was strikingly good looking. His eyes focused on her, taking in every detail. He worked with very sick mostly dark African people; and her well-dressed appearance, white skin, crystal blue eyes, blond hair, and fit, healthy tanned body filled the room with light. He wasn't too busy to notice every feature as she stood before him.

One of the little boys who came with his sick mother looked at Damaris and asked his mother innocently, "Is she an angel, Mommy?"

She looks like one, thought Dr. Hoffman.

Mr. A introduced them and asked if they could possibly get a pass to tour the hospital.

"I wish I could show you myself," he said, looking straight at Damaris.

She felt faint. Was it the heat of the room? He wrote out a pass and then made them an offer to meet him tonight around six at Brian's Pub near the port in Cape Town. Patrick wrote his address and phone number on a prescription pad, folded it, and pressed it into Damaris's hand, his touch sending shivers up her arm.

"Here's a hospital pass too. The Khayelitsha Hospital is not like American hospitals. Don't be shocked. We are understaffed and underfunded. You can see the huge slum in the distance, and this is who we serve. I am getting behind now. I want to finish by five so I won't be late for our dinner. Until tonight, Damaris?"

His smile was seductive, and Damaris thought to herself, *I could fall in love with this man.*

The hospital was a beehive of activity where patients lay in gurneys hooked up to IVs, unattended outside surgical rooms, not a nurse or doctor in sight. Mr. A and Damaris stood inside the entrance of the emergency room, seeing patients bleeding from car accidents, gunshots, and stab wounds. The doctors and nurses fought valiantly for lives as more people were brought in by ambulance, and the smell of alcohol and blood made Damaris nauseous. No private rooms here, just large dormitories filled with sick or injured patients.

Damaris asked Mr. A, "How do the workers do it? How do they work in these conditions?"

"My guess is they have superhuman strength, perseverance, and a dedication to heal. Doctors Without Borders is very demanding and selective about who works in these places. They work hard to save lives, and they also teach people how to take better care of themselves. DWB is very concerned about tuberculosis and AIDS, which are ravishing the African population. We'll learn more about what Dr. Hoffman does tonight at dinner. Until then, let's explore this lovely city and its environs. Raphael will drive. There is rampant crime. You would be a juicy target."

Mr. A narrated their tour. "Cape Town, the oldest city in South Africa, had its origin in 1652 when the Dutch East India Company established a refreshment station for its ships, a magnificent location beneath the precipitous walls of Table Mountain. The Dutch and the English wrangled over it. It was the site of the first European settlement in South Africa and therefore is known as the country's mother city. The policy of apartheid began under British rule. Today's Cape Town is a multicultural city, from high-rise buildings like the modern Civic Center to historical buildings, the national parliament house, the University of Cape Town with its white-pillared colonnades stretching across the facades with Table Mountain and the Twelve Apostles mountain range as its backdrop."

They all agreed the university was magnificent.

Mr. A talked about the demographics of the university. "During apartheid, Black students weren't admitted. Now the university student population is 70 percent Black and 22 percent White."

Mr. A thought this was a positive sign for the future of the Cape Town area. They drove by many mosques, which were spread across the city. The beauty of the city was also in its white-sand beaches as well as the impressive mountain ranges which wrapped around it.

After the brief tour, Mr. A took her back to the ship so she could shower and dress for dinner with Dr. Hoffman. She was excited about getting to know the handsome and dedicated doctor. She dressed in her most feminine silk dress and took special care with her hair and makeup. She piled her hair up loosely with a few bobby pins with soft stands loosely framing her face, hoping the style would make her look older and more sophisticated. Assessing herself in front of the full-length mirror, she wondered if Patrick would find her attractive. Mr. A knocked on her door and looked appreciatively at her beauty. He was sure Dr. Hoffman would be enamored by this vision in white.

"Damaris, I'm not going to be able to join you tonight. There are some serious issues I need to address here in Cape Town. Raphael will drop you off at the restaurant and remain close by. Enjoy Doctor Hoffman. Have a great time!" he said as he gave her cheek a gentle pat.

The restaurant was rather dark, with dim table candles giving off faint light. The room was designed like an English pub and smelled of chips and ale. Patrick sat in a corner booth, hidden by the darkness, thinking about the difficult cases today at the clinic; and at first, she didn't see him. She looked around; and as she stood, she radiated light in that dark room like she did in the clinic, with an air of innocence blended with a natural sexuality he knew wasn't contrived. She overflowed with life. The men in the room held their glasses of ale in midair as she passed by them, appreciating the beauty that Patrick saw. It had been a long, hard day for Patrick, and just the sight of her eased his tension. He stood up and waved to her. He liked the way she walked and held her head up high. She was a luminescent and angelic light in that dark English pub.

He wanted to learn about her tonight. He wondered about her as woman. He was very particular. Sometimes women as beautiful as Damaris were empty headed and shallow. She was on the *Queen*

Mary alone. Was she a spoiled rich girl? An heiress? But there she was, approaching him with a shy, sweet smile. She nervously sat down next to him in the booth, not knowing how to start the conversation. She told him Mr. A wasn't coming. The conversation started with him asking questions about her trip so far. He could tell she appreciated beauty. Her descriptions and observations were perceptive and detailed. He discovered she was very mature for a girl of nineteen. He was nearly thirty. The age difference didn't matter to him. He asked her about her favorite port stops. She told him she had met his parents and actually been to their home in Perth and they had given her about a two-hour photo show of his life.

He laughed. "That's my mother. She loves to tell people about me. You probably know more about me than the people I work with! I do know you met them because she telephoned me a few days ago and told me about you. She had a feeling you might come to the clinic for a visit."

She loved his smile, the dimple in his left cheek, his straight white teeth, and his long dark, almost-black, hair, casually styled, looking like he had just run his fingers through it instead of using a comb. He looked like a movie star.

"Can I interest you in a specialty South African drink? In fact, I'll give you two choices. The first is a glass of Van Der Hum liqueur, which has a nice citrus taste. It's called the 'white lightning' of South Africa, or you can choose the famous Witblits, a grape-fermented brandy. Americans say it's similar to moon-shine and is very strong. Even a sip can knock your socks off. Of course, you don't have to choose either."

She told him to choose, and two Witblits were set in front of them by the bartender. She never had anything stronger than wine on the ship, and one drink of this set her throat on fire.

"Just sip it, Damaris." He laughed.

After an hour of conversation, the Witblits fire hit her head-on. She felt dizzy and a little silly. She didn't remember much after that. It was midnight. He drove her back to her ship in his Volkswagen and asked if she'd like to spend the whole day with him tomorrow. He was due vacation days because he had worked seven days a week for several months with no break. He promised he would show her the lovely places outside of Cape Town. She quickly agreed but reminded him she had to be back on the ship by midnight because the ship was leaving early the next morning. She was still a little tipsy from the Witblits as she sat on her balcony with a tall glass of ice water, looking out on beautiful Cape Town, glittering gold on the outside but covering mistrust, fear, and hatred on the inside. She still felt the touch of Patrick's fingers on her arm and the light touch of his lips as he stood by his car saying good night. She asked the Lord to help her make good decisions regarding Patrick because she quickly felt a deep infatuation with this handsome South African doctor who apparently felt the same about her.

He picked her up in his Volkswagen at 8:00 a.m. the next day, rested and ready to be her tour guide. She could tell he needed a serious break from his hard work, and she vowed she would make his day lighthearted and fun. She dressed in her sportiest clothes and most comfortable shoes and brought a pink flannel sweatshirt and matching sweatpants in case it was chilly. Patrick wore a dark-blue T-shirt with the logo for the Cape Town Spurs on it, a very popular soccer team, and athletic shorts showing off his muscled legs. He looked like an athlete and not a doctor.

"Damaris, Cape Town is one of the world's best cities for driving. We'll take the scenic route with the best panoramic views. I grew up here and have happy memories of the places I'll show you. We'll drive out to Cape Point first. Every part of the road is a picture-perfect view. Table Mountain is the huge landmark here, which proudly stands above Cape Town, a massive mountain with a flat plateau often covered with clouds on the surface, making it look like a white tablecloth and therefore the name. We'll drive along Chapman's Peak Drive, which hugs the coastline with occasional stopping places where you can observe Hout Bay."

Damaris was in in a dream world of wild ocean and mountains. At the bottom, he headed inland to the other coast for Simon's Town. They found a cute place to eat lunch and spent two hours at the Boulder Beach, where a massive colony of two thousand African penguins lived and played on the shore. Damaris took many pictures of Patrick and selfies of them together. He brought some folding beach chairs and, at a place called Foxy Beach, placed them on a viewing platform. He held her hand and occasionally moved his hand up her arm provocatively as they watched the penguins waddling to and from the water. Patrick liked hearing her intelligent observations, and her questions showed she had an eager interest in learning about the world. The weather was temperate. The gentle sea breeze blew her hair in all directions, and Patrick had thoughts about how her hair would look spread out on one of the pillows in his apartment. They laughed and shared stories. It was easy to talk to him. She told him about life in her small Midwest town and how hard it had been to lose her father as a young teenager. He told her about the challenges of medical school, and she shared her dream of becoming an architect. She bragged about her brother's musical talents, and it surprised her when she learned he knew and liked one of her brother's songs he had heard on the radio. They pulled up a You Tube video on his phone and listened to Bryan's Top 100 Billboard hit. Patrick was impressed.

They moved on to Cape Point on a more rugged road than the previous one. They parked and hiked to the top of the hill to the lighthouse, where the view was breathtaking, as if they stood on the top of a tall skyscraper, looking down on the ocean below. They took the funicular, a mountain escalator, back down the hill, then drove around the Cape of Good Hope, which she had read so much about in her history books! The most southwesterly point of Africa! The coastline was jagged with loud, churning waves. Patrick warned her of the baboons who lived there and liked to look for food in the car if they could get into it. They were sneaky, always watching for an opportunity to grab food and even hiding under vehicles. They watched the baboons with amusement.

It was getting late in the afternoon. They returned to Cape Town by Chapman's Peak Drive again. The light from the setting sun shone down on the coastline, creating magic. They pulled over into a scenic view area, and Patrick turned off the motor. She could tell he was thinking about something.

"Your ship leaves in the morning, doesn't it?"

"I'm afraid so," she said sadly. "I really haven't had enough time here. I don't want this time with you to end," she admitted sadly.

"Damaris, it doesn't have to end. This morning, I did some research about how a cruise passenger can leave a cruise earlier than planned. You could do it, but there are some hurtles. You wouldn't get much of a refund for your final three weeks, but you could do it, Damaris. I also checked with my clinic, and I could take a leave of absence for a week."

"You're saying you want me to cancel the rest of this cruise and stay with you for a week?" She was surprised by his offer.

"More than anything in the world."

She knew it could be done. They couldn't keep her on the ship, and she had enough money to absorb the cancellation costs. But what if one week turned into a longer stay? There was her mother, her brother, her plans for Linn, and her new home. Could she make those sacrifices for a man she hardly knew? If she stayed with him, she knew for a fact there would be sexual temptation. Just the touch of his fingers on her arm or the feel of his lips on her cheek created deep arousal. Her intense sexuality had awakened when she saw Corey bending over the engine of her Corvette, but she was proud of being a virgin. She and Mr. A had talked about sexual temptation and how to stay away from it. He listened to Damaris's arguments but reminded her she was given free will and she was alone in making these difficult decisions.

She truly desired to save herself for her future husband, especially now that she had submitted to God. Yet here was Patrick, an unbelievably handsome, intelligent South African doctor offering himself to her. Every part of her wanted physical intimacy with him. But what if she became pregnant? More complications and problems. They were from different worlds. He was as comfortable in his world as she was in hers. She would have to give up her dreams. But his dream was working as doctor who could save lives, and it would continue. What if she stayed here permanently just to be with him? She couldn't volunteer with DWB because of the lengthy screening process. She couldn't drive around Cape Town alone. It was too dangerous. There was no future in this relationship. Sure, she could spend a week with him and would probably lose her virginity and maybe become pregnant. Would this be where she would want to raise a child? Behind high walls and barbed wire? Would she want to bring a child back to Linn with no father?

"Patrick, let's have dinner somewhere. I need to think about this."

"After dinner, let me show you my apartment before you go back to the ship. We can talk privately there."

As he talked, he put his arm around her and seductively held her other hand. She could feel his leg pressing against hers. The Witblits had lowered her resistance. She wanted to go with him to his apartment. She didn't care if she had only one night with him. Her whole body was filled with physical longing. She remembered in an instant the story of Adam and Eve and the snake tempting them to disobey God, promising they wouldn't be hurt in any way.

Mr. A, help me. I need you! her spirit cried out.

She was weak. Her body fought against her spirit. Patrick was leading her into a situation that wasn't right. She knew that. Then a miracle occurred in her spirit. She was given the strength to say no.

At dinner, Damaris took a deep breath before she shared her true feelings with Patrick. (She didn't see Mr. A watching around a corner of the restaurant.) "Patrick, you are the most amazing man I have ever met. You are a young woman's dream. For so many reasons, I can't stay. I don't want just a one-night stand with you. If I stayed here with you for a week, I would be tied to you. I don't want to live in Cape Town, as beautiful as it is. It just isn't in the cards for us. You are committed to your work, and I have many plans for my life in America. I'm not going to your apartment. I am this close to going over the edge with you because you're so desirable. It would be easy, and I know it would be wonderful! Just the touch of your fingers on my cheek is enough! I will never forget the last two days with the handsomest of men in one of the most beautiful cities in the world! I took pictures of you and I together, and these memories will have to do. Saying no to your offer is a difficult decision, but I know it's the right one."

At the pier, she gave him her address in America. They stood by his Volkswagen as he gently held her in his arms. She could feel his heartbeat. She wanted to stay with him.

"Please don't leave, Damaris," he begged, taking a strand of her hair and wrapping it around his fingers. "Please stay with me," he pleaded.

As he pressed his lips softly against her neck, her body silently cried out, *I want to stay, Patrick, but I can't!*

She broke away from his arms and ran to the ship. Later that night, before she showered, she touched her silk shawl to her face, his musky smell still on it and wept, still questioning whether she had made the right decision.

*****

She made the arrangements and cancelled the rest of her cruise. She settled her room charges using her credit card. Even though it was thousands of dollars in charges, she paid the bill as easily as she now paid a utility bill. They would bill her for her cancellation fees. The cruise director hoped she would change her mind—she was such a beautiful and exciting addition to passengers and crew alike. She walked one more time through the exquisite ship and thanked all the people who made this voyage so special. She put a ten-thousand-dollar tip on her credit card to be shared generously with her butler as well as the waiters and bartenders, housekeeping staff, casino workers, and spa staff. She booked a one-way ticket to New York, then on to St. Louis, leaving tomorrow at 10:00 am on Qantas Airlines from Cape Town International Airport. She called Bryan and told him she was coming home early, probably around April 16, and would tell him later why she made this decision. He was excited about seeing her! She heard a knock on the door; and Gerard, her butler, asked if he could enter. He brought her a bottle of champagne in an iced silver bucket as he did on the first day to welcome her.

"This one is a goodbye gift," he said sadly.

She asked if she could give him a hug because words could not express her gratitude for the service he gave. He was happily embarrassed because he normally didn't get heartfelt hugs from beautiful American girls on this very British ocean liner.

The next morning, she woke at 6:00 a.m. and dressed in her most comfortable and tasteful clothes. The *Queen Mary* would leave the harbor at 8:00 a.m. She would be at the airport by then. She wanted to get away from Cape Town as soon as possible before she changed her mind about Patrick. Damaris stood on the balcony, the gentle breeze softly blowing her hair, offering her spirit a sense of peace as the porters came to take her bags off the ship. She wondered if she would ever see Cape Town again. As she stood waiting for a taxi to the airport, she looked up at Table Mountain with its lacy tablecloth of clouds and the jagged silhouette of the Twelve Apostles mountain range and thought of Patrick. He didn't know she was flying to New York in three hours; and as he stood on his apartment balcony, coffee in hand, he heard the three blasts of the *Queen Mary*'s air horn as it left the harbor. His heart ached as he watched the elegant ocean liner sail out of the harbor and into the ocean, thinking it was carrying the woman he loved from the moment he saw her in the clinic. He wasn't going to give her up this easily.

42

Home to America

Damaris settled into the soft, comfortable leather first-class seats with her bag, camera, journal, *Gone with the Wind*, and Bible—plenty to keep her occupied during this eight-thousand-mile, eighteen-hour nonstop flight to New York. Because of her cancellation, she would miss Namibia; the Canary Islands; Madeira, Portugal; and Vigo, Spain. She didn't care; she was tired of cruising. January 3 to April 12, three months and ten days of cruising, was a long time to be away from home! She looked at the photos in her camera, starting with New York in January until now—the beautiful ship, the food and entertainment, the lovely ocean and landscapes, mountains, coral reefs, waterfalls, exquisite architecture, glittering cities, white-sand beaches, rainforests, churches and cathedrals, history, world-class art museums and galleries, the Sydney Opera House, the glittering modern skyscrapers of Dubai, bike rides, the helicopter ride, driving along coastal cliffs in a quad vehicle, riding a thoroughbred racehorse through the ocean, and watching the penguins on a sandy beach. She remembered also the orphanages with abandoned children, their eagerness for love and affection, the hunger, their loneliness, and the squalor and hopelessness of the poor. She had a wonderful trip but also wrote down the ministries' names Mr. A showed her. She would remember those who existed to serve and not be served. God had given her the means and a new heart to serve with them.

She looked through the pictures, happily reliving her trip, but then…where were pictures of Mr. A and Raphael and of the limousine? She scrolled through her camera, feverishly looking for any photos of them. She knew she had taken many, maybe hundreds. She was never without her camera. There were pictures of her smiling and happy but none with them. It couldn't be! Did she accidentally delete them? She had pictures of herself and Patrick but not of Mr. A or Raphael! What about the lunch in the outdoor café in Barcelona? What about the snorkeling trip in Dubai? They were all in the ocean together, and she snapped pictures of them sunning on the white-sand beach. What about dining in the Queen's Grill with him? She knew she took pictures! She checked the photos again. How could she tell her stories without him and Raphael in the pictures?

Then again, how could she tell her stories with them? No one would believe her!

She shrugged her shoulders. Mr. A always told her, "You'll find out later." Maybe later she would understand this mystery. She would ask Mr. A, the next time she saw him, why he wasn't in any pictures in her camera. She looked out the window, seeing below her the last vestiges of unforgettable South Africa. Her horizons had broadened, and she was no longer the same small-town girl that left Linn three months ago. She didn't see Raphael sitting in the last row.

Flying into JFK, she could see the magnitude and size of this great metropolis of eight million people. She thought of Shanghai, China, with its twenty-six million—three times the population of New York! She booked a room at the Ritz-Carlton, less than a mile from Carnegie Hall, for $900 a night and took a limousine to the hotel. Tomorrow would be the day she went to the Steinway showroom on Fifty-Seventh Street to buy a grand opening gift for Bryan's new recording studio and for a future performing arts center in Linn. She dressed in her best and took her camera. The hotel limousine drove her to the showroom in bumper-to-bumper traffic, car and taxi horns honking incessantly. The showroom reminded her of a luxury hotel lobby hung with oil paintings. The walls were covered with embossed wallpaper and velvet drapes. Sparkling crystal chandeliers reflected the sun's rays onto the richly covered floors. The salespeople dressed in tailored suits. There were magnificent grand pianos spaced around the room with their lids up, and a central area with comfortable chairs and sofas provided potential customers with a place to listen to the pianos being played. She told them she was interested in purchasing a nine-foot Model D Steinway for her gifted brother who once was asked to attend Juilliard, the golden idol of music schools. They showed her that model on the showroom floor, and she asked if someone could play Mozart for her, Bryan's favorite composer.

A gentleman sat at the piano while Damaris listened intently. This was the piano of her brother's dreams. All the salespeople as well as potential customers and tourists were enraptured by the resonant sound of this meticulously crafted instrument. When finished, the room was silent for a moment, the vibrant sounds still reverberating throughout the hall.

She looked at the salesman and said simply, "I'll take it."

She called her bank and initiated a money transfer to Steinway and Sons of almost $200,000, including tax and shipping. She was assured their company could deliver the piano to Missouri within two weeks. Damaris asked if they would give her a tour of the Steinway factory in Queens, and immediately a two-hour private tour was arranged for the next day. Steinway picked her up in a limousine the next morning for her private tour. The factory felt like a church. The workers were focused and serious. One worker told her each piano had its own personality because the people who made them put their hearts and souls into their construction. Each piano's tone was different, just like each human being was different. Sadly she was not allowed to take pictures for Bryan. She was told her brother could watch the documentary *Note by Note* to see the craftsmen and craftswomen who built these amazing pianos. She learned Steinway supplies 95 percent of the world's concert pianos. Steinways are totally made by hand, and their tone makes them superior to all other pianos in the world. Bryan knew about Steinways. He didn't know that, within two weeks, a large truck with the black letters "Steinway and Sons" would drive toward Linn on Highway 50 looking for his recording studio.

The Steinway limousine took her back to the Ritz-Carlton. She decided she would jog through the lovely Central Park, where she spent the afternoon. Joggers, walkers, and families of all races enjoyed themselves in this iconic and beautiful park in the middle of this astounding city of eight million people. She watched a movie being filmed in the park with Cameron Diaz and thought it must be boring for the actors because of how tedious the process. She spent hours watching people and listening to musicians sitting on benches and lawns playing for donations. She had a wallet full of one-hundred-dollar bills, and when she heard a talented musician, she dropped a bill in his hat or music case, which brought a huge smile of appreciation. Damaris wasn't aware Raphael walked close behind her as he had done from the beginning of her journey. As she headed back to her hotel, her phone rang. It was Patrick calling from South Africa. She hadn't spoken to him since she said good-bye in Cape Town. She told him how she had flown back to America from Cape Town and why. She could tell from his voice that he was somewhat stressed about his job at the clinic. He asked where she was and when she would be home. She told him she had flown to New York to buy a Steinway for her brother. He told her he loved her and that he was making plans to come to America as soon as he could. Her hands were shaking as she held the phone. Was this what she wanted really? Is he truly the one? She told him she was having many thoughts and conflicting feelings. He said he would call again and told her he loved her. She said goodbye without saying the same to him. She didn't understand herself. She had actually considered staying in Cape, but now back in America, the vision of Patrick soon faded. She felt as if she had just finished a fairy tale story and set it back on the bookshelf. Would it gather dust? Would she take if off the shelf later and dust it off? Would she try to read it again? She was a realist. She knew many women see their potential boyfriends or husbands through dark glasses, blinding them to their man's faults, thinking they can change their man after having sex or getting married. They see their man's good qualities—attractiveness, a good income, loyalty to their family—and ignore bad tempers, selfishness, impatience around children, and his lack of faith. Patrick's good looks, his accent, his education, his dedication as a doctor, his smile, and his intense brown eyes initially overshadowed the fact that he wasn't a believer. Pastor Dave had counseled her about becoming "unequally yoked." She knew Patrick's lack of spirituality could be a contentious issue for them down the road. Pastor Dave had warned her that many Christian women believed their man would find God later in their relationship. Their prospective men might or might not attend church with them. They might not read the Bible, but they would later. Or so they thought.

Damaris wasn't going to be one of those foolish, delusional women. She would keep her eyes wide open. She prayed in Cape Town for God to help her withstand the sexual temptation she had with Patrick. She knew he wasn't the one. She wanted the whole thing the way God meant it to be. She was willing to wait.

The next day, she flew to St. Louis from JFK. Little did she know that Pastor Dave was keeping tabs on her whereabouts and had organized a parade for her as Bryan drove her back from St. Louis. As she flew, she thought about all the money she spent and felt guilty. She had been financially destitute for so long she wondered if she was being foolish and materialistic. She had a Prada handbag and a Gucci travel bag, which together cost $1,000! Before her win, she bought her purses and bags from Goodwill for $2 each. She now had $400 million in funds to invest and maybe $11 million left for pocket change after all the spending she had done, but the habit of worry often haunts for a lifetime, no matter how secure the present environment. She thought of Scarlett in *Gone with the Wind* and how financially insecure she felt even after she married the wealthy Rhett Butler. The scars of poverty were still etched in Damaris's heart; and she prayed, one day, God would erase them. She called Bryan and shared her feelings. He understood. He told her he felt God was going to use the recording studio in powerful ways.

"What's this about God, Bryan? I have never heard you mention His name."

"Damaris, after you left, Pastor Dave would come over to the studio and hang out occasionally. He asked me questions about my life, and we had interesting conversations. What he said made sense. About a month ago, I was putzing around the studio, and a white limousine parked in front. The chauffeur, a nice-looking young blond guy, about thirty, opens the door for a well-dressed older man who introduced himself as Mr. Armstrong and his chauffeur, Benjamin. He said he had met you on the cruise and happened to be passing through Linn and wanted to meet me. He was pretty honest and said you had some kind of spiritual awakening in South Africa and that you were reading the Bible Pastor Dave gave you. He knew about the recording studio and said he came here to talk to me. We sat in the reception room as he talked of music existing as a powerful tool for good in the hands of the right people. He told me I had already touched lives with my music, but soon I would be touching lives that would live on in eternity. I didn't know what he meant, but he talked to me as a friend. It was a weird encounter, but it made me feel happy and peaceful. We shook hands, and he said he would be talking to me soon again. As he drove away, I wondered what the people of Linn were thinking as this beautiful white limousine drove through town. Maybe they thought the president had come to visit me! I didn't know then that someone more powerful than any president had just talked to me.

"Anyway, Pastor Dave asked me if I could sing one of my songs at his church the next Sunday. I agreed, and later that day, I wrote a guitar song called 'Who Are You?' Maybe it was about Mr. A. I don't know, but for sure, I was wondering about God. I told the church about my conversations with a man named Mr. Armstrong who had met you on the *Queen Mary*. Word had gotten around town I would be at the church, and it was packed. I felt this song deeply. It was a more honest song than I had ever written. I shared the struggles I was having with God. I wasn't a member of their church, didn't profess to be a Christian, and I knew there was some resistance to me as a rock musician. I've heard the gossip. Before I sang, I confessed to the church I was open to learning about God. I turned and looked at that beautiful stained glass with Jesus beckoning to the little black sheep outside the gate as if He was reaching out His hand to me. I was the lost black sheep.

"I strapped on my guitar and played a long introduction before I sang. It was a unique situation, and I felt something I had never felt at my concerts with all that clapping, shouting, screaming, and jumping up and down, most people high on marijuana or in various states of inebriation The people actually listened to the words! They weren't smiling, Damaris, but they were listening intensely! They were still and silent, and I didn't understand the silence. Did the song touch them in any way? There was no applause after I finished. I sat there on that stool, my head bowed, the light filtering through the stained-glass window with Jesus calling with his outstretched hand. There was this hush. It felt sacred as if time stood still. I can't explain it.

"Pastor Dave walked over and stood next to me on the platform. He called the people to come to the altar and gather around me. Someone was playing soft guitar music in the background, and the entire congregation walked quietly in slow motion to the front and laid their hands on me gently as they prayed out loud. I never heard words like that, Damaris, words of love, comfort, and encouragement. They didn't want anything from me. They wanted to bless me. My body felt warm, like there was power in their prayers, and that power was infiltrating into my body. All of a sudden, I started crying. You have never seen me cry have you, Damaris? Even after dad died? Maybe all the pain I stuffed inside was finally releasing into this place of love. My tears were like a dam breaking.

"Maybe it was minutes or hours, I don't know, but the people kept praying. Pastor Dave's arm was around me, and I thought of our father and his love for us. As they prayed, all the hurt and grief began to melt like chocolate left outside on a hot summer day. Voices lowered to spoken whispers. Pastor Dave asked the congregation to pray the Lord would use my talents in real and powerful ways for His kingdom. He asked that, as a congregation, they would encourage me in my faith and help me grow into the image of His Son by the power of His Holy Spirit.

"That was a month ago. I haven't been the same since. My band had played to so many audiences, but not one performance made me feel the way I did in that church." He looked at her with tears in his eyes, wondering what she would say.

"Bryan, I had a similar experience in Durban, South Africa, in a church, a worship center. I was shaken to my core."

She told him her story, and he smiled in agreement.

"I am reading the Bible now. Are you?"

"I am," she said, "especially before I sleep each night. Do you know that Mr. A told me that you and I have broken the chain of unbelief that has run in our family for generations? Isn't that amazing?"

"Yes, it is, Damaris. Maybe now we can share with others that we've both won the biggest lottery prize of all, the gift of faith!"

43

Parade Time

Linn was buzzing. Bryan Kelly had just picked up Damaris at the St. Louis airport in his new van. In a small town, word gets around like wildfire. The day before Damaris's return, the whole town knew she was coming home; and the city council and the mayor, as well as the police and sheriff's departments, were ready to greet them in front of the courthouse. Restaurants were stocked with food, and Casey's brought in a good supply of beer and wine. Linn loved parades as much as the travelers on Highway 50 hated them. There was no way to go around the parade route, Main Street. Linn parades usually backed up traffic for hours. Linn didn't care! Any reason for a parade was fine with them.

A new school bus had been delivered, as well as a state-of-the-art fully equipped ambulance and firetruck. They had huge red bows tied around them like Reggie's Jeep Gladiator, with big thank-you signs on the front. New sidewalks made the town look new. All the utilities were now underground along Main. No more telephone poles with electrical wires dangling from them. The wrought iron benches next to the new old-fashioned lampposts with flower planters wrapped around them made the businesses look inviting. The old pool area was filled in with dirt. The snack bar was torn down, and sod was placed over the whole area, hiding any indication there was ever a pool there. The large white gazebo was built, and benches were installed as well. The Bible verse Jeremiah 29:11–13 was etched into a beautiful granite slab in one corner surrounded by flowers. It said:

> "For I know the plans I have for you," declares the Lord, "plans to prosper you and not to harm you, plans to give you hope and a future. Then you will call on me and pray to me and I will listen to you. You will seek me and find me when you seek me with all your heart."

It was her special verse because it was God's promise to her. But it was also an encouraging verse to anyone who was confused about the direction they were headed in life. Knowing God had a plan and a purpose for every single person would eventually give people hope as they read the words. Now Main Street had two beautiful white gazebos for gatherings and entertainment. The city council named the new gazebo area Osage Park. Now that spring was here, the pool contractors had broken ground for the new McGuire Park pool and promised it would be finished before summer started. Fifty shade trees lined Main. The old-timers in town who did not like all the changes were assured the city council had given their approval because they knew it would help business in Linn. Damaris hadn't seen any of these changes, and the town hoped she would be happy. A podium was set up with a microphone for speeches.

Cell phones alerted the crowd that Damaris and Bryan were just outside of town near the Caspar's 66 station and restaurant. People lined up two and three deep near the courthouse to wait for their arrival. Damaris and Bryan couldn't believe the crowd turnout. Media cameras, local news stations, and newspaper reporters lined the street. They even had a police escort with lights flashing! Damaris looked for Corey, but he was nowhere in sight. She was disappointed. They parked in a space next to the podium, and Pastor Dave smiled at her as he pointed toward his church as the electronic bells played a hymn from the new white steeple.

Damaris smiled as he opened the car door for her and led her up the steps to the podium. There was an audible gasp. This was the plain, tomboy Damaris Kelly—the shy, plain bookworm who waited on them at BJ's? That cleaned houses and babysat their kids? This shapely, well-dressed, manicured vision of beauty? The mayor gave her a fervent handshake as people clapped.

"I'd like to thank everyone for welcoming Damaris back to Linn. We know now she went on a round-the-world voyage on the *Queen Mary 2*, and she might want to tell you some good news about her trip. The whole town thanks you, Damaris, for using your winnings to help our town be the best it can be. Now I'd like the president of Missouri Tech to say a few words. Sir?"

He came to the microphone and told the crowd that Damaris had contributed $2 million to their trust fund to help students who couldn't afford tuition. The audience gasped, then clapped enthusiastically. He also announced that Bryan Kelly's new recording studio was going to work in conjunction with the college to add sound recording to the curriculum, thereby attracting more students. More clapping. Legends Bank thanked her for allowing them to be her investment advisers. Pastor Dave was asked say a few words since he and Damaris were good friends. As he came to the podium, Damaris cried as she put her arms around him.

"I missed you so much!" she whispered.

"Good afternoon, people of Linn. This is a happy day. Damaris just returned from a three-and-a-half-month trip around the world on the ocean liner *Queen Mary 2*. She told me she kept a journal and took thousands of pictures, and in a couple weeks, she is going to have a slide presentation in the high school auditorium. She'll make an announcement in the next few days about the day and time. I know she will have interesting stories to share. She wants the people in Linn to share in that experience, especially with the children, because she wants history and geography to come alive for them. She is going to have large maps so you can vicariously share in her travels. I want to say that I am proud of her for thinking of Linn, and I hope you like what she has done for our city. Every time our bell rings in the new church steeple, I say a prayer of thanks. She also told me on the phone that she wants to help all the churches in Linn with any pressing needs."

Enthusiastic clapping.

"So again, it's good to have you home, Damaris!"

Loud applause and cheers.

"Damaris, would you like to say a few words?"

She looked beautiful, standing confidently as she spoke to the crowd. How she had changed! Before, she would not have been able to stand up and speak like this.

"Gosh, hello, everyone. I am looking at how beautiful you have made this town since I've been gone. This makes me so happy! My heart is full now, and I'm glad you all are here. I can't tell you how happy I am to be home! I didn't expect this reception. I expected to come home and immediately crash on the little bed I've slept in my whole life over there on Benton Avenue. I missed this town. Truthfully I almost considered staying longer in some of the beautiful places I visited, but this is my home. I can't wait to show you pictures of the *Queen Mary* and the lovely places I saw. I met an older man on the ship, and he became my traveling companion for much of the time. He showed me not only the beautiful places but orphanages, homeless shelters, and slum areas that would make you cry. I plan on telling you about some special organizations that might interest you during my slideshow. I need to go home now and rest. It's been a tiring week. Again thanks for welcoming me back. I haven't done anything but get lucky and shared some of my luck with Linn. It's you, the people of Linn, that make this a great town. So again, thank you! God bless you!"

Wild applause.

She didn't see Corey out of uniform standing next to an attractive brunette near the courthouse, intently following Damaris with his eyes until she drove off, then walking with his date into BJ's for a hamburger and a beer, wishing it could be Damaris going in with him.

44

Dreams Come True

Steinway and Sons promised Bryan's Steinway Model D grand piano would be delivered from New York City to Linn. A week earlier, Damaris had an interview with an *Unterrified Democrat* reporter, telling him about this fabulous piano she had bought for Bryan in New York City, but he wasn't to print the article until after the piano was delivered. When the Steinway and Sons truck came into Linn, she called the newspaper reporter so he could capture the moment at the newly named Exodus Studios. Bryan didn't know the piano was coming.

Steinway called Damaris when they were close to Linn. Word of mouth brought a large crowd of people to the studio. Many had seen the truck driving toward Linn, and cell phones got the word out. As the truck pulled up, Damaris asked Bryan to come out in front because he was getting a special delivery. When Bryan walked outside and saw the black letters "Steinway and Sons" on the side of the delivery truck, he looked at Damaris in surprise. When the drivers opened the back, there was something large wrapped with thick blue blankets encased in a huge wooden crate. Damaris proudly told Bryan that one of his dreams just came true.

As the crowd watched the men unload this magnificent piano and carefully bring it into the studio, Damaris told the crowd about her trip to Steinway and Sons in New York, her tour of the factory, and the purchase of the two-hundred-thousand-dollar piano, including shipping costs. She promised she would take pictures of it inside the studio and post them on YouTube. The four men carefully carried the piano into the building on dollies and took hours to set it up and tune it as Bryan looked on in disbelief. This piano of all pianos was his?

The piano tuner had followed the truck in his Mercedes from New York and spent the afternoon making sure the tone and action were perfect. Bryan held Damaris's hand tightly with tears in his eyes as he looked at this magnificent instrument being readied for him to play. He watched the tuner intently as he worked. He asked questions, still in a daze that this instrument, used by the most acclaimed concert pianists in the world, was now part of his studio. One day, it would be placed in the performing arts center he and Damaris would build. For now, it was his to play.

When the tuner finished, Bryan, Damaris, and the band members sat on the studio chairs as Bryan sat on the piano bench. He placed his hands on the keys and pressed one white key. The sound resonated for many seconds. He played a chord. The harmonics were perfect. The tuner wondered if he knew how to play. Damaris whispered that Julliard Music School was once interested in him attending their school. Brian wasn't afraid to start playing. He didn't feel worthy. He knew that human hands had made this instrument. It wasn't factory made. The personalities of the craftsmen were in it, which made it so beautiful. They were counting on him to make this instrument sing as it was meant to sing.

Before he began playing a Mozart concerto, he asked the tuner if he would deliver a message to those men and women who handcrafted this piano. "Tell them I am playing for them today with gratitude and thanks."

Eventually the craftsmen in the Steinway factory would see the YouTube video of him thanking them and hear him play Mozart. The acoustics in the studio were perfect for this concert grand. He began. Never had Bryan played an instrument like this. One of the band members recorded the moment on You Tube, and a million viewers were mesmerized by the piano's tone and resonance as well as Bryan's playing ability. As Damaris watched Bryan play, there were tears streaming down his face as if he were a lost child who had finally found his mother.

After everyone left, Bryan played into the night, alone in the studio but not totally alone. Those who handcrafted this piano were in there with him. When Damaris came by the next morning, he had fallen sleep hunched over the keyboard, as if the concert grand had totally consumed his passion and left him exhausted. The studio was consecrated that night during his moments of playing. Bryan would never be the same as a musician. He had reached great heights in the night that no one heard but his Creator, and there was much more to come.

45

New Beginnings and Final Goodbyes

A few days later, Damaris began sorting through huge piles of mail from the last three months, a time-consuming job with so many people asking for money. She threw away most of it, kept the important stuff, and was glad when the grueling task was finished. She dressed casually, opened the garage door, took off the car cover, and smiled as she saw Baby (the new nickname for her car) parked there calling to her, *Drive me!*

She ran into the house, grabbed her keys, and drove out to Bryan's studio. She loved the name Exodus Studios and the sign he had made with tasteful gold letters above the front entrance. The building was modern in architecture with simple lines, functional yet attractive. There were quite a few cars in the parking lot. She walked through the front door, smiling. Inside, the Rogues were practicing as two sound engineers worked the soundboards. Bryan told the band to take a break as he ran to her, then led her around the facility with enthusiasm, ecstatically happy his years of dreaming had finally become reality. She had yet to see the whole facility. Bryan had built bedrooms with bunkbeds and a kitchen, plus men's and women's showers and restrooms. Musicians could stay there as long as they were recording. The lottery money had built one of the best equipped recording studios in the country. His Steinway was safely moved to one corner of the main studio and covered until further use. She had put her money to good use. The entire music world would benefit from her generosity and Bryan's Exodus Studios.

She met with an architect that afternoon and sketched out how she would like her house built. It would be a three-story, ten-thousand-square-foot modified version of a European castle built with Missouri rock and stone. Inside, a huge spiral staircase would lead to four second-floor bedrooms. The third floor would hold the huge master suite overlooking the future grotto area through large floor-to-ceiling windows. Every window in the house would have electronically controlled privacy screens. One turret, connected to the master bedroom, would display a huge library like the *Queen Mary's*, with leather chairs and opulent brass lamps. The other turret would be the office for her future charities. The inside of the house would be luxurious but homey. She wanted six bedrooms. The basement would contain two of the bedrooms and two baths, one for Bryan and one for the future housekeeper she would hire as soon as her home was completed.

A four-car garage was a must. She wanted a tree-lined driveway from the highway entrance to the front of the house. When she talked to the landscape designers, she told them they had no limits on the cost. She showed them pictures of varieties of flowers, trees, and plants and lush green lawns and trees like the jacarandas and eucalyptus in Australia. The back of the house already had the forest as a backdrop, but her dream was to put in huge grotto areas with water-falls. She contacted Lucas Congdon of *Insane Pools*, a television show she liked to watch, and budgeted $1 million for the pool area of her dreams. When his crew came into town, they stayed at the Stone Hearth Inn and ate at local restaurants, continually signing auto-graphs on napkins or restaurant menus. When the house was completed, the whole property, including the sound studio, would be enclosed by an attractive tall black wrought iron electrified fence. She wasn't paranoid, but she knew both her house and Bryan's studio could be possible targets for thieves. They both would install state-of-the art security systems, and Damaris would hire a full-time security guard to patrol their properties. Damaris made sure they were both heavily insured. She ordered another Steinway for her huge great room on the main floor, not as expensive as the concert grand but good enough.

When the architect finished the plans, Damaris and Pastor Dave looked them over, and construction began. She was promised the construction would take less than a year. She wanted most of the materials and labor to come from local sources if possible. This home was a far cry from their little home on Benton Avenue. She still felt she was in a dream and would soon wake up from it and be back in the difficult circumstances of the past years.

With the help of a local technology expert, she created an interesting slideshow of her voyage, complete with music and narration. The gymnasium held five hundred, and they had to turn people away. So Damaris promised she would do another presentation the next night with the school's permission. The people were astounded at the pictures Damaris took. The last few pictures were of her and Patrick during the two days they were together exploring the beauty of Cape Town. She told them he was a doctor she had met who offered to show her around. She didn't make a big deal of him because she knew how rumors flew in this town. At the end of the second night's show, as she talked to people congratulating her on her presentation, she saw Corey approaching from the back of the auditorium. She gave him a smile as he walked toward her. He wore a T-shirt and jeans, and his hair was longer than when she had last seen him. He had dark circles under his eyes, and she wondered if he felt well. She didn't know he was spending sleepless nights thinking of her, frustrated about their relationship.

She was happy to see him, but the first thing he said to her, with a bitter voice, was "I especially liked the part about the doctor showing you a good time. Now I understand."

"Understand what?"

"Come on, Damaris. Do you think I'm stupid? Do you think I don't know you?"

"Corey, I'm sorry about our last conversation on the ship. I never wanted to hurt you in any way."

"Well, you did. I can't begin to tell you how much."

Damaris didn't know what to say except "Well, you have a real cute girlfriend now. Someone told me you were with her at the parade."

He looked at her with contempt. "Do you really think I care at all about her other than she was a pretty girl who was as lonely as I was? Do you really think I could just turn off my love for you and forget it never existed?"

"Can we talk somewhere else, Corey? There are people around, and it's embarrassing."

"Why, Damaris? What good does talking do? I came here tonight because…I guess I came here to see your slideshow. That's all. I've seen it. Good night. I'll see you around town, I'm sure."

He turned his back on her and left the auditorium. Her heart told her to call out his name and beg him to come back to her, but she didn't. Maybe it was her pride. She remembered the soft touch of Patrick's hand on her arm and the light brush of his lips on hers, but wasn't Patrick a faded, disappearing fairy-tale dream? Her conflicting emotions confused her; could she love two men at the same time? For different reasons?

46

Good News,
Bad News

Harris House, the alcohol recovery center in St. Louis, called Damaris and said her mother had used her time productively and achieved their goals. She was free from alcohol and the desire for it. They said her joy was infectious, and she was well liked and looked forward to life in the real world. The counselor said her mom had some good news and wanted to tell Damaris before she left the rehab.

They put her mom on the phone; and she cried out, "Damaris, my darling, it's so good to hear your voice. I can't wait to hear about your trip. I have had such an insightful and healing time here. You'll be glad to know I'm moving on from grief. Your dad and I had a wonderful relationship, and I value those twenty years. After all, we made you and Bryan! The news is I developed a friendship with one of the counselors who came in for special classes, and we seemed to have a healthy connection. Now that I am going to be released, he has asked me to marry him. He's a good man, Damaris, a loving man, and he cares for me deeply. He's anxious to meet you and Bryan. What do you think?"

Damaris was surprised but told her mom, "I just want you to be happy, Mom. That's all I ever wanted. If he's the man, I'm all for it."

"That's great to hear, Damaris. He has a house in a suburb of St. Louis, and he wants us to be together. Could we come to see you in a week? His name's Jerry. How's that house of mine doing?"

"I'm living here for now, Mom, but I bought ninety-five acres outside of town, and they're beginning the construction of my new home. If it's okay, I'll live in our house until mine is finished, then you can sell the old house or whatever you want to do with it."

"Of course, you can live there. I will probably stay with Jerry in his home here in St. Louis, but we will get married first, okay? We can celebrate when we come next week."

"I'm happy for you, Mom, truly. Does Bryan know?"

"I'll call him after we hang up. I want to hear about your trip and your plans for Linn and Bryan.

Here's Jerry's cell phone number. I love you, my daughter."

"I love you too, Mom. This news is as good as winning the lottery!"

Her mother had been such a worry to her for so many years. Damaris had carried too many burdens as a teenager. She thanked God that her mother was finally at peace. She hoped Jerry would let her pay for a beautiful honeymoon for them as a wedding gift.

Later that day, her phone rang as she relaxed on the sofa looking through interior decorating magazines. She was surprised to hear the voice of Amelia Hoffman, Patrick's mother, calling from Perth, Australia.

"Damaris, this is Patrick's mother. James is on the other line."

"It's so good to hear from you! How are you?" she said, genuinely happy to hear from them. "How is Patrick?"

There was silence on the other end, then Damaris heard Amelia sobbing.

"Amelia, what's wrong?" Damaris had no idea.

"Damaris," said James, "We have something to tell you, something sad, devastating, and heartbreaking."

Damaris heard the pain in his voice.

"A few weeks after you left Australia, Patrick called and told us he had met the most beautiful woman in the world. He thanked us for steering you to the clinic and told us you had two lovely days together. He also told us he asked you to stay in Cape Town. You gave him many reasons for not staying, and when he saw the *Queen Mary* pull out of the harbor, he decided after he fulfilled his two-year contract with DWB, he would leave South Africa to be with you if you wouldn't come there. He told us he loved you, and we were happy that you might one day become our daughter-in-law. We hoped, maybe one day, you and Patrick would get married, and our dream would be for you to live in Australia near us. We aren't too old to be grandparents."

She paused as if trying to find the right words.

"One of his responsibilities was to occasionally oversee small clinics outside Cape Town, making sure there were enough supplies and staff for these poor small villages. They think he was bitten by an infected mosquito. When he returned to the clinic, he started getting the chills and a high fever. Then he would return to normal and keep working without rest. He would get another fever with bad headaches, nausea, and vomiting. The staff checked him into a hospital in Cape Town which had more services available. By this time, we had flown there to see if we could help. His joints and muscle pain were unbearable. He was so fatigued he couldn't even lift his arms. He began breathing rapidly. His heart rate went crazy. The last thing he said was 'Tell Damaris I love her.' He died, Damaris, in that Cape Town hospital. Our only son, a healthy, vibrant, young, dedicated doctor who fought to cure disease. They think it was malaria."

Damaris sat in shock.

"We are walking around like living corpses with no children now and no potential grandchildren. The services were held in Perth where our friends live. We received so many letters praising him as a dedicated doctor. I'd like to send you copies of these. We wanted you to know, Damaris, because you gave him his last few days of happiness."

Damaris was in disbelief. How could this handsome young doctor be dead?

She spoke gently to Mr. Hoffman. "I lost my dad unexpectedly when I was fifteen. I understand grief. I want you to know that I took many pictures of Patrick those last few days. I promise I'll send you copies, and we can grieve together. I should have stayed in Cape Town. We could have had more time. Maybe he wouldn't have gone into those villages if I was there."

She was crying too.

"You aren't alone, Amelia and James. I want you to know I was minutes away from staying in Cape Town with him. I cut my cruise short so I wouldn't be tempted. I was falling in love, but it wasn't the right time or place. I am so sorry for your loss. I have an idea. I'm building a new home which should be finished by next spring, and I would like to have you come for a visit. I'll have some nice rooms for you by then, and hopefully it will be a place where you can heal. You could meet the pastor of the church I am attending. He has helped me so much. What do you say?"

Mr. Hoffman said, "Call us when you are ready for us, Damaris."

She said to them lovingly, "James and Amelia, cast all your cares on Him, for He cares for you." She heard them weeping.

She wondered if she would ever again feel the way she felt for Patrick in the two magical days she knew him. Could any romance match those brief hours in Cape Town? She would soon have her answer.

47

A New Life

Her house was finished. It truly was the showcase she had dreamed of and designed, as elegant as anything she had seen on her trip. The *Insane Pools* company had done what they promised. It was a forest paradise of waterfalls and grottos with an outside kitchen, grass areas for volleyball, and beach areas for sunbathing. The lighting at night reminded her of the Magic Fountains of Montjuïc in Barcelona. She scoured bookstores and the Internet for classic books to fill her library. She bought many interior design books and realized she had an astute flair for decorating. She hired an interior decorator to assist her with furniture, drapes, window coverings, floor coverings, bedroom linens, and towels, all of the best quality and the best money could buy. She ordered a smaller Steinway grand for her great room and loved it when Bryan visited and played for her.

The Linn facelift was complete, and it lifted the spirits of the townspeople and gave them a new sense of pride in their town. One of her dreams was to build a five-star restaurant in Linn for fine dining, much like the Queen's Grill on the *Queen Mary*. She bought property as close as she could to the college so they could use the restaurant for restaurant management and culinary school training. She hired one of the best chefs in the Midwest to create a menu that would astound the people in Linn and surrounding areas. Some residents in town thought she was wasting her money. But after a slow start, business picked up, and eventually it was hailed as one of the finest five-star restaurants in Missouri, drawing people from all over the area. There was a first-class wine selection and an elegant bar. Now people in Linn had a place where they could celebrate anniversaries, birthdays, and other special occasions with candlelight and soft classical music. People in Linn enjoyed having a fine restaurant like this for important occasions. Reservations had to be made months ahead.

College students were trained as waiters and became as skilled and professional as those on the *Queen Mary*. The kitchen was huge, designed for preparation as well as storage for fresh food. The culinary students were trained in the art of cooking exquisite food, which looked like pieces of art and tasted even better. She hired a maître d' who was also the manager who greeted the guests and checked each table throughout their time there. Damaris instituted a dress code for men and women. At first, people were dubious about this. Many men in Linn didn't want to wear a suit coat. The women loved it because it gave them a chance to dress up. She named the restaurant Queen's Grill, after the dining room on the *Queen Mary*. Eventually she had to enlarge the parking lot. The restaurant not only paid for itself; it made a good profit. She donated 25 percent of the profits to the college scholarship fund. If someone complained about the prices, she reminded them some of their money spent on dinner was going to the college scholarship fund.

The McGuire Park Pool was finished and made a great addition to the town. There were four life-guard stations and two diving boards. Across the way, Damaris built a large snack bar with cooling fans for the workers and a large shaded area for swimmers and families to eat. High school students were paid an hourly rate to work at the snack bar, and any profit was theirs to use for school programs. Each swimmer paid a dollar for the day to help with expenses in the summer, and Damaris said she would pay the city for any loss of money. Missouri musicians used both the gazebo parks for concerts and had to reserve ahead at the Chamber of Commerce. Musicians loved being able to gather together. Dulcimer and fiddle players, banjo players and vocalists, singing groups repre- senting all age levels and abilities, and cloggers and tap dancers—all loved to come to Linn to perform. Damaris installed lights inside the gazebos for night- time concerts, which were very popular. The newly planted trees along Main provided much needed shade; and more people walked through the town enjoying the trees, flowers, and benches. Established businesses spruced up their exteriors, and some new businesses filled previously empty office spaces.

Damaris set up a fund at the bank for those who were having a hard time paying their rent or buying food. She remembered her days of hardship, and she vowed no person in Linn would ever have to lose hope or feel there was no one to turn to in a difficult situation. All these improvements brought new business into Linn and a new sense of pride. The Stone Hearth Inn operated at nearly 100 percent capacity. Damaris bought some land near the college and made a deal with Best Western to build a hotel and small convention center, which the town needed.

Damaris volunteered weekly at Grace Community, helping with the food distribution to the needy. She attended weekly Bible studies with Pastor Dave and continued to grow spiritually. She met with the bank regularly. The amount she received after taxes was $422 million. She would live on the interest from $400 million, which was about $600,000 a year after taxes. She made new friends and met new people, which pulled her out of her basically shy shell. She had spent fifteen million of the twenty-two million on all the capital outlays in Linn. Six million she gave to the charities Mr. A had told her about or shown her. It seemed to her that, as she blessed others with her finances, she was blessed a hundred times over! All this should have made her happy, but she was lonely. She missed Corey. He would pass by her in his sheriff's car without a smile or a wave. If she went to BJ's and he was eating there, he picked up his sandwich and walked into the back room without a look or a smile. They both attended Pastor Dave's church, but he sat in the back pew. At the end, he would slip out of the service without even acknowledging her. Pastor Dave saw this from the lectern and was saddened for the breach in their friendship which had once looked so promising. He prayed for them but trusted God had a better plan for both of them.

48

Corey

This November afternoon, the assorted red, orange, and yellow leaves fell like large colored raindrops on the property now rented by Crazy Charlie or, as he now called himself, Chief Red Cloud. He was out of prison again on parole, renting an abandoned farmhouse for $200 a month with no running water, heating, or air-conditioning. He filched water from various sources and powered fans in the summer and a heater in the winter with a rundown portable generator. He lived on welfare and profits from selling methamphetamines throughout Osage County. He painted a huge red-and-white circular target on his roof because he said the cops had made him a target. He wore a camouflage fishing hat hung with rusting lures, pulled down over his stringy, greasy hair; a dirty tie-dyed T-shirt; and filthy ripped jeans and rotting sandals. He smelled bad and washed his clothes and took baths by jumping into Pointers Creek with all his clothes on. The Osage County sheriffs and Linn police kept an eye on him. They suspected he cooked meth somewhere outside his cabin, down an overgrown path about a fourth of a mile away.

On this day, the dry leaves had caught fire. The closest neighbors called the fire department, which answered the call immediately, and the sheriffs decided to come along just in case Charlie caused trouble as he usually did. When they arrived at the property, they extinguished the fire while Charlie barricaded himself inside the crumbling cabin.

Corey and his partner, Jack Kellerman, parked in front of the shack; and Corey yelled, "Charlie, come out of there now! We want to talk to you about how this fire got started."

Charlie yelled back, "Come on, Corey. You know how. But it wasn't me who did it!"

"Then who?"

"I ain't tellin'. That's *my* business. And you ain't callin' me by my new name, Chief Red Cloud."

"Okay, Chief Red Cloud. You're breaking the law, so now it is my business. I've asked you to come out here, but if you don't, I'll have to kick in the door in and haul you out!"

"Just try!" Charlie yelled. "And if you come in here, you are gonna get a real big surprise!"

"Do you have a gun, Charlie?"

"I sure do. Remember? And I know how to use it," he yelled back.

Corey signaled for Deputy Kellerman to sneak around to the back door.

"One!"

"Hey, Corey," he yelled through the closed door, "how's that pretty girl that won all that money, the daughter of that slut of a mother? I hear you two aren't a thing anymore. Did she get too rich and too uppity for a poor cop like you? Tough luck, huh? You could have gotten some of that money!"

"Two!"

"I guess she didn't want a lapdog or a poor cop eatin' the crumbs off her table."

"Three!"

Corey kicked down the door, then backed up as Charlie walked outside pointing a .22 pistol which he had loaded with hollow points for maximum damage. Corey yelled to Jack to get to the radio and call for backup.

Charlie warned, "Oh, no, you don't. Stay right where you are. If you move, Corey's a goner. We all know at this point in time I'm goin' back to prison, so I don't got nothin' to lose. What I really want is to shoot both of you dead. I'm tired of you cops stickin' your noses into my business."

They heard police sirens in the distance. The ambulance had radioed there was trouble at Charlie's place. Charlie looked down the gravel road, and in an instant, Corey made a lunge for him.

Charlie pulled the trigger, aiming for Corey's head. In an instant, something strange happened.

Apparently some kind of force pulled Charlie's gun to the right, the bullet hitting Corey in the left shoulder and bursting an artery. Corey fell back, blood spurting from his shoulder area. Deputy Kellerman threw himself at Charlie, and he hit the ground, stunned.

After a scuffle, the sheriff cuffed him and called on his radio for assistance, yelling, "Officer down! Officer down!"

Corey had already lost too much blood from his artery and was losing consciousness.

"Hang on, Corey. Hang on!" yelled the deputy as he applied compression.

The target Charlie painted on the roof helped the medivac helicopter from Jefferson City find the place in twenty minutes. The ambulance returned, and paramedics frantically applied more compression and tourniquets. At the hospital in Jefferson City, Corey was put on a life-support system. The whole town immediately knew he was in a life-or-death battle. Phone calls came into the hospital. People volunteered to donate blood. The town began to pray. They loved Corey. He was one of theirs.

Damaris was out by her pool listening to the radio when the news flash came on their local station that Deputy Corey Gardner had been shot and was in critical condition at St. Mary's.

Damaris froze. *No, not Corey!*

She ran into her house, grabbed her car keys and purse, jumped into her Corvette, and headed for Jefferson City.

As she drove gripping the steering wheel tightly, disregarding the speed limits, she prayed over and over, "Lord, please don't let Corey die. I love him. I know that now. Please save him!"

At the hospital, Corey's parents and Pastor Dave prayed in the waiting room outside the intensive care unit. They didn't know that the whole city of Linn had quickly organized prayer vigils—all the churches. A kind of hush fell over the town, and people traveling through Linn on Highway 50 felt a strange pall along the road, the quiet stillness of a town praying for a life and a miracle. The vigil lasted two days as Corey and the doctors fought for his life. Corey had lost too much blood. His upper torso and shoulder area were wrapped tightly. Tubes and IVs connected him to blood bags and fluids. Oxygen and ventilators kept him breathing. Before the shooting, Corey was a vital, healthy young man. Now he was gaunt and pale, his breathing labored. They allowed Damaris and his parents to visit for a few minutes. Mrs. Gardner was crying. She had already lost a young daughter to cancer. Corey was all they had left.

Damaris touched his hand, bent over him, and whispered in his ear, "Corey, this is me, Damaris. I'm here, touching your hand. I'm so sorry for the way I've treated you this past year. I wasn't ready for your love. I'm ready now. Fight, Corey. Fight for the sake of your parents. Fight for our future together. Please, Corey! I need you like flowers need rain."

She picked up his hand and pressed it lightly to her lips as her tears fell. The nurse reminded them time was up. She touched Corey's hand softly and said goodbye. She said she would be at the hospital as much as she could. As she walked out of the room, she noticed tears falling from his eyes onto his cheeks. She prayed that it was his way of showing her he still loved her and would fight for their future.

*****

Corey lived! The town rejoiced. He spent a week in the hospital gaining strength and was brought home by ambulance to his parents' farm and advised he was not to do any kind of physical labor or use his arm at all. He had fractured his shoulder and ripped muscles in his upper arm. He was on strong painkillers for his excruciating pain. Damaris called his parents on his second night home and asked if she could come for a short visit.

As she drove up the drive to their lovely farmhouse, Corey sat in a large rocking chair on the wraparound porch, holding a glass of sweet tea. He had lost so much weight and was deathly pale. His hair was longer. He needed a shave. He was not the clean-cut, muscular deputy he once was. He wore his Exodus Studios T-shirt and sweatpants and was barefoot. She always thought he was handsome, and even now as he recovered, she thought he looked very European and quite desirable. The intensity of his love for her still showed in his eyes as she sat on the rocking chair next to him and handed him a bouquet of flowers, which Mrs. Gardner quickly brought into the house to put them in a vase. They sat comfortably in silence for a while. He grimaced in pain whenever he made any kind of movement.

"Crazy Charlie did a number on me, didn't he?" He tried to smile, but the pain was too deep. "Stupid me. I didn't wear my bulletproof vest that day. I'd gotten lackadaisical about it. The chief just told the whole department that, from now on, no one was to leave the station without wearing one. Big mistake, huh?"

He took her hand gently and gave her a sweet smile. She looked beautiful sitting there. How long had it been since he sat so close to her?

"Damaris, I want to ask you something. Was I dreaming on that hospital bed? Did I hear you say you loved me?"

"I did say it, Corey." She smiled.

"Have you changed your mind?" he asked anxiously.

She brought his hand up to her lips and kissed it. He winced. Any movement in his left arm caused extreme pain.

"What made you say that to me?"

She looked directly into his eyes. "Corey, when I saw you lying there with the chance you might not pull through, I thought how hard it would be not having you in my life. I couldn't bear that, Corey. I remembered your faithfulness, your honesty, your morals, your sense of humor, your dedication to your job and to the people of Linn, your love of music, your love of fishing, hunting, and the outdoors, your sensitivity to my feelings, the feeling of protection I have when I'm near you, and, of course, your love for me. You are also very attractive, even now. I realized, at that moment, you are the jewel in my life. Maybe I was too young in the beginning.

When I saw you lying there hooked up to all those machines and IVs, I remembered all the conversations I had with Pastor Dave and Mr. Armstrong, the nice elderly gentleman I met on the ship, about God's plan and purpose for my life, and I knew, at that moment, with surety, that you were part of that plan. I'm sorry that I rejected your love. I know it hurt you. Can you forgive me?" she pleaded.

He stood up and pulled her gently to himself with his right arm, his lips seeking hers.

Mrs. Gardner looked out the living room window and, seeing them together, said to herself, *Finally*!

As they stood there holding one another for a brief moment, in her mind, she saw the fairy tale Patrick standing in front of the *Queen Mary* waving goodbye to her; and for some reason, it felt good to let go of that brief dream. She knew Corey was the real thing, the one who was the perfect fit for her life and plans for the future.

"It'll be a while before I'm back to normal, but I want to ask you this, Damaris. When I'm healed, will you marry me?"

She didn't have to think about her answer. She knew.

"Yes, Corey. Yes, a lifetime of yeses!"

"I'm really tired now, Damaris. I need to lie down. You're not going to change your mind, are you?"

The next day, when she visited Corey, she accepted the lovely engagement ring he had bought for her two years ago, the night he brought her the necklace with the two hearts entwined. He placed it on her finger there on the porch as the colored leaves fell in profusion over the yard, the white puffy clouds drifting across the brilliant blue sky and the rich, spicy smell of fall permeating the air. She never forgot that moment. They would be married, and it would be right. There would be no doubts in either of their minds.

His mother put the engagement announcement in the *Unterrified Democrat* the next day, and the town rejoiced, echoing his mother's thoughts—"Finally!"

Later that week, Deputy Kellerman came to Damaris's house to tell her something about the shooting. They sat in her huge living room in front of the fireplace.

"Damaris, I know you're going to think I was just seeing something that wasn't really there, but Crazy Charlie had the gun pointed right at Corey's head when he pulled the trigger. Behind Corey stood this tall blond guy. I glanced at him for a brief moment when he reached out his hand in front of

Corey's face, as if trying to protect him, and it made the bullet move to the right, in slow motion. I really saw it, and then this guy just disappears, and the bullet hits Corey where it did, saving his life. What do you think? Do you believe that I really saw this? Do you think I'm crazy?"

Damaris laughed. "Of course not. In fact, what you saw was reality. I'll tell you one thing, just between you and I. That man was sent to protect Corey. He was real. Trust me. Thanks for sharing that, Jack. Did you tell Corey about it?"

"I already told him, and you know, he repeated what you just said."

"Jack, there are many mysteries on this world. We live in the real world, but there is a supernatural world that we are not often aware of because our flesh hides the truth from us. What you witnessed was a supernatural occurrence. Accept that and be thankful you witnessed a true miracle."

49

At Last

Damaris's mother did not relapse. She was happily married to Jerry and loved living near the bustling metropolis of St. Louis. When Damaris asked her to help with the wedding, she was honored and thankful her daughter once again trusted her. Her mother was the happy mom of five years ago. She discovered her mother had organizational skills, creative ideas, and an eye for beauty. The planning brought them closer together as never before. The days of mourning for Phillip were over, and together they shared only happy memories of a husband and father.

The wedding was set for June. They had waited six months so Corey's shoulder could heal. Damaris and Corey went through marital counseling with Pastor Dave, and during that time, they learned more about each other. Pastor Dave knew theirs would be a good marriage. It started in the right way, both of them remaining chaste until their wedding day. Damaris didn't want to leave anyone out, so she announced an open invitation for all residents of Linn to attend the ceremony and reception. Pastor Dave's church was too small for a thousand wedding attenders. The city council donated the use of the entire Mcguire Park at no charge. Huge rented tents spread across the park area. The ceremony would be held under the largest of the white tents, where a long, raised platform surrounded by flowers would hold the wedding party and the band. The band! Bryan's band would play the wedding music. Damaris asked for Irish music and old rock and roll tunes for the reception.

Damaris's rented portable dressing rooms were placed for the bridal party. Large linen-covered tables displayed three multilayered cakes, each in itself a work of art. The culinary students from the college created these masterpieces with the supervision of a specialty baker Damaris hired. Other tables held champagne and fruit punch, teas and coffee, and platters of exquisite hors d'oeuvres prepared with utmost care by the Queen's Grill chef and his staff. Potted blue forget-me-nots lined the aisles. Damaris and Corey asked that no one bring gifts but instead donate to a fund they had set up at the bank to help people who struggled with their rent or house payments. Linn being Linn, giving gifts was part of its nature. Of course, many donated to the house fund; but quite a few made Corey and Damaris beautiful quilts, needlepoint, tatted lace tablecloths with matching napkins, hand-painted birdhouses, and crocheted blankets, learning ahead of time what colors she used for decorating. They gave to Damaris and Corey what couldn't be bought but was worth more than money—the time, effort, and love that went into their handmade gifts which would one day be their children's heirlooms. After their honeymoon, they opened these gifts made with such love and care and wept for the beauty and thoughtfulness that went into their making.

As she and her mother planned the wedding, Damaris had misgivings. Would it be too ostentatious? Did Damaris look like a show-off? She asked respected people in the community what they thought. Most thought that, if she could afford it and invited everyone in Linn, then why not? It would be one of the best parties Linn ever had. Corey and Damaris were loved, and Bryan Kelly and the Rogues would provide the music—definitely a first for a wedding in their town.

Damaris wanted to be a beautiful bride for Corey's sake. She was giving herself to him—body, soul, mind, and spirit, her wedding gifts to him. She and her mother drove to Kansas City in her Corvette to the best bridal salon. Georgia was scared at first at the rumbling power of this car; but after a while, as she grew more comfortable, she began to enjoy the ride. The dress Damaris chose was simple but elegant, trimmed with pearls and lace, and Renaissance in style with long transparent flowing sleeves. A light and airy veil would be embellished with fresh dainty-blue forget-me-not flowers, the color of the bridesmaids' dresses.

When she stood before the mirror, her mother cried with tears in her eyes. "You are so beautiful, Damaris. There could never be a lovelier bride. Your father would be so proud."

The wedding day—perfect weather, blue skies, and a soft June breeze. The groomsmen were Corey's fellow deputies, looking handsome and proud in their dark-blue suits. The bridesmaids, Damaris's fellow waitresses from BJ's, dressed in coral-sea-blue silk dresses with fresh blue forget-me-not flowers, honored to be part of this historic wedding. Bryan would give Damaris away as her father would have done. How she wished her father were alive now! He would be proud of Bryan and Corey and would be the beaming father as they danced the father-daughter dance. She had done all she could to prepare. The rest was in the Lord's hands.

As the chairs filled, Bryan's band played softly in the background. Pastor Dave went into both dressing rooms and prayed for the entire bridal party as well as the bride and groom. There was always a sense of holiness in his prayers, as if God Himself was speaking to them, and the rooms flooded with His spirit.

Bryan's band began playing an old Irish love song their father had sung to them as children, and the procession began. Each bridal party couple walked with solemnity to the altar. As Damaris waited, she looked to her right, and there were Mr. Armstrong and Raphael standing next to him near the white limousine parked by Damaris's Corvette in the grass. Two other men stood with them, a redheaded young man and a blond-haired one, all dressed in dark-blue suits. She serenely smiled at all of them and waved. She began walking slowly up the pathway. The crowd stood, enthralled by her otherworldly ethereal beauty. Corey stood next to Pastor Dave, his eyes intently focused on Damaris, as Bryan sang a lovely Irish love song as he played his Roland keyboard. The crowd knew brides were beautiful, but there was something spiritual in the way she walked toward Corey, as if she was surrounded by celestial light.

Corey stood transfixed, handsome, and a little nervous in his dark-blue suit. He couldn't believe this lovely woman he had loved for years would finally be his. They had saved themselves physically for one another, thanks to Pastor Dave's and Mr. Armstrong's counseling. It hadn't been easy for either of them. They were young, healthy, and filled with life and strong, passionate love and desire for one another; but they stayed away from situations where they would be tempted. They wanted the best for themselves as a couple. As she approached him, he could barely breathe. When she stood in front of him as the music played softly, Pastor Dave was sensitive to what was going on between them. Bryan stopped playing. A hush fell over the crowd—even babies and toddlers stopped fussing. Damaris and Corey were in a heaven of their own now, in a vortex of love, their longing for one another showing on their faces. People remembered their own feelings on their wedding day and smiled. Pastor Dave began the service with a tender and deep-felt prayer. He loved them both. He knew God would be the third person in their solid, lasting marriage.

Each had written their wedding vows, which the pastor handed to them. As they read their words to one another, the crowd listened in hushed silence to the poetry of their love as they clasped each other's hands and touched their foreheads as they bowed their heads in prayer. Corey whispered his love for her, and she did the same. Their words silently rose into the trees, and the warm breeze of love wrapped itself around every guest. Like a floating silken parachute, silent love hung in the air. Pastor Dave laid hands on both of them, praying a benediction.

Then in a booming voice, he said, "I now pronounce you man and wife! Kiss your bride, Corey, and let's get on with it!"

Everyone laughed, and as Corey kissed her deeply, the fragrance of her perfume wrapped around him like a soft blanket.

Damaris and Corey didn't know the Rogues had been practicing Irish dance tunes all week. They bought Irish instruments, which they would store at the studio for other occasions—an Irish fiddle, a tin whistle, a flute, a concertina, a button accordion, and the famous bodhran drum, a large framed drum covered with goatskin beaten with a stick. They had listened to the Gaelic Storm Irish group from the *Titanic* movie and learned to play tunes on the unusual instruments tolerably well. They moved their regular band instruments as quietly as possible during the vows, secretly replacing them with the Irish instruments. The attendees didn't know what was in store for them. When Pastor Dave pronounced the couple man and wife, the band surprised Damaris and Bryan as they burst into a joyful Irish dance tune, John Ryan's polka, the bodhran drum beating triumphantly and Bryan playing the button accordion.

As Corey and Damaris danced down the aisle, the whole crowd stood, shouting and responding to the music. Little children danced with abandon, swinging each other around. Corey triumphantly brought Damaris down the aisle. Cameras flashed, and the wedding ceremony was posted on YouTube later that evening. A few Missouri and also national newspaper reporters were there and wrote about the wedding with Damaris, the big jackpot winner, and Bryan Kelly and the Rogues. A hired crew moved all the chairs, and a huge portable dance floor was quickly and expertly placed. The Irish music continued joyously, and many attendees responded with smiles and dancing, not a typical response in a town steeped in conservative German traditions and self-contained expression.

Damaris and Corey walked over to the limousine where Mr. A and his three friends stood. Mr. A introduced his friends—Jacob, with the blond hair and piercing blue eyes, and Benjamin, a cute redhead with lots of freckles—all dressed in tasteful dark-blue suits. Damaris wondered what Mr. A was up to, but she had promised she would always trust him. Mr. A said they wouldn't have missed the wedding for the world. After all, they knew many of the attendees. He told her he wanted to talk to her about some issues but would wait until after their honeymoon. The three men stood by the limousine the entire night, watching the proceedings intensely. Damaris asked Mr. A to dance with her several times, reminding her of their happy times on the *Queen Mary*'s ballroom floor. The Linn residents had never seen better ballroom dancers. The reception went in full swing, and by the end of the evening, the limousine and Mr. A's friends had disappeared. The Rogues played Irish music, old rock and roll dance tunes, and some of their hits, which received loud applause. The cake was cut, the hors d'oeuvres eaten, and the toasts made. The reception lasted until dark, and no one wanted to leave.

Damaris and Corey were excited as they sat in her silver Corvette hung with dangling streamers and balloons. At least fifty cars lined up behind them, honking their horns as they drove through Linn. Residents who couldn't attend the wedding waved and honked as the procession drove through town. Damaris and Corey opened the electronic gate to the house and pulled into the driveway. Corey attached a "Do Not Disturb" sign on the front door They would leave for Florida for their honeymoon in two days but spend two nights in Linn first, enjoying the newly decorated house and amazing grotto and waterfall area in the back. Corey was scheduled back as a deputy in two weeks, so they weren't in a hurry.

He carried her across the threshold, and they both walked up the spiral staircase hand in hand. Soft piped-in music played throughout the house. They entered the master bedroom and lit candles. Damaris changed into one of her silky negligees, and Corey wore the soft robe she had bought him. They stood on the balcony listening to the night sounds of frogs and cicadas as fireflies lit up the night and the colored lights from the grotto reflected on the water. Corey took the pins out of her hair and let it fall loose around her shoulders, then lifted her hair and kissed the back of her neck as he held her close. She was twenty-one and had saved herself for her husband. She didn't know what to expect. Corey, too, had saved himself for her, and his love and desire for her was like a bomb inside ready to explode. Damaris never knew her own desire could rise to this extent, so intense and consuming. He lifted her onto the bed. Their bodies, souls, minds, and spirits became one that night on their king-sized bed as the cicadas sang their song. Their togetherness lifted her to heights she never knew existed.

The next day, they stayed in bed until five o'clock in the afternoon, exhausted from the wedding and their lovemaking. Corey brought her coffee in bed on a tray with flowers, just like her father used to do for her mother. They dressed and drove to McGuire Park. All the tents were gone, the dressing trailers hauled away, the platform disassembled, and the tables and chairs delivered back to the rental place. Even the trash had been emptied. They shared memories of the night before as they walked through the park holding hands. Bryan and his band were a big hit at the wedding and were back in the studio practicing for their big concert in St. Louis in six days. The people Damaris hired did a good job of cleaning up. The hundred potted plants filled with blue forget-me-nots were given away to the guests as thank-you gifts. There was no indication a wedding took place the night before. The park looked bare. But it wasn't bare of memories, and their hearts were full of love.

By this time, they were famished. The Queen's Grill was open for dinner. Corey could be happy with hamburgers. But she had opened this restaurant for fine dining, and she wanted to celebrate. They stopped at their now jointly owned beautiful home and dressed in better clothes. Corey put on the blue suit coat he wore to the wedding. The restaurant was full of patrons, and many applauded as they walked in. The restaurant was beautiful, the waiters efficient, and the food superb. The chef came from the kitchen to ask Damaris how she liked his food. She complimented him with enthusiasm. He loved having her as the restaurant's owner. Her expectations were high, and she wouldn't settle for less.

After dinner, they sipped some South African liqueur Van Der Hum. She had ordered cases from South Africa, and the waiters sold many glasses to the customers. This was a religious town, but people did not object to having fine wine and liqueurs before and after their dinners.

Corey asked her, "Did you eat like this every night on the *Queen Mary*?" He looked at the menu again. "You can't even pronounce the names of the food!"

"Corey, we're training these college kids to pronounce the names correctly and know the ingredients and how they are prepared. After working here, they will be trained well enough to work in some of the finest restaurants in the world, and they need to be knowledgeable."

"Most of them are farm boys!"

"Many of them see the preparation of good food as an admirable profession. They are also learning how to give good service and make the patrons feel important."

"I suppose so. I have to admit the food and service were great!"

"Did you notice there are no televisions to discourage conversation and eye contact with one another and only classical music is played in the background? This town deserves a five-star restaurant. Do you know food connoisseurs are coming from all over Missouri now to eat here? Also I have been talking to Bryan about playing his classical guitar here occasionally just to bless the dinner patrons. He's busy, but maybe every now and then, he could find time."

Corey was thoughtful. "Damaris, we have been so busy with this wedding we haven't really talked much about anything else. As we sit here in this peaceful place, I want to discuss some things that are bothering me. I knew your having all this money would cause issues between us. Crazy Charlie said I was collecting crumbs from under your table. I know what he said shouldn't matter, but he's not the only one who thinks that. It feels weird living in a million-dollar home with a million-dollar grotto and pool area in the backyard which I didn't pay for. It feels strange calling it 'our house.'"

"I didn't pay for it either, Corey. The money was a gift," she reminded him. "It's our house now. I'm putting both our names on the title."

He changed the subject. "I think this restaurant is a great project for you. You're passionate about it, and I think people really appreciate it. You paid for Bryan's studio, and his earnings are keeping it running. He is independently wealthy now, and he earned most of it with his music. I think it's great you're volunteering at Dave's church and helping with food distribution. Those are good things. What I do mind is my not working. After the honeymoon, I'm going back full-time to the sheriff's department. That's my profession. I feel I'm contributing to the community by keeping guys like Charlie off the street. I don't like you paying for stuff. It makes me feel less of a man. By the way, how much did our wedding cost?"

"I guess about $100,000, including our honeymoon."

"That's two years of pay for me!"

"The bride usually pays for the wedding, if that makes you feel any better!"

"That's not the point, Damaris. When we go out to eat, I want to pick up the check and leave a tip, not you."

"I don't pay for our meals here. So you can leave a tip tonight, okay?"

"You're still paying for the meal, don't you see? I have to be a self-sufficient man and not rely on your money."

"Corey, I won this money. We're married now. This money is ours now, together. Your shoulder is still sore. I see you winching at times. You aren't ready to go back to work."

"After a night like last night, you, of all people, should know how well I am."

They both smiled.

Damaris teasingly said, "I must admit you have gained back your strength and vitality." She winked at him.

"Yes, I have, when it comes to you, especially." He leaned over and kissed her softly on her cheek. "I want to tell you some things you might not know about me. You know my parents are pretty well off. Do you know they own three thousand acres of prime farm and grazing land and several apartment buildings in Linn? I am their only heir. So you haven't married a poor deputy from a poor family. I have a college education in criminal justice. The department says it has eventual plans for me to work in a supervisory position. I want to work. I am not good at sitting around."

"Corey, I'm afraid you'll get hurt again. If something happened to you, I couldn't stand it. I almost lost you before."

He put his arm gently around her, understanding her fear. "That was a freak accident. I'll wear my vest from now on and be safe. After all, I have a guardian angel, don't I?"

She wondered if one of those men standing by Mr. A at the wedding might have been his.

"Furthermore, I am not your lapdog like Crazy Charlie yelled. I'm a man. I want to support my wife and eventual children. I'm proud. I want us to have a strong marriage, a lasting one. I hope this money thing doesn't get in the way."

Damaris was surprised. Why didn't Pastor Dave counsel them about this? He didn't mention these feelings in their marriage counseling sessions. She changed the subject.

"Corey, here is a card for the day after our wedding with some gifts written on a paper inside the card. I asked some of the deputies what you would like for a wedding gift. Please don't be mad at me, okay?"

He wondered why he would be mad. He opened the card and read her words of love and kissed her deeply, then unfolded the sheet of paper and read the words out loud, "You are now the proud owner of a brand-new white 250-horsepower, twenty-one-foot Ranger Comanche bass fishing boat and also owner of a brand-new white four-wheel-drive Toyota pickup truck with 5.7 liter engine, a tow bar, and boat trailer, along with a side-by-side, double-trigger Kimber shotgun. Most importantly, you are the owner of Damaris (formerly Kelly) Gardner's heart. No returns allowed. I love you, my precious and adorable husband."

He read the paper several times. "Are you kidding? This is about $200,000 worth of stuff!"

"Corey, if you're too proud to accept these gifts, I'll cancel the orders. Would you like me to do that?" She smiled.

He acted like he was thinking long and hard about his answer, then said with a grin, "Are you kidding? I'm not *that* proud! It's a good thing we have a four-car garage! When will I get to see these?"

"After our honeymoon. For now, I don't want to share you with a fishin' boat!"

He gave her a deep kiss. "Thanks, Damaris. Would you go fishin' with me sometime in our new boat? I'd like that."

"Of course. Let's go home now, Corey, to our home."

Damaris signed the bill; and Corey generously tipped the waiter, chef, and bartender.

"By the way, what did you get me for a wedding present?"

"You'll find out when we get home," he said seductively.

That night, he asked Damaris to wear one the flowered bikinis she bought for their honeymoon on Amelia Island, Florida. They swam in the grotto and made love under the stars. His love was the greatest wedding gift he could give her.

50

Honeymoon
AMELIA ISLAND

Corey wanted to go deep-sea fishing in the Atlantic Ocean. They stayed for a week at the Ritz-Carlton on Amelia Island off the east coast of Florida, thirty minutes north of Jacksonville. They chartered a luxury 380 LXF Boston Whaler deep-sea fishin' boat for four days, coming in each night for food at the Ritz's Salt restaurant, five-star dining at its best. Corey laughed as he reminded her to say fishin' instead of fishing. They saw many sharks and even caught a few. Damaris remembered the experiences she had in the Great Barrier Reef and still had a fear of the ocean. Corey's dream was to catch a swordfish or a tuna. In three days, he caught three swordfish, two he had to throw back because of legal restrictions. The one he kept weighed four hundred pounds. The whole crew was excited as he fought to land this amazing fish. They would process the fish, freeze it, and send the meat back to Linn for her restaurant.

She loved riding on the boat with Corey and laughed at his excitement. In the beginning, she read, sketched, and watched the ocean wildlife; but after the second day, the crew encouraged her to at least give fishin' a try. The crew was especially attentive to Damaris in her pink bikini and surfer-girl good looks. Corey was proud of the attention they gave her and wasn't jealous because he had absolute trust in her. On her first day of fishin', with the crew's help and after a two-hour tiring battle, with all the muscles in her arms, back, and legs straining with every ounce of strength in her, she caught the prize—a 350-pound bluefin tuna. She screamed with delight! The crew was amazed at the strength of this strong, fit beauty. Corey was proud of her. She did get a little help, he reminded her later as she bragged about her trophy fish.

In five days, they caught two tuna and the swordfish, as well as wahoo, mackerel, barracuda, cobia, and triggerfish. Corey promised they would have one bluefin tuna mounted and hung in their large great room in memory of their honeymoon. The rest of the fish would be processed, frozen, and sent to Linn to the Queen's Grill. Corey told her every night as they lay in bed that, even if he caught the biggest trophy fish, she was the biggest trophy in his life. Her muscles ached and Corey rubbed Amish cream over her body to ease the pain. His shoulder also ached, and she did the same for him. They fell happily asleep curled up in each other's arms. She told him every night he was a keeper! As a fisherman, he truly appreciated that comment! The last two days, they rented a small fishin' boat and did Salt River fishin' near the island and caught some largemouth bass and trout. When they weren't fishin', they rented bicycles and/or walked around the beautiful fourteen-mile-long, three-mile-wide island. Corey loved the ocean and vowed they would return to Amelia Island for more vacations. He told her there was only thing he liked better than fishin', and that was lying in bed with her wrapped in each other's arms.

*****

After the honeymoon, on one of Corey's days off, Mr. A, Raphael, and Jacob pulled up in their driveway in the limousine. They sat on her comfortable leather sofas as they visited. Mr. A complimented her on her decorating taste and told her this was more than a social visit.

"Damaris, when I met you in January of 2015, you had begun your world cruise. Starting from the second night, you let me be your tour guide with Raphael as our companion. You didn't know who we were or where we came from, but you trusted me. I taught you many things and showed you some great needs in this world. I introduced you to eight different charities and ministries in different countries who were doing God's work. Would you believe me if I told you Raphael has been with you, Damaris, since you were a child, and Aaron has been with you as well, Corey? He was the one that kept the bullet from entering your brain. They both have protected you from many dangerous situations even though you didn't know it. One day, I'll tell you both about some dangerous moments that were prevented because of my two companions.

"The wise decisions you have made in your life are because you listened to my voice. I'm not your conscience but more of a guide and truth teller. I am intimately involved with those who love the Creator and His Son and have surrendered or will surrender their lives. We can be seen at times and not seen at others because we are spiritual beings with specific jobs. Tonight I am reminding you of the organizations you learned about as we traveled. I introduced you to people who demonstrated Christian faith in action. There are many organizations in America who do that, but America is a wealthy nation. We have many of the same issues as these countries, but the number of the poor and destitute in those foreign places is astronomically larger than in America. There are millions dying because there is not enough money, food, people, or government agencies ready to help.

"You have done many good things for the city of Linn. You have been generous. Now I am asking you to think globally and do even more. You're beautiful, intelligent, well spoken, and now well-traveled. You were once a shy wallflower content to sit in the shadow of your brother's success. God has a greater purpose for you and Corey as your husband. Damaris, you have proven you can create a professional slideshow with music and narration describing these ministries. Pray about it first. This new slide presentation I am asking you to create is what you have been gifted to do. Also I want you to start a foundation which works toward saving lives and giving people hope by leading them to God. I know you can motivate people to give because the needs are so great and you have seen firsthand what they are.

"I wrote a list for you just as a reminder. I'll read the list to you, and then it will be yours as you do what your heart tells you to do. Let's review them again, for Corey's sake.

"One, Stephen's Children Ministry in Cairo, Egypt, run by Mama Maggie Gibran, the Mother Teresa of Cairo, which ministers in appalling slums and helps rebuild children's lives.

"Two, Phu My Orphanage in Ho Chi Minh City, Vietnam, ministering to handicapped children who have been abandoned.

"Three, the Annunciation Orphanage in Saigon, Vietnam, with fifty children and two nuns. The children have no family support. They need money and more toys.

"Four, the House of Hope in the Henan Province of China, ministering to abandoned orphans.

"Five, the Exodus Foundation in Sydney, Australia, which feeds the poor and ministers to the homeless.

"Six, Doctors Without Borders, *Médicins Sans Frontières*, which receives no government help and relies on charities. You have seen yourself the doctors and medical personnel saving lives.

"Seven, the AMG Ministries in Athens, Greece, which concentrates on at-risk youth.

"Eight, the Durban Christian Center or Jesus Dome in Durban, South Africa, a biracial nondenominational church ministering to spiritual needs by bringing people closer to the Lord. This is where your heart was opened up to God, Damaris. You were told about these places because of their great need."

He handed her a business card and the list. "Here is the name of a man who will help you set up a foundation for these eight ministries. Corey, Damaris once asked me how any one person or organization could possibly make a difference in the suffering of the world. I told her the brief story of the boy who walked along a beach with his father looking at thousands of starfish stranded on the beach from a great storm as the tide receded. As he walked, he'd see a starfish moving as if trying to get back into the ocean, and he would pick it up and throw it into the ocean. They walked some more, and the boy would find another struggling starfish and throw it back in.

"His father looked at him and said, 'Son, there are thousands of starfish on this beach. You can't possibly make a difference and save them all.'

"As the boy picked up another and threw it back into the ocean, he looked up at his father and said, 'Well, at least I made a difference to *that* one!'

"No one group or individual can meet all the needs of the suffering human beings in this world, but each of us can make a difference. I know you both will make more of a difference than you already have. I will always be with the both of you for advice if you need it. My boss has sent Raphael and Jacob to watch over you. Most of the time, you won't know they are there, but they will be."

Corey sat holding Damaris's hand, trying to process all he had heard. "Are you God?" he asked sincerely.

"There are three distinct beings that make up the one true God, the Father, the Son, and the Holy Spirit. It's a mystery to many people on earth, but it seems normal to us because our life is in the spiritual world."

Corey was mystified. "Who are Raphael, Aaron, and Benjamin?"

"Who do you think they are?" He smiled broadly.

"Are they angels? Are they our guardian angels? You said it was Aaron that kept that bullet from entering my head."

"I'll tell you what, Corey. The answer is in His Word, Luke 4:10. Look it up!"

"Another thing I want to know is why you travel around in a white limousine if you are spirits."

"That's a good question. Sometimes we appear in human form, and I figure, since I spend so much time on earth teaching truth and traveling from town to town, I might as well be comfortable!"

He laughed heartily, and Aaron and Benjamin laughed along with him.

"We'll be on our way soon. But first I have some really good news for the both of you." He smiled the mysterious smile he usually had before sharing one of his truths.

"What kind of good news, Mr. A?" asked Damaris. She knew that smile well.

He paused, creating anticipation. "You and Corey are going to have a child. You heard it here first, my precious friends. We'll be going now. Remember everything I've said."

They looked at each other in disbelief. The next day, Damaris went to the pharmacy and bought a pregnancy test.

Damaris should have known. Mr. A knew everything, and He never lied.

51

Bryan Kelly

Right before the baby was born, the news exploded in Linn that Bryan Kelly and the Rogues were nominated for a Grammy for best alternative music album, putting them in the same category as U2, REM, and Nirvana. A Grammy! People in Linn were proud. When Grammy night came, Bryan and the band were in Hollywood standing backstage waiting for the shapely actress to announce the winner. A large crowd gathered at BJ's and at Damaris's new home to watch the awards on television, including her mother and new husband. One commentator described the award as honoring artistic achievement, technical proficiency, and overall excellence. Alternative music was described as embracing progression and innovation.

"That's Bryan!" everyone shouted.

His music was also described as a less intense version of rock, considered more original, more eclectic, and more musically challenging. Bryan's creative and fertile mind knew no limits. His music was especially popular with college students and millennials.

The actress carefully opened the envelope and announced slowly, "And the winner is...Bryan Kelly and the Rogues!"

The crowd went wild. Everyone in Linn went crazy! Pastor Dave's church bells rang loud and clear. The band members came to the stage joyfully, accepting their trophies. Bryan stood before the microphone, thanking the band; the city of Linn; his sister, Damaris; and the Missouri lottery for enabling him to build one the best recording studios in America in his hometown. He ended by thanking his Lord for giving him a gift for creating music. How the Hollywood establishment hated any acknowledgement of God at an awards ceremony, but Bryan said it with such a charming Irish smile he won people's hearts. The applause was surprisingly enthusiastic!

Linn was ready for another parade after the Grammys. As Bryan and the band returned to Linn down Main in their huge tour bus, the crowd cheered. The band members waved, and their driver parked the monstrous bus in BJ's parking lot. Of course, the mayor had to make a speech as well as city council members. Bryan and the band stood waiting to say a few words, as well as Damaris and Pastor Dave. He laughed about their town now being nicknamed Lucky Linn. The travelers on Highway 50 parked their cars wherever they could and joined in the celebration. Again media people from all over the Midwest snapped pictures and interviewed the residents of Linn.

Damaris planned a catered celebration at her home that night for invited guests. The band was there and brought wives or girlfriends. It was a cold January, so there was no poolside entertaining. But the fireplace was comfortably blazing. Pastor Dave gathered them in a circle for prayers of thanksgiving for the many blessings given to all of them. Bryan played some quiet jazz on the Steinway as people sipped eggnog, hot cider, or wine and ate the delicious hors d'oeuvres. It was a joyous celebration! Corey had a few words to say.

"You know, I am so lucky to have Bryan and his band in my life. They have become my friends. I consider Bryan a brother as well as a brother-in-law. The Rogues have held together for seven years, which is rare for most bands. Bryan had rules. No drugs. No drunkenness. No inappropriate relationships with girls. Strict practice times. Ethics in all their business dealings no matter what it cost them. They deserve this Grammy. Their songs are heard on radio stations all over the country, in shopping malls, doctors' and dentists' offices, Sirius XM radio, local and national AM and FM stations. Their music is everywhere. Their concerts are sold out. Bryan told me that their manager booked a concert in Dublin,

Ireland, for next year! You guys are truly a success in every measure possible. Let's have a toast to the Rogues and their future success as well!"

After the party, Corey, Damaris, and Bryan sat in front of the warm fire. Bryan wanted to talk as he drank a glass of wine. He said he was in the process of rethinking his priorities. He didn't have much time anymore to write, compose music, or even just play. He was frustrated. He was a creative being, not a businessperson. He had hired a man to manage the band and the recording studio, which took a load of responsibility off his shoulders, but Bryan didn't want his musical expression to feel like a business. He hated the business details. Building the studio was a huge energy-depleting amount of time and labor. Concerts were sapping his energy. He needed a vacation. It was taking a toll on who he was as a musician and an artist.

He already talked about these feelings with his band members. They were disappointed that, at the height of their popularity, Bryan was considering a new direction; but they understood. They were still Bryan's band and decided as a group they would hire a girl singer as Bryan stepped back. Bryan had been listening to tapes and watching videos of some promising, attractive young women who sang with strength and depth and who also had confident stage presence. It was a difficult time for them after just receiving a Grammy, but the decision was made they would continue as the Rogues without Bryan's name or as their lead singer, just for a while. He needed to recharge. He wanted to pursue the depth of his musical abilities and concentrate on his four loves—piano, guitar, composition, and experimentation in recording.

Bryan spoke to them honestly. "My music was never about notoriety or money. It is who I am as a person. I'm not for sale. There's still so much musically inside me that I haven't been able to express. The band was limiting and defining me. I want to be true to who I am. I don't know where my thinking will lead me, but I am open to God's leading. I'll display our Grammy proudly in the studio office. I'll work with the musicians who rent the facility, but I'll be secluding myself as much as possible. I'll have more time to experiment and write really good music. I'll work hard every day and hopefully get inspired. When I'm not creating, I have no peace. I want to create the music of His spirit, and I want it to be beautiful, good, and truthful. That's the rock I want to stand on."

They all sat there in silence, watching the embers burn lower and lower. What could Corey and Damaris say? This was Bryan's path, not theirs.

Ariana Marie Gardner was born exactly nine months from Corey and Damaris's wedding night, a beautiful, smiling child from the beginning. Bryan left for Ireland soon after she was born, rented a cottage in the small-town of Galway, and, with his guitar and an electronic keyboard, wrote many songs, which he planned to record when he returned. Ten of the songs would be part of his album the *Ariana Lullabies*, his gift to his newly born niece. He liked to hang out in the Irish taverns which had live music and attend local music festivals. He loved Irish tavern music and was contemplating a Celtic rock album. When the pub customers learned Bryan Kelly was in the audience, he was always asked to play and sing. He tried out his new songs on these audiences and would always close with the words "Now tell me what you think." Afterward, many people gathered around him, and they would drink Guinness together. He knew they recognized honest music. He took their suggestions to heart as well as their compliments. He respected their sensitivity to authentic music. Later he would record the songs written in Ireland and have great commercial success. He lived in Ireland for a year and grew as an artist as he tapped into his Irish roots.

52

Damaris

It was a warm summer evening as she sat next to the pool, the waterfalls reminding her of the cruise through the Milford Sound in New Zealand. She had just put her darling Ariana to bed. She and Corey had been married for a year, and Ariana was the little love of their lives. She sipped a glass of wine as she wrote in her journal. Bryan would soon return from Ireland. She had missed him terribly. Her mother was happily married and came to visit her little granddaughter as often as she could. Corey enjoyed his job and always remembered to wear his bulletproof vest. Damaris prayed daily for his safety. Their romance and passion was as intense as ever, and Corey often went home on his lunch hour to the delight of his fellow deputies.

When they asked him what he had for lunch, inevitably he would laugh and say with a twinkle in his eyes, "My beautiful wife, of course!"

Although she had spent millions of dollars, her financial advisers wisely invested her money, and the interest alone provided money for Damaris's many good works.

The city of Linn was doing well. Pastor Dave's church bells rang regularly. Residents didn't have to look at their watches or phones to know the time. People could walk the entire length of the town from one end to the other on wide sidewalks with comfortable benches and shade trees. Legends and Osage Parks were continually in use by musicians from all over Missouri. McGuire Park pool became a popular place in the summer months. Storefronts were painted, and new business signs made. The new Best Western Hotel and Convention Center was in continual use. The Stone Hearth Motel thrived, often with 100 percent occupancy. Damaris donated money to any church who had a pressing need. College students came from all over the country to Missouri Tech to acquire a sound recording degree using Exodus Studios or a restaurant management / culinary arts degree using the Queen's Grill as their laboratory.

Damaris honored Mr. A's wishes and created slide shows for the new Armstrong Foundation, which helped fund the eight ministries Mr. A had shown her. She spoke at least once a week to a community or church group either locally or nationally, always prefacing her presentations with the story of her lottery win. She went from a shy wallflower to a confident speaker. Not only did she give generously to the foundation, but she raised millions of dollars for these charities which helped meet the physical and spiritual needs of thousands. She knew the money given to these ministries often meant life or death, and her speaking engagements were undergirded with power as she spoke passionately about them. Americans are givers. After hearing her speak, they gave generously, and volunteers rose up in large numbers, people willing to minister to the needy in foreign countries. Children were fed and educated, and families found decent shelter.

She donated to organizations that provided clean drinking water to the oppressed who lived in large crowded cities. Mr. Armstrong had predicted that she would one day become a hero in the eyes of many. She gave her money quietly, without fanfare. She never felt she was a hero. It was a lucky day when she won the lottery. She used that luck to help others. She thanked God daily for that day when she rode her bike to Casey's to pick up a gallon of milk which she could barely afford. She had changed little these two years except grown more lovely and more at peace. She had transformed into the beautiful woman of God that Mr. A had spoken about, with a gentle spirit and a kind and loving heart.

She still rode her bike into Linn on the new sidewalks or walked Ariana into town in her pink stroller, and just like Pastor Dave, always had time to talk with people she met along the way. She and Corey loved to dance at BJ's on nights when there were live bands. They were country people, and humility was their trademark. She knew Mr. A would always be nearby when she needed sound advice and that her family was protected. She had seen the protectors. She knew their power. She believed all would be well. They both found faith—a real, true faith based on God's love, forgiveness, and acceptance. They were new creations, born not of flesh and blood but from the spirit of God.

Above all else, her trip opened her eyes to a world that desperately needed hope. Mr. A taught her many wise lessons on her world cruise, which she remembered and put into practice. She learned from him that racial prejudice in any form destroyed the lives of both the conquerors and the marginalized. She witnessed different cultures and religions and became more tolerant of divergent views and cultural lifestyles without compromising the truth. She stood firm in her faith and had a passion for sharing the truth. Her travels exposed to her the spiritual darkness in the world, and she prayed daily she could be a light shining brightly in that darkness.

Sadly life's challenges often break into lives unexpectedly even in the midst of joyous, peaceful pauses. Corey and Damaris had no way of knowing another tsunami would soon head their way.

53

Ariana

Corey fished whenever he could in his new bass boat
and liked to drive to the Lake of the Ozarks, about
seventy-five miles from Linn. When he came back
in the afternoon, he would give the largemouth bass
and crappie to Sofia, their housekeeper and cook,
who would prepare delicious fish dinners. Damaris,
either pregnant or eventually with a new baby, had
only fished with him off the coast of Amelia Island,
Florida, where she caught her 350-pound bluefin tuna, which they had turned into the fiberglass
mount which hung on a large wall in their great room
as a reminder of their fantastic honeymoon. Damaris
finally agreed on this warm September day to come
with him and bring Ariana for her first ride in their
boat. She and Sofia, their housekeeper, packed a
cooler full of turkey sandwiches, homemade oatmeal
cookies, and sodas.

Ariana was two now, full of life and enthusiasm. She never sat still, wiggled her way through
life, and spent time kissing Damaris and Corey on
the lips. She was the main source of laughter in their
home and was a perfect combination of Corey's and
Damaris's good looks and vibrant health. Her deep
dimples on both cheeks and flashing brown eyes
endeared her to all who came in contact with her.
She looked like the child star Shirley Temple with
the same ebullient personality. She knelt every night
beside her small bed, her palms pushed together
pointing to the sky, an angelic look on her face. She
prayed for everyone and every situation in her life,
sometimes taking fifteen or twenty minutes. Her
parents knew God heard her prayers because of her
persistence and sincerity of heart. When her Uncle
Bryan came to visit and played their Steinway, she
sat close to him, listening and watching every note
he played. He taught her to play simple tunes, which
she repeatedly played throughout the day. She loved
romping with their new black Labrador retriever
puppy, which Corey would train to take the place of
his old Labrador retriever, Sam, who had just died
from old age. Ariana hated wearing any clothing but
her pink panties. Damaris constantly dressed her in
shirts and long pants, only to find them five minutes
later thrown on her bed. Ariana was a free spirit.

*****

This day, the lake was busy and quite choppy because it was Saturday. They hadn't arrived until 11:00 a.m., and the partiers already had begun drinking heavily and skiing at dangerous speeds across the lake. Corey found a quiet fairly small cove nearby where there wouldn't be so much noise to scare the fish away. Ariana was excited about everything she saw, and they had a hard time settling her down. Corey bought her a little plastic fishin' pole and secured a big fat white marshmallow on the end. She watched her daddy fish and then tried to copy him. Corey secretly secured the plastic fish to the end of the pole when she wasn't looking; and when he yelled, "Pish, Ariana, pish!" she jerked up the pole and screamed with delight at the plastic fish hanging from it. Of course, she wanted to do it over and over again, and Corey had to delay his own fishin' for a while until she lost interest. Damaris snapped great pictures and laughed as Corey looked at her with appreciation as boat drivers sped by and whistled at her in her turquoise-blue bikini. He smiled back at them and gave them a thumbs-up, indicating he appreciated her too but that she belonged to him. Childbirth had not scarred her stomach or ruined her figure. He leaned over and kissed her neck as she took pictures. His passion for her had not ebbed in their two years of marriage. She still appreciated his muscular physique, and his deep love for her fired her passion for him.

Under a shade tree near the shore, they ate lunch while watching Ariana giggle at the fish in the live well. Neither one of them saw Raphael, Aaron, and their new friend, Elijah, their guardians, and protectors, standing on the shore as Corey pulled out into the main channel. By this time, many of the boaters were drunk. It was a party lake. The previous year, there had been five deaths due to boating accidents. Jet skiers, wakeboard riders, and high-powered pleasure boats were loud and obnoxious. Corey was aware of the boat traffic and the level of inebriation of many young people on the lake. He was feeling protective of Damaris and Ariana, as was Raphael and friends who stood near the shore. Unbeknownst to Corey, a 400-horsepower ski boat driven by a tattooed drunk, as inebriated as all of his five passengers, male and female, was driving seventy miles per hour directly headed toward Corey's boat. The driver stood behind the wheel looking back at his passengers, a beer in one hand, laughing and yelling cuss words. In a moment, he hit a huge wave from another boat, causing him to lose his balance and jerk the wheel hard to the right. His boat keeled over, even scaring the drunk passengers as the boat tipped steeply.

Corey was careful to look both right and left as he entered the channel. Suddenly he heard the roar of a wide-open engine to his left. His Ranger was capable of speeds of a hundred miles per hour, but he could not escape the inevitable crash of the large boat speeding toward him. When the boat hit, the whole ski boat

lifted over the top of Corey's boat, the propeller making deep gashes and shattering the windshield. Ariana's
head hit the side of the boat, leaving a deep bloody
gash in her forehead and ejecting her violently into
the lake facedown. Raphael and friends jumped into
action, swimming toward the child and then keeping
the baby's face out of the water so she could breathe.
The violent impact threw Damaris against the inside
of the boat which broke her arm and severely bruised
her body. Blood splattered all around them as Ariana's
little body was thrown into the lake. Damaris screamed
for help as she desperately reached out for Ariana to
keep her head above water. Corey had some deep cuts
and contusions but no life-threatening wounds. He
frantically swam to the other side of the boat to help
his family as Damaris tried, without luck, to stem the
flow of blood from the side of Ariana's head. Her only
child, her baby, was unconscious.

Luckily the caring Midwest people acted in uni-
son. Two medivac helicopters were called to the lake
from Jefferson City. In record time, five ambulances
were there with assistance. Four people in the drunk's
boat were killed from the impact. The driver's life was
spared, but he had many serious injuries. Later he
wished he could have died in that accident because of
what followed. Both boats were destroyed. Damaris
and Corey weren't seriously injured; but the doctors
told Damaris that a brain injury like this could leave
Ariana brain dead, paralyzed, or in a permanent veg-

etable-like state. There was a chance she would never walk or speak again. The whole of Missouri began praying for this innocent child.

As Damaris and Corey sat next to her in the ICU, they were in shock. Damaris's broken arm was in a cast. She thanked God she and Corey weren't so injured that they couldn't take care of Ariana if she survived. Damaris had been through this with Corey. She couldn't believe she was reliving it again with her daughter. Mr. A told her guardian angels would protect them. They weren't protected. Her daughter was going to die. She was told the driver wasn't killed.

Why not? she asked herself.

He deserved to die, not her innocent daughter. Yet she could hear Mr. A's voice saying she must forgive.

"Mr. A, we need you! Please help my daughter. And forgive me for having such hatred for this man. I'm begging for a forgiving heart."

A stranger stood in a dark corner of the room. He was Elijah, Ariana's angel, praying deeply. He wished he could have done a better job of protecting her; but he couldn't see into the future or know the plans God had for this little girl. Mr. A would know why this child's life would be spared, and Damaris's family would know soon. He had to trust Him.

One night, Mr. A came into Ariana's hospital room. Raphael, Aaron, and Benjamin stood next to him. She and Corey asked him directly why Ariana wasn't protected. Where was Ariana's guardian angel, sleeping on the job?

"Why couldn't he steer the boat away from my family?" asked Corey in frustration.

"Did anyone in the other boat have a guardian angel?" Mr. A asked.

"I don't know," said Corey.

"How many people were killed? I'll tell you. Four out of those six people were killed in that ski boat. Their families will never see them again. Your lives were spared. Damaris had only a broken arm, and you had only a minor concussion and scrapes and bruises. Those boats were destroyed! Don't you think that's a miracle? Can you see divine intervention in that situation? I understand your frustration, but you were protected. Can you recognize that? Look at all the people who came to your rescue, who made phone calls, who ministered to you in the ambulance and the helicopters who helped save lives. Just because you don't understand doesn't mean you aren't being protected. It's not a formula. Some people die under the protection of their guardian angel. That is one of God's mysteries."

Like Corey when he survived his gunshot wound, Ariana miraculously recovered after spending three weeks in the hospital with the best care and thousands of prayers. She opened her eyes one day as Corey and Damaris held her hand and smiled.

"Mommy, Daddy, hold me."

The sweetest words they could ever hear! The doctors x-rayed Ariana's brain and saw some strange brain activity they had never seen before. They gave her an MRI and a CAT scan so they could study the unusual darkened areas in her brain. They decided to let her go home. She was talking, laughing, and walking nicely. They wanted to continue to study and monitor her brain activity and document the growth or decrease of the dark masses on her tiny brain.

Back at home, she liked to watch Irish dancers on television and DVD's and she copied their moves. Her chubby little legs looking like Shirley Temple in her 1930s movies. She loved to sing—morning, noon, and night. Her uncle Bryan had just returned from a reunion tour with the Rogues and the band's new female back-up singer, Alessia Nolan, who turned out to be a powerhouse singer with a wide vocal range and the ability to sing a soft, endearing love song as well as powerhouse rock ballads. They no longer were solely an alternative rock band. They were incorporating Irish instruments into their repertoire and this new style was becoming popular with their fans. Bryan had new hopes for his band, and the comeback from his seclusion musically refreshed him. He returned from the tour as quickly as he could and hurried to Damaris's home to see his young niece, grateful she was alive and happy. He and the whole band had been praying daily for her recovery. Ariana ran to him joyfully when he came to visit on this day and planted her famous kisses all over his face.

Bryan picked her up gently and sat her on the piano bench next to him while a Mozart concerto quietly played in the background through the sound system.

She leaned her head sweetly on his shoulder and pointed her finger to the speaker in the ceiling and shouted, "Mozart!"

Brian was surprised. Damaris pulled up another song, Beethoven's *Pastorale* symphony.

"Beethoven!" she shouted with joy.

They tried several songs, and she pronounced the names of the composers with confidence. She was only three years old! She could barely talk! Brian was astounded. Damaris told him she was showing musical gifts like he did as a child, and she asked Ariana to sing her favorite song. She slid off the piano bench and, with a voice that carried through Damaris's large home, sang in tune the whole "Jesus Loves Me," both verses in full voice and perfect pitch. They knew she believed God loved her with no doubt in her mind. Bryan asked her to play something on the piano. Damaris brought the little electric piano from her bedroom. Ariana sat down on her small stool, pushed some buttons on her own, turned up the volume, and played a child's version of Mozart with violins in the background.

Bryan jumped up from the Steinway as she played. "Why didn't you tell me she was doing this, Damaris?"

"You've either been gone or too busy."

"Bring her over to the studio tomorrow, could you? I want to try some things with her."

"She's only three, Bryan."

"This is when it began with me."

This is when it began with Ariana Marie Gardner. Her accident somehow tweaked a creative part of her brain, at least that's what the doctors told her parents later on. They didn't know, that while little Ariana lay in that comatose state, she entered the gates of heaven, a place so beautiful and peaceful that she experienced absolute comfort and happiness. Mr. A was there and told her, as she sat on his lap, that one day the world would hear the voice of an awe-inspiring singer who would raise the spirits of millions of people around the world and it would be hers. Ariana smiled because she knew it, too.

At eighteen, Damaris Kelly had won the $950 million lottery. She listened to Pastor Dave's advice and spent the money wisely, using it to bless thousand of others. Her greatest blessings in return were her husband Corey and daughter Ariana. She couldn't predict Ariana's future, but both she and her brother, Bryan, saw the seeds of greatness in her as a singer and musician even at this young age. They couldn't predict exactly the musical heights to which she would ascend, but they knew Ariana would fulfill her destiny. After all, Mr. Armstrong was her best friend.

About the Author

Julie Garrett is a retired teacher, former worship leader and songwriter, newspaper editorial writer, a Civil War reenactor for twenty years, and a well-traveled explorer and adventurer. Presently she is the keyboard player for her church, an avid American history student, and a journal writer for over sixty years.

She is the wife to Mark, also a retired educator and writer. They live a busy and fulfilling life in their home in Saddlebrooke, a few miles north of picturesque Branson, Missouri.

The sequel to The Lottery Winner is soon to come. Look for Ariana in the months ahead.

"Ad astra per aspera"
A rough road leads to the stars

CPSIA information can be obtained
at www.ICGtesting.com
Printed in the USA
LVHW100046091122
732695LV00018B/102

9 781685 263300